FAVOURITE CAT STORIES

FAVOURITE CAT STORIES

Foreword by Nerys Hughes

COMPILED BY
LESLEY O'MARA

ILLUSTRATED BY
WILLIAM GELDART

PAN BOOKS
LONDON, SYDNEY AND AUCKLAND

First published 1992 by Michael O'Mara Books Limited

This edition published 1993 by Pan Books Limited
a division of Pan Macmillan Publishers Limited
Cavaye Place London SW10 9PG
and Basingstoke

Associated companies throughout the world

ISBN 0 330 32771 2

· 1 3 5 7 9 8 6 4 2

A CIP catalogue record for this book is available from
the British Library

Printed in England by Cox & Wyman Ltd, Reading, Berks

Contents

Foreword

NERYS HUGHES

There were two small orange kittens in the RSPCA Cattery eight Christmases ago. We chose the shivering tiniest one, and his brother stared at us in a lonely bewildered way as we left. On Boxing Day we went back and got him. My daughter Mari-Claire, who was four at the time, called the little one Cuddles – a name which did inhibit me a bit when I was desperately calling his name up and down our street when we lost him once. Fearless and loyal, more like a dog than a cat, he follows Mari-Claire everywhere through thick and thin and even through snow. My son Ben called the other kitten Twm-Twm (Welsh for Tom Tom) after a much-loved long-ago cat my Auntie Gwen befriended in Wales.

Having muttered and grumbled about cats' hairs in favourite chairs, settee backs used as scratching posts, and tortured mice by the kitchen door, I was taken aback by the total desolation I felt when Cuddles got run over, and we thought we were going to lose him. His sense of adventure and curiosity had taken him along the road to play dodgems with the traffic, and he got knocked down by a motorbike, breaking some bones and shattering his pelvis. We were all sobbing as we left the emergency vet's that night, having been told to leave him overnight so that the vet could test if his bladder had been pierced, if so he wouldn't survive. The next morning we were stricken to be told that he hadn't passed water, so the vet feared the worst. As we were going out of the door, gazing at him with love and despair, he smiled at us, gave a little bark, and relieved himself hugely and copiously all over his cage. We whooped and cheered and took him home. Patrick, my husband, made a little hospital cage out of an old cot and some wire netting so we could restrict his movements for a few weeks. He made a complete recovery, growing muscle tissue instead of bone over his pelvis, as cats do, and is now as daring and as lively as ever. Cuddles the Survivor. Perhaps that is why I identified so strongly with Doris Lessing in her beautifully written story about Rufus, her orange cat. The subtle but determined inroads that cats make into our hearts and homes! The doors that have to be left just ajar, creating thin draughts, the chairs that are forfeited, the meals on wheels and company that has to be organized when we go away, and the cross orange backs that are turned on me when we get back.

Certainly Doreen and Charles Tovey adjusted their friendships and lifestyle to accommodate two very naughty cats, I'm not sure I would have the patience to live with the beautiful and wicked Siamese Solomon and Sheba! Charles Dudley Warner celebrates the life of a mysterious and exceptional cat called Calvin. 'Incident on East Ninth' is a clever thriller – but then all the stories are evocative and readable.

If you don't like cats you'll enjoy reading this book. If you like cats you'll love it.

The Cat That Could Fly

STELLA WHITELAW

IT BEGAN on a curiously still morning when not a leaf stirred and even the butterflies seemed to hover over the flowers without moving. The dead elm stretched its ashen branches skywards waiting for the chop that was a long time in coming. A mile up a chartered Tri-Star ferried yawning early starters to a package holiday in Majorca, its gentle hum followed by vapour trails in the sky.

Leopold trod the dew-hung clover with delicate paws. He was a big ginger and white cat with a wide, surprised face and fluffed cheeks. His eyes were very green and brilliant which added to his startled look. He lived an uncomplicated life: he ate and slept; he caught the occasional bird or shrew just to keep his hand in.

The family that he lived with were what Leopold called sleek. They had everything – two cars, two colour television sets, a video recorder, wall to wall stereos, a deep freeze that could take a whale, every domestic appliance on the market, and yet they were as mean as a cross-eyed snake. They bought him unbranded cat food, a mish-mash of wet cereal and unmentionable animal parts; he never got a taste of fresh liver or fish. They drank the cheapest coffee, bought broken biscuits, and cut all the 10p-off coupons out of the paper. They were sleek all right.

They were sleek on affection too. If Leopold jumped on to a vacant lap, he was hastily brushed off.

'Gerroff my suit! I don't want your hairs all over me. Shoo. Shoo,' said the sleek man impatiently.

The sleek woman was as bad. Her clothes were also uncat-able. The one person who liked Leopold was the daughter, Dana, but she was preoccupied with O levels and boy friends, and the only time Leopold saw her was when she came in late from a disco and they shared the cosy quietness of a 2 am kitchen.

As Leopold took his early morning stroll down the garden, he heard a faint chirp, chirp. The sound made his stomach contract. He was hungry. Last night's supper was best forgot-ten, and they would not give him a breakfast until he had been outside for at least an hour. Leopold did not understand these rules. It was another of their odd ways. He noticed that they ate broken biscuits whenever they felt like it.

Leopold crept up on the sound. It was a baby thrush, softly speckled brown and white, a big fluffy, helpless creature, looking straight at Leopold with bright, trusting eyes. It stag-gered a few inches and fell forward on to its plump breast. Leopold's surprised expression sharpened with delight. This was obviously some sort of game. He patted the soft feathers with a tentative paw. The bird chirped encouragingly and hopped another few inches. A few trees away, the mother bird heard her baby's call but was not alarmed. It had to learn to fly by itself.

Suddenly Leopold pounced. The baby's neck hung limp between his jaws. Leopold growled, a low rumbling jungle sound echoing back from his wild ancestors. He paraded his victim, the feathers stuck out round his mouth like an Air Force moustache. He crunched the tiny body thoughtfully, blood on the short white fur under his nose.

The mother bird went crazy. She flew from branch to branch in distress. She swooped over the ginger cat and what was left of her baby, her cries loud and distraught. But it was too late. There was nothing she could do. She took one last look at the big cat and flew blindly into the empty air.

There was a great oak which Leopold liked to climb. He never went very far because he knew his limits. But today the baby bird lay heavily in his stomach, and Leopold climbed higher, hoping to leave the uncomfortable feeling behind. The thick tangled branches gave no hint of how high he was climbing. He went on, up and up, leaping from one claw-hold to the next. Because there was no wind, the branches barely moved, again giving Leopold an unfounded sense of security. When a broken branch revealed a glimpse of the land below, Leopold was quite amazed. He could see the tops of other trees, padded with green-like cushions beneath him. The garden of his house was a smudge of blurred colours. In the distance was the church spire, almost eye level. A helicopter whirled into sight, coming straight towards the oak, its rotor blades clattering discordantly.

Leopold leaped back. He forgot he was on a branch, up a tree. He took off backwards, falling head between heels, somersaulting through a cascade of leaves and broken twigs, the wind rushing through his whiskers, flashes of sky and earth alternately in vision as he hurtled towards the ground.

He spread his paws helplessly in a gesture of supplication to the great cat god in the sky. He closed his eyes tightly. He did not want to see what was coming to him.

Leopold first became aware of a change when the swift rushing wind in his ears slowed to the merest whisper. He was still falling, but no longer that shattering, pummelling plunge earthwards. He seemed to be drifting. Perhaps he had died.

He opened one eye the merest slit. He saw the Japanese maple, a beech hedge and below him a bed of button dahlias, prim and tight-headed. He landed right in the middle of the flowers and shook himself.

'Gerroff my dahlias!' the sleek woman yelled from a bedroom window.

Leopold extracted himself from the damaged flowers with dignity and walked away, a curled yellow petal behind one ear like a Hawaiian hula dancer. He had too much to think about to be worried by appearances.

After breakfast he sat looking at the oak tree. It did look very high. What had happened to him? How could he have fallen all that way and survived? He knew that cats could fall from the roof of a house and land unhurt on four paws, but that tree was at least three houses high, or so it seemed to Leopold. Eventually Leopold wandered into the wood to the far end where it was secluded and the blackened stump of a tree struck by lightning stood lonely and unloved.

He climbed the black stump, sniffing the lingering smell of sulphur. He sat in the fork and looked down on the carpet of pine needles below. It was about eight feet high. He could either scramble down the charred bark, or he could jump.

He jumped. He expected to land on the bed of needles in about one and a half seconds flat. But strangely he seemed to float. It took four seconds to land. It was puzzling.

He thought about it for a time, then decided to climb the stump again. He jumped off from the fork. This time it took six seconds and he landed some yards away on dry bracken.

Leopold was beginning to enjoy himself. After all, what harm was there if he wanted to spend the afternoon jumping off an old tree? What the hell! He climbed again, rapidly, like a Red Arrow. He jumped again, quite merrily, paws spread, wondering where he would land.

Suddenly he saw a clump of nettles right below him. Despite his thick fur, he knew all about nettles. His pink nose was particularly vulnerable. He stretched wide his paws in horror and sailed over the top of the clump. Without thinking, he lifted both his right legs and wheeled away in a shallow curve towards an open patch of ground.

When he returned that evening, the family scolded him and said he was too late for supper. They sat round the television, dunking broken biscuits into watery coffee. Leopold licked at the dried bits still stuck on his breakfast saucer. His drinking bowl had not been changed and the water was practically growing algae. He jumped on the draining board and stretched his neck towards a dripping tap.

'Gerroff the draining board, you wicked cat,' the woman shouted. Leopold obligingly removed himself. For a split second, as he jumped, he almost spread his paws but an inner caution stiffened this action and he landed awkwardly, unbalanced.

'Now don't do that again! I won't allow it.'

He sat on the front steps in the dark until Dana came home from her date. She was sniffing into a twisted scrap of handkerchief and her mascara had run into panda smudges. She made herself a mug of milky cocoa and poured a large saucerful for

Leopold. She knew where her father kept a hidden packet of chocolate biscuits and she helped herself, spreading out the remainder so that he would not notice the difference.

'Of course, I can never tell them about Roger,' she said to the cat, stroking his ears. 'They wouldn't understand about him not having any money, or a job. They'd never understand.'

Leopold daintily mopped up the fallen crumbs. No, they would never understand. The next morning, he was at the door, waiting to be let out, and streaked through the moment there was a crack. He spent all day practising, graduating from tree to taller tree. It was exhilarating. By mid-afternoon, he acknowledged what he had been wondering about ever since his miraculous escape from the big oak.

It was not simply this new skill which filled him with joy and excitement, but the fact that it held the key to something far more important – escape. He walked back to the house quite jauntily, not caring that his supper would not make up for missing breakfast.

'Caught yourself a little mouse for breakfast, did you?' asked the sleek woman, scraping the last globule of mush from the tin. 'There's a good pussy.'

Good pussy swallowed the revolting food. It was important now to keep up his strength. When he saw the family go out for the evening, he climbed on to the roof of the house, skirting the television aerial and leaping up on to the flat top of the chimney. He sat there for a long time, his tail neatly curled over his feet. It was not that he lacked courage; it was just that this was the first time he had contemplated jumping from anything other than a tree. And it might be that trees were a vital ingredient . . . however, he would never find out just by sitting.

He stepped off into space, automatically widening his paws, claws outstretched, tail stiffened, lifting his head. These movements slowed his free fall, then he leaned carefully into a wide arc, his brilliant eyes almost crossed with concentration. He glided across their garden, passed the dahlias, rising over the hedge, then soaring up as he came face to face with an overgrown rhododendron bush. The evening air was cool and peaceful as he locked into a pure, straight, calculated climb, his whiskers twitching as the wind resistance began to increase. He winked as he passed two alarmed starlings flying home to roost. As he topped the climb, he closed his paws, tucked his head down and streamlined his descent on to the flat roof of a neighbour's garage. Shaking with relief, he sat down and began to lick back his ruffled fur. He had done it. He did not need a tree.

After that, there was no stopping Leopold. He jumped off anything and everything. His greatest day was when he managed to climb into the church belfry and then up the narrow ladder that was steel-pinned to the side of the spire. There was precious little room at the top for him and the weathervane. The dim metal cock spun round, creaking, obviously out of control, almost knocking Leopold off his perch. Leopold took off in a perfect swallow, levelling out at about 100 feet without any effort. The thermals of air took him up higher and he gloried in the feeling of space and freedom. Below the neat rows of houses and gardens stretched for miles. Dark green patches of woodland were all that were left of the great forests which had once covered the hills. He flew over the top of the ugly grey gasometer, tracking for fun the snake-like train that swayed along the line. People were so small, wobbling along on matchstick legs, heads down, wrapped up in their worries and dreams. No one noticed a large ginger-and-white cat flying casually overhead.

He began to get more adventurous, exploring the countryside and neighbouring towns. He followed the river Thames to London, but did not stay long among the high-rise flats and skyscraper office blocks. The air traffic bothered him and the pigeons were rude.

'I've just seen a cat fly by,' said a stunned window cleaner in a cradle at the 21st floor of some offices.

'Fell out a winder,' said his pal morosely, wiping a dark mirrored pane of glass. 'Probably pushed.'

'It was flying. It was a ginger cat.'

'We gotta little tabby. Company for the missus.'

The window cleaner screwed up his eyes against the sun. Whatever it was was almost out of sight, skimming over the top of St Paul's dome, the cross sparkling in the bright rays.

Perhaps it was a ginger bird. He clamped his mouth shut and turned back to his work. He did not want to get his cards.

Of course, Leopold could not keep his secret forever. He began to get careless. The family gave a party with watered gin and cut-price whisky to celebrate the sleek man's latest promotion. As they cleared up, Leopold slid among the chairs looking for morsels of cocktail snacks. If they were anything like the general standard of catering in the house, most of the guests would have dropped them. He found a pathetic shrimp on a soggy toast finger stuffed behind a pot plant. It wasn't bad. The cheese they had used had been so stale and crumbly, it had parted company from the cubes of pineapple and there were lots of bits on the floor.

The sleek woman had also lashed out on a dip made from dried chicken soup and tinned cream. Not many people had dipped so there was a lot left. As she was scraping it all together and wondering if she could turn it back into soup, a big dollop slopped off her finger and fell on to the carpet. Leopold raced to the rescue.

'Gerrout the way! You damned cat! Look what you've made me do,' she stormed. She swiped at him with her morocco-bound visitors' book. (Someone had signed: 'Unbelievable party, darling.')

The book caught Leopold on the side of his head. Swift as a flash he spread his paws and leaped to the safety of the pelmet. The woman was furious and did not notice anything unusual about the ascent. She lashed out at him again and he took off, flying right across the room to a shelf on the other side.

'You wicked thing,' she shrieked, wondering if she had watered the gin enough.

'Mummy,' said Dana, opening the french doors to let out the smoke-laden air. 'I think Leopold can fly.'

Leopold soared out into the night air. He shared a gnarled oak with an old owl and contemplated the future. They knew now. Perhaps it would not matter. After all, what could it possibly mean to them? Habit was hard to break and, at breakfast time, Leopold nodded to the sleepy owl and took off for home. He flew down into the garden and sauntered up to the back door, casually twitching his tail.

'Darling,' cooed the woman, scooping him into her arms.

'Darling Leopold, you've come back to mummikins! Nice pussy, come and have some lovely milk.'

Leopold was thoroughly alarmed, squashed against her second-best jumper with the sequin buttons. She smelled of musk and face cream. He struggled but she was holding him very tightly. He heard the back door shut and it was the thud of doom.

They sold him to a circus. As he was being driven away in the back of the circus owner's Cortina estate, the sleek family was hugging each other with glee, waving the fat cheque and planning to buy more cars, more televisions and a holiday in the Bahamas.

Leopold quite liked the circus for about two days. They put him in a large cage that smelt of bear, and people came and looked at him, bringing delicious things like fish and chips, beefburgers and anchovy pizzas.

Then the circus owner put him on the scales and declared a diet. Leopold must not gain a single ounce. Aerodynamics he called it.

Leopold did not understand the circus. It was so bright and noisy with strange animals growling in the night. They did feed him better food than he was used to, though he suspected it was left over from the lion's share.

The trouble started when Miss Dora, the trapeze artist, refused to carry Leopold up the ladder to her platform high in the roof of the big tent. She absolutely refused even to touch him.

'I shall come out in a rash all over,' she said, every rhinestone on her brief costume quivering with indignation.

The circus hands rigged up a basket affair in which to hoist Leopold up to the platform. Leopold hated it. He felt sick as it swayed and jerked higher and higher up into the dim black regions of the roof. He stepped out on to the narrow platform and looked round politely. It was very high up indeed. Miss Dora stood as far away from him as possible.

'Shoo, shoo,' she said, her feathered headdress nodding with each word. 'Go away.'

Someone switched on a spotlight, blinding Leopold. He stepped sideways to avoid the brilliant white light and, disorientated, he fell off the platform. He fell, paralysed with fear, like a stone, and landed with a bounce in the safety net, all four paws and his head stuck through the mesh; it was very undignified.

'Now, Leopold,' said the circus owner, speaking slowly and deliberately. 'When you get up there on the platform I want you to fly across to the other platform.' Leopold looked back at him with puzzled green eyes. 'Fly across, like Miss Dora. Only you're a clever pussy and you don't need a trapeze bar.'

Miss Dora scowled. 'I don't like sharing my act with a cat. It's ignominious.'

Again Leopold was put into the elevator and swung up to the platform. Again he fell into the net. The sweat began to come out on the owner's brow. He had gambled a fortune.

This time Leopold rolled over and got into such a mess in the netting they had to cut it to get him out. He tried not to look smug as he returned to his cage.

'Please, pussy,' said the circus owner the next day, wringing his hands. 'Fly for me. I gotta lotta money tied up in you. You wouldn't want to see old Joss go bankrupt, would you?'

Miss Dora had covered her body thickly with an antibite ointment in order to protect herself from Leopold's deadly rash. The smell was awful. He couldn't stand it for two seconds. He launched himself off the platform at speed, did two fast circuits of the arena then, spotting the exit sign, made a beeline for the opening. He dipped stylishly over the big top before heading off towards the far country. He felt the faintest twinges in his paws as he climbed higher in the sky. He had never reached this altitude before. His tail streamed out behind him, his fur filled with air and the loose flaps of skin under his armpits belled out like a parachute.

Leopold was looking for the sea. He had had in mind for some time to learn to fly properly. He was a bit afraid of going to the mountains to find an eagle or a condor. They were so big and unpredictable. But seagulls, now they were a different kettle of fish. And there was no doubt about it, they could fly. Leopold's capacity would be one of an ardent observer.

He was quite surprised when he eventually found the sea. It was not at all as he had expected, just miles and miles of heaving wet blue waste. But the seagulls were there in their thousands, screeching and diving and squabbling among themselves. Leopold particularly admired their precision take-offs and landings on water.

He went down to the pebble beach to practise a few low-level take-offs, but each time he nose-dived straight into the sea. It was horrid, and he soon discovered that he could not fly very well if his fur was wet.

'Scram, scram,' shrieked the seagulls as Leopold went head-long into the waves yet again. He gathered his dignity round him like a wet bathrobe and climbed into the heather to dry off.

When he found the cliffs, he knew he had the answer. Their sheer height was impressive; the grandeur of the craggy rock face filled Leopold with quivering pride. This was going to be his home. He was going to be a cliff cat; he saw himself leaping about the rock face as sure-footed as Tarzan, catching his food among the gorse on the headland, sleeping in a small cave. He could watch the seagulls all day and learn their secrets. He would practise diligently from his cliff-top take-off, experimenting, and adapting their flight to his. It was going to be wonderful.

The seagulls were a bit alarmed by this peculiar, flying ginger thing. They knew cats ate birds but what sort of cat was this? They resorted to a Mafia-style protection racket, dropping Leopold the odd, freshly caught mackerel in return for paws-off. This suited Leopold admirably. He did not fancy a mouth-ful of wet feathers.

Leopold ate well. Fresh fish, rabbits and mice; the dew to drink from fragrant morning puddles shot with silvery sunshine. He was very happy.

His flying improved. He could stay in the air for much longer and with a lot less effort. He could glide in for touch-down with fanatical precision. He experimented with stalling in the air, letting himself fall, heart in mouth, then pulling himself out of it moments before hitting the waves. He skimmed along the surface of the sea with carefree abandon. He learned to loop the loop, to power dive like a blazing meteor; he perfected a victory roll, coming out of it to soar up into the blue sky until everything was so translucently blue that he could no longer tell which was sea and which were the heavens.

He was sailing along on one such routine flight, his thoughts to himself, when he discovered he could no longer see land. He circled around, his green eyes searching the horizon. He could see nothing solid or familiar. He flew slowly, wondering in which direction to make tracks. He had no idea how far this sea stuff went.

He began to get tired, flying in ever wider circles. Then he realized that the sun had gone and it was getting darker. He was not alarmed by this as he could see very well in the dark. But this was not the night. It was another kind of foreboding, grey gloom; the gathering of thunder clouds laden with rain.

Leopold looked up as he heard far-off rumbling. There was going to be one heck of a storm, and he was going to be caught in it. He knew what would happen when his fur got wet. He knew what would happen if he had to land on water. Zwat. Caput. End of Leopold.

He flew on bravely, his body aching. The first big drop of rain hit him squarely between his eyes. He blinked and adjusted his speed. He had to keep his head or this thing would beat him.

He tried to climb higher to get above the storm but it was too late. The thunder clouds were dark and menacing; flashes of lightning lit up the rolling masses of horror. He began to wish he had stayed with the circus, or perhaps even the sleek family.

The storm gathered into a seething black mass overhead; the rain began hitting him like sledgehammers. In minutes he was soaked, his fluffy fur plastered to his skin. He lifted his head, trying to maintain height. Fiercely Leopold fought to hold his own, relying on the months of practice to come to his aid now. But he was losing speed and losing height. The dark water below was surging in great white frothed waves, deep gullies sucking and swallowing each other. One bedraggled ginger-and-white cat would soon disappear beneath that hungry sea.

Leopold could hardly see now. His lids were glued by the onslaught of rain. He began to fall. As he fell, he mewed piteously . . .

'Jumping Jehova, if it isn't raining cats and dogs! There, my fine fellow, don't struggle. Mike Kelly's got you safe enough.'

Leopold found himself caught by strong arms that took the impact of his fall. It was a miracle. He must have fallen straight into the arms of a saint.

The saint was wearing glistening yellow oilskins and a brimmed sou'wester off which the rain was dripping. His lined and crinkled brown face had a pair of the bluest eyes Leopold had ever seen.

'And where did you come from? I suppose you done drop out of one of them aeroplanes? My word, we'd better take you down below and dry you off before you catch your death.'

Mike Kelly carried Leopold down into the tiny cabin and began to rub his coat with a rough towel. It was the smallest room Leopold had ever seen, cat-sized in fact. He looked around with interest. The room pitched and rolled in the strangest way, but it did not seem to disturb the man so it must be all right.

'Well, you're stuck here now,' Mike Kelly went on. 'Whether you like it or not. I'm sailing round the world and I shan't make landfall for weeks. You can get off then if you want to, or you can come back to Ireland with me. Please yourself. I'm easy. What do you think?'

Leopold had already made up his mind. No one had ever consulted him before, or treated him as an equal.

'I'm needing a ship's cat and a bit of company,' said Mike, opening a tin of evaporated milk. 'So you dropped in just right. You'll earn your keep and I reckon we'll get on . . .'

It was the beginning of a lifetime of devotion and mutual companionship. Leopold sailed all over the world with Mike, following him round strange foreign places and wintering sometimes in Southern Ireland in Mike's cottage while his catamaran was docked for repairs or maintenance, and the next voyage was planned.

The circus owner sued the sleek family for misrepresentation and the wrangling went on in court for years. Eventually the judge dismissed the case, saying it was useless to go on when neither party could produce the evidence, ie, the cat in question. The costs were enormous and the sleek family, who had spent the cheque, were rather silent as they made an appointment to see their bank manager. Dana did not go. Instead she ran off with Roger and went to live with him in a caravan.

Leopold did not entirely give up flying, though it took him some time to get his nerve back after that terrible storm. He made sure he did not fly too high, or too far away, realising that navigation was his weak point. He even perfected a new technique of a low level approach for a deck landing.

If Mike ever noticed his cat flying round the masthead, he was too tactful to mention it. Occasionally he was heard to mutter unsaintly comments about the Blarney Stone, or wonder if it was the Irish whiskey.

One day he vowed he'd write a book about Leopold, but then, who would believe him?

Cats of My Childhood

MAY EUSTACE

T HE NOSTALGIC longing for childhood days superimposes itself on everything I write.

> Why do I write,
> What sin to me unknown,
> Dipt me in ink,
> My parents' or my own?
>
> *Alexander Pope*

Looking back on my yesterdays is to me an exercise in solace and inspiration. No other human experience fills me with such delight. When I reminisce I forget all the cares of the world. I forget that I am getting old. I forget that I am now nearly altogether alone. I forget that I have tax forms to fill in and pension books to sign. I forget all the irritations of the present and enjoy again the old familiar haunts, with the old folks and the animals who first taught me how to live.

> I remember, I remember,
> The house where I was born,
> The little windows where the
> sun,
> Came peeping in at dawn.

Yes, those were the days. Clearly, as through a looking-glass, I see the old home, the gardens, the paddocks and rivulets. And I see the pathway, too, which leads to the river and the woods carpeted with bluebells, primroses and cowslips. And then – as if I ever could forget – I see my mother and father again. Mother's long black skirt is trailing in the dust and my father's moustache seems longer and bushier than before. They are speaking in whispers, as if they still have some unfinished business in hand. It was the business of love and sex. Our family was not yet complete.

And, fortunately for us children, our parents were so taken up with each other that they left us very much to our own devices. Within reason we could do what we liked. The same good fortune followed the cats. They were everywhere, males and females together, just living their own lives in their own sweet ways. I know that mother never had a kitten destroyed and there were many of them coming and going in all directions. If I had today's official standards of points I am sure I would have found, amongst them, Rexes and Havanas, Silver Tabbies and British Blues and Bi-coloureds galore.

I was only a small child when the seeds of cat enchantment were sown within me. Not in a namby-pamby way but in a studious and interested fashion, more becoming to an older child. And I repeat again that cats were everywhere. On a sunny day they came out in number, each selecting its very own sheltered and sunny spot. Ostensibly, none of these outdoor cats could claim from us a roof for their heads. We had our own recognized cat dynasty, which included the cat belonging to Rosey, our old housekeeper, and one or two others who scrounged their own kind of living. But we had plenty of surplus rations which we handed out freely to the strays.

But how many of these multi-coloured or self-coloured cats were really strays? There was one little tabby who always had her afternoon nap on my window sill. She basked in the sunshine like an oriental goddess. She felt and smelled good. Her ears stood up sharply and she had wisdom written all over her little striped face. She had a cute black nose which seemed to direct her always to the sun. I would not say that she was an over-friendly cat. she did not permit too many familiarities— one or two little rubs, a tickle under her chin, a gentle touch to her little thick tail. No more. She let me know she did not like my overtures and stood up and went away. I thought that an apt name for her would be Winny Silly.

Our next sunbather was the doorstep cat. He was pure black

and every inch a male. I was sure of this because I often heard Rosey using bad language towards him; nevertheless, he sat it out though his noxious presence angered the humans. He was quite an agreeable old fellow and permitted me to rub him down and tickle his chin. We called him Steptoe, not after the TV character we know today, but because of his location preference and also after our uncle. He was a very rich farmer and came to Kilkenny once a year. He did not trust anyone to do his buying and selling and when he came down the road on a fair day he had the biggest herd of cattle of all the farmers. He specialized in the Herefordshires and congratulated himself on being a quality breeder. He had only one weakness: he always celebrated a good sale with a good drink. He liked his whiskey neat and always ordered it in doubles. Mother did not seem to mind for she said it was his own money he spent and he could do what he liked with it – his pockets always bulged with £5 and £10 notes. When my father helped him into his cart he just dropped down in the straw like an asphyxiated pig and the pony went along home without any direction, keeping to his own side of the road and negotiating his entrance to the drive carefully.

But Steptoe held onto the step no matter who was coming and going, so long as it was sunny and warm. You were at liberty to step over him but not to displace him.

The barn cat was a black and white one and the most determined sunbather of the lot. He was not so distinguished-looking as Steptoe. His coat was rather coarse, there were odd smudges of white on his tummy and the tip of his tail was white for a good half-inch. He was domesticated, too, and never objected to having his whiskers pulled. Like the others, whose names were associated with their own selected habitat, we found that Barny was a heaven-ordained name for him. He always hung round the barn and it would appear that he had a special friendship for the little black Kerry cow who was house-bound until her calf was born. She was known to wander and had her calves in the most unlikely places. Once she actually gave birth while standing in a stream. Only by the merest fluke was she found in time. In the meantime, if the sun shone, Barny came out to enjoy it and, if the weather was bad, he went into the straw with the cow. Sometimes we did not see him around for a couple of weeks. He did not smell so much of cat as of cow dung.

With regard to smells and scents country folk are more discriminating than those born in towns. The scents of lilacs and roses could never obliterate the smells associated with animals. But Rosey had a town nose, really, and particularly disliked tom cat odour. If she got the slightest whiff she was away for the dog or for her switch.

Then there was the most beautiful of all the cats – the white Persian. I say 'beautiful', but I ought to have said 'could have been beautiful', for her coat was always very dirty. Her lovely fan-like tail was trailed in the dirt too. I am absolutely certain that she had blue eyes which she used to advantage – if ever a cat winked an acknowledgment it was Persi. Her favourite haunt was the stable where we kept the big brown stallion. He was an enormous fellow and generated a special kind of heat which appealed to cats. Persi did not have to cuddle up to him; you could always see the perspiration coming from his body. Though he was a noble beast, full of puissance and fertility, the occasion for him to prove himself never arose.

Besides those named there were also more cats hiding in the hay lofts and it only needed the sun to bring them out. It was interesting to see how the various cats reacted to weather changes. I do not know what Kilkenny weather is like now but I remember that, half a century ago, it was always raining. My mother pointed out that the ever-green grass and the lush vegetation everywhere was the result of the pleasant moist climate. She loved the rain. Once she went on a holiday to her brother in Wembley and she said the weather was too clammy and dry; she longed for the drip, drip, drip, that seemed to be going on forever round our old home. I can remember standing so often in the porch waiting for the sun to shine and my pal and I chanted the popular dirge, 'Rain, rain, go to Spain, and never come back again'. During these wet periods the cats disappeared altogether. All, of course, except our own cats who had managed to sequester themselves in some quiet corners. But no stray cats were allowed the comfort of Rosey's kitchen. She did not keep her hearth so beautifully polished and the surrounding brasses so exquisitely radiant and shining to dazzle the eyes of the strays. This inviting spot was hers and for her little cat alone. Even the house dogs on the payroll were not encouraged to loiter in the comforting glow from the turf fire and the logs.

It was really Nan that set our project in action. Nan was one of the songsters who was with me singing in the rain. She was also one of my best school friends and had a big heart for all cats.

'Where is Winny Silly today?' she asked, seeing the vacant corner.

'Funny you should ask as I was just wondering the same myself. Every time it rains she goes away. Suppose we try to find out where her second home is?' I replied.

'Yes,' said Nan, 'we will run after her next time she comes and decides to leave.'

'And there are others, too, who sit around in the sun for days at a time and as soon as the weather breaks – away they go. It would be fun to find out where they all live.' And there and then we embarked on a project which would establish for all time the true homes of all our visiting felines.

It was quite a few days before we could get our plan started. The weather had been most inviting and we saw all the cats in their sunbathing haunts. I told Nan that mother had prophesied that the low clouds now in the sky meant that rain was on the way. And she was right. Nan had barely arrived when the first drops fell. The first to really get the message was Winny Silly. She was away in a flash with the two of us after her. She jumped over the garden gate like a born athlete, wound her way along the hedge, through the woodside, in and out amongst the trees. We were both out of breath trying to keep up with her. To make matters worse Nan fell down a marshy slope and commenced to cry, 'I think I will go home. We'll never catch her, and I am so tired.'

But I dismissed her complaints and she soon stopped them and came running on with the same zest as she had at the start. We had Winny in sight when she took a sharp turn into the lane leading to the priest's house. We watched her let herself in through the window with such aplomb that we knew she was home. We waited round for a bit and she did not come out. So that was that. Our first query was solved: Winny Silly was the

priest's cat. Sunbathing on my windowsill meant nothing to her. She was there because she liked the shelter it afforded her. She had no love for stray humans. When life suddenly became hard, and the cruel winds of winter buffeted her about, she knew where she could find comfort – on the welcoming knees of the priest's housekeeper. Here food was plentiful and warmth abundant.

Finding Steptoe's domicile took a more exhaustive search. In the first place a few drops of rain were not enough to displace him. We watched him while he crouched miserably against the wall, while the rain lashed all about him.

'Come on Nan,' I whispered, 'I think he has had enough.' Yes. That was so. He was moving. First, he looked appealingly into Rosey's kitchen. The fire was sending out rays of warmth and light which made Steptoe's skin tickle in anticipation. But before he had as much as put a foot forward Rosey was after him like a ton of bricks.

'No stray cats here, please!' said Rosey in a language that Steptoe understood. He walked sulkily away. We wore heavy rain wear and Wellington boots and continued in Steptoe's wake. Once again he took the same route as Winny, but this time he passed the priest's house and went in the direction of the river. It was like a funeral march for, rain or no rain, Steptoe was in no hurry. He stopped several times for a smell of this and that. Then, quite unexpectedly, he stood in front of his own halldoor but this time it was not the usual kind of door – it was a door that one had to jump over and this abode was a houseboat of sorts. There didn't seem to be any welcoming hands coming out to fondle him; nevertheless, he climbed into the cabin, displaying a proprietorial air, and sat himself down. It was evident that this was his real home. No matter how desolate and dreary everything looked in the rain, we were satisfied that this was where Steptoe lived. Later, mother told us that an old fellow known as Joxer had laid claim to the boat after the death of the real owner. He was known to be respectable and did odd jobs for the farmers. He did quite a good bit of fishing, too, and if anyone wanted a nice fresh trout Joxer was their man.

We were very pleased to have found Steptoe's home. Now we had traced back two of our sunbathers. After that I often purloined some of Rosey's cat food for poor Steptoe because I felt he had a lean time on the boat. Miss Winny Silly needed no extra rations for she lived the life of a lady when she was not on our windowsill. She was well fed and well nourished from the generous table of the fat parish priest.

Now for Barny. His conduct was not always predictable. Sometimes for days he disappeared and then we saw him surreptitiously climb through the window of the cow shed. It was certain there was some sort of affinity between the little Kerry cow and him. When we did approach him he was always amiable and we were sure that he was not an abandoned stray. He was never ravenously hungry like Steptoe, so Nan and I agreed that he came from a good home. Yet we had not a single clue. Finding his home would be a hit-or-miss matter. Unlike Winny and Steptoe he was not driven away by the rain. When his sunbathing was disturbed he just went inside and played the waiting game with the little cow. He lay comfortably in the straw as if time did not matter. Nan and I decided that all we could do was wait. Surely this was wise, for by waiting we found out all we wanted to know about Barny. We were coming home from school one day when a little fellow called Tommy Docherty asked us if we would play a game of marbles with him. As we had never before been asked favours from boys, we agreed to do this.

'Hold on a minute,' said Tommy, 'I see Jimmy, our cat, coming home for his dinner.' And at that very moment we looked into the eyes of Cowshed Barny. So that was that, Barny – alias Jimmy – had a good home.

As we walked back Nan and I congratulated ourselves on establishing the real identity of Cat Number Three – Barny of the old barn – a cat who had fallen in love with our little cow.

The fourth cat, the dirty white Persian, was the most difficult of all to trace, for she never left the stable. When she was not sunbathing on the roof she was inside with the big horse. She really was a homeless stray as she never left our yard and she was the one cat that was never missing. She was always hungry and ate ravenously in a manner more becoming to a waif and stray than to her Persian forebears. I could never catch her. Nan and I saw her several times a day and we decided that, if we could catch her and clean her up, she would gain entry in to any society – and most certainly into Rosey's kitchen. The word 'Persian' was magic.

We told mother of the lovely white cat we saw in the stable and we were sure she was a Persian.

'Persian, indeed,' said mother, 'and how could a Persian cat be turned into a waif or stray?'

So 'Persian, indeed' was our most difficult quarry. To trace her was not going to be easy.

About this time Nan and I started our education proper at the convent school. No more frolics with Tommy Docherty and his kind. Every morning we walked nearly two miles, along footpaths, leafy lanes, through the woods and fields, passing the old church and graveyard, and up the hill to the convent. A little later mother got us our own pony and trap and we took him to school every day. It was very difficult getting permission to tie him up at the back gate and there was one thing we had to promise and that was that we must clean up every evening. The little nun who was in charge of the roses welcomed the good manure we placed so liberally on her rose trees. Driving backwards and forwards to school, with a car full of scholars, was amongst the proudest and happiest experiences of my early school life.

And soon, very soon indeed, there occurred the last and final key to our cat project. Reverend Mother's first address to the assembly included a request pupils to keep an eye out for her own very special white Persian cat, which had been missing for about a month.

'Did you hear that, Nan?' I whispered, 'could it possibly be Persi?'

Trembling all over I put my hand up to speak. 'Please, Mother, I think I know where there is a white Persian.'

'Speak up, child,' was her reply but I was not able to speak any louder and I was summoned to the table.

Then everything changed. Suddenly her voice sounded more kindly and the next thing I knew was that I was being sent home with big Alice, the convent cook. Yes, she immediately identified Fluffie, the convent cat. While the chase was on she told mother that she was a very special cat, having been imported (or rather smuggled in) from the home of a viscount in Le Mans – a special gift to Reverend Mother for services rendered to his daughter while boarding in the convent. Then Alice took mother aside and said that, being a female, she was becoming a real annoyance, especially when the male cat population of the town serenaded her all night. It took quite a little while to catch Fluffie as her month's freedom and life as a waif and stray had whetted her appetite for adventure. With the whole of our working staff guarding every exit from the stable, Alice dived headlong under the horse's belly and emerged with a much-bedraggled Fluffie.

Instead of settling down to be the angelic, white-robed creature she used to be, her stay in the outside world had unsettled her. She was no longer content to listen quietly to the angelus bells and the clanking of the rosary beads as the nuns came and went from their devotions. Celibate and happy though her owners might be, Fluffie was now rebellious. The quiet of the convent was shaken. After a serious conference in the community it was decided that Fluffie would have to move on – not as a horse's mate in a dull and depressing stable but as a companion for someone of importance in the town.

When Reverend Mother's wishes were made public the convent bell rang loud and often as hopeful hearts sought ownership of the most important cat in town. From several applicants Fluffie was presented to the mayor, for who better than the first citizen to win such a prize?

But now the real fun started. On the night of arrival Fluffie escaped up the chimney and it looked as if she would be impossible to catch, so the First Lady sent out a series of SOS. The mayor himself was quickly on the scene and, when he looked up the chimney, he was soon blinded by soot that had been displaced by the cat. More and more SOS to civic dignitaries and others. The district nurse outran the doctor and arrived in time to shout: 'Oh, your Lordship! Your poor, dear Lordship! Water, soap, castor oil and brandy! Quick!'

It did not take Ellen, the district nurse, many minutes to get things under control. She cleaned up the mayor, cheered up the mayoress, nipped the wee brandy and went after the cat. By this time Fluffie was in a more agreeable mood and was not so difficult to catch.

'You may take her if you want,' stammered the mayor, 'she is too much for me with my civic duties.'

And so Fluffie became the nurse's cat.

It is so many years ago that I cannot remember all the details but I know that, after her weekly bath, her coat was as white as snow. She was as sweet as she was handsome – and nurse watched carefully over her morals. The occasional tom who picked up her trail ran for his life if ever he saw nurse appear, so there were never any little Fluffies to carry on the name.

And that was how it was in my youth. Cats and everything to do with them were so much fun.

A Vet's Life

JOHN BOWER

'**M**RS JONES is on the telephone. Apparently her cat has just jumped off the sofa and its tail has dropped off!' My very able nurse had never delivered a more unusual or macabre message than that. At this stage I decided to speak to Mrs Jones myself as obviously there was some mistake – such a thing could not happen. It had! Mrs Jones's description of the furry object, about nine inches long, which was no longer part of Blackie the cat, left me in no doubt at all. I suggested she should bring both parts of Blackie in to my surgery where I hoped I could resolve the problem.

Blackie had indeed jumped off the sofa and lost his tail. About three weeks earlier, Blackie had been involved in a road accident from which he appeared to recover fairly rapidly. He had not regained the use of his tail, however, due to a 'stretch fracture' at the base of the tail. This type of fracture is caused by a car tyre trapping the tail while a cat is still crossing the road at speed. This had, in this case, led to the death of the tail but not of Blackie. A minor cosmetic operation was needed to tidy up what was left of Blackie's tail and Blackie was as good as new – certainly a few inches better off than a Manx cat.

Cats do have problems with their tails. They seem to pay dearly for the extra bit of balance that the tail may give them. I always think of tail injuries as happening to cats that nearly got away with it. The tail, as I mentioned, is a fairly common site for a road accident injury. It is also often involved in injuries sustained in fights with other cats – presumably, either in cowardly cats which were running away at the time (too slowly), or possibly in cases in which the aggressor unfairly pounced from behind.

In the surgery, cats can be more difficult to handle and restrain than dogs. If a dog is a little fractious it is possible to muzzle it to prevent a bite and, of course, its claws are relatively harmless. A cat, however, can only be muzzled with extreme difficulty and usually distress is caused. The result is less co-operation than if it were not muzzled, and its claws can inflict most unpleasant wounds to the veterinary surgeon, the nurse or the owner. To reprimand a dog when necessary can help; in the case of cats it only makes the situation worse. Patience is the only real answer apart from a sedative when really necessary. Luckily for the profession, the attitude of the owner of an unco-operative cat is usually sympathetic to the veterinary surgeon. This varies from the mild, 'Do be careful, he may bite and scratch you', to the blunt, 'Don't trust him— he's a tiger.' This latter type of cat is usually brought in to the surgery trussed up in a small bag with perhaps his head protruding. One client of mine brings his cross-Siamese (very cross Siamese!) into the surgery from the waiting room by holding onto the scruff of the neck only. In this way the cat is brought in with all four legs and eighteen claws rigidly extended, teeth bared and a continuous, meaningful, warning growl coming from its mouth. I was horrified the first time this happened and tried to explain to the client that there were better ways of carrying his cat. However, a short abortive attempt to demonstrate other ways with his cat convinced me otherwise! I now see this cat only at his home, where he is considerably better behaved.

Some cats are great believers in the saying that attack is the best method of defence. The minute they are placed on the consulting table they make a determined attempt to climb up the person examining them. This is a highly effective method of avoiding an examination. Equally effective is the raised attacking forepaw when a hand comes anywhere near them. But once the cat is restrained by the scruff of the neck gently on the table, then it is usually possible to carry out a thorough examination.

A separate waiting room for cats away from their canine cousins is a sound idea in a veterinary practice, although this is not always possible owing to shortage of space. Certainly cats are more relaxed in such surroundings than sandwiched between a great dane and a wolfhound. It is always much safer to bring a cat to a surgery in a cat basket or zipper bag than just to carry it or wrap it in a towel. This minimizes any risk of escape which we all know can and does happen, and also ensures that the cat does not obtain such a close view of his neighbours in the waiting room.

I recall one escape with amusement now but great concern at the time that it happened. The surgery had finished and I was just contemplating a quiet evening when the door bell rang. At the time I lived above the surgery so there was no escape during off-duty hours. I answered the door and found a client holding her cat closely to her without even so much as a towel wrapped round it. The owner had misread the surgery hours and was presenting the cat for a routine check on a fractured leg which I had encased in a plaster cast the previous week. The poor cat took one look at me, realized immediately who I was and took off. The owner struggled to hold it but to no avail and within three seconds the cat had disappeared down the path, limping at lightning pace. I say limping because a quick look at the owner revealed that she was still holding the plaster cast! This was the one part of the cat that she had grasped when he struggled, to try to prevent him from escaping, but the Houdini had pulled his leg out of it and bolted! The story has a happy ending which is why I can now look back on it with amusement. Houdini limped straight home and was promptly returned to the surgery in a zipper bag. I applied a further plaster cast and within four weeks his leg was as good as new.

The most astonishing escapologist I ever handled was a ginger tom called Sandy. Sandy lived in a small coastal fishing village and, true to form on a Saturday evening, ate a piece of mackerel which unfortunately still contained the hook. This inevitably caught in Sandy's throat and my services were needed. This was no simple matter; the hook was anchored firmly in the throat and Sandy was in no way appreciative of my efforts to remove it. There was no alternative but to take him back to the surgery for a general anaesthetic in order to remove the hook. Sandy was popped into a strong wicker basket and placed in the back of my estate car. The sliding windows of the estate were closed. After a few miles I decided to telephone the surgery to make sure there were no further urgent calls on the way back. Luckily there were not. On my arrival at the surgery, I lifted the basket out of the car and noticed that it was surprisingly light. Sandy had gone! The car, of course – he must be in the car! But I could feel myself beginning to panic. Mislaying a patient is not a common occurrence and I was hoping that this was a false alarm. It was not – Sandy was not in the car either. One sliding back window was now open. While I had stopped to make the telephone call, Sandy had escaped from an escape-proof basket (I have since decided that no wicker baskets are escape-proof!), opened one of the sliding windows and absconded. All of this at least ten miles from his home, on the wrong side of a very wide estuary, and with a fish hook in his mouth. I think it was at this stage that I nearly joined the Ministry – and not the Ministry of Agriculture at that!

How was I to explain this to his devoted owners? I decided that there was no substitute for the truth, which I proceeded to tell them over the telephone. The news was received with unbelievable calm and equanimity, and apologies for not telling me that Sandy would open sliding doors, cupboards and windows. I assured them that I would alert all the other veterinary practices, RSPCA and police. This I proceeded to do but, of course, none of them at this stage could help.

Three weeks later the RSPCA inspector arrived out of the blue with Sandy (dear, lovable Sandy) whom he had just picked up on the other side of the estuary from that on which he had been lost. I cannot explain to this day whether Sandy is a strong swimmer or had, in fact, jumped out of the moving car nearer to my surgery than I originally thought. Anyway, Sandy was back and looking fat and healthy at that, but with the fish hook still firmly embedded in the back of his mouth. He had obviously managed to eat well despite the presence of the hook. I rapidly administered a general anaesthetic and removed the hook. Sandy was then returned to his surprisingly

grateful owners and I exchanged all my wicker cat baskets for fibreglass ones.

I suppose this escapology is one aspect of intelligence in cats. It varies from cat to cat and my own three Siamese demonstrate quite clearly how the application of intelligence can vary. Guilia and Sadie are mother and daughter, and make up a very efficient door-opening team. They cannot open a door with a round knob but are experts at door handles. Sadie, being younger and fitter, jumps up at the handle and pulls it down with both forepaws as she falls to the ground, while Guilia, with precision timing, scrapes at the base of the door when the handle is depressed and opens it. They are so good at this that I have had to reverse the door handles of rooms which are forbidden to cats. The lounge falls into this category as the cats regard the lounge suite as their scratching posts. Rudyk, our third Siamese, has found an answer to this door provided we are in the lounge. He has noticed that, when the front door bell rings, we open the lounge door to go to answer it, which is when he nips in. He has also noticed that, in the bedroom upstairs, is an old-fashioned tassel pull to a bell which used to summon the maid in some past era, and that both bells sound alike. Amazingly, he has put two and two together and, when he wishes to come into the lounge, he runs upstairs, pulls the tassel, waits until one of us opens the lounge door to answer the front door and into the lounge he goes. We had not the heart to disconnect this bell.

Some of the more amusing incidents in the course of a working day are concerned with the sex of the cat and the problems arising if the owner is wrong about it. I see male cats called Sue and females called Jason but, luckily, a substantial proportion of Fluffys and Blackies, names which could apply to either sex. Owners can become quite indignant if told that the cat is not the sex that they thought it was. I recall a huge, obviously masculine, tabby with the typical male development of the cheeks and wide head, being presented at the surgery for the spay operation. I pointed out tactfully that spaying was the term applied to the female operation but that the male operation was called castration. To this the owner pointedly replied that she was aware of this and her cat was, of course, female. I rapidly checked that my original impression of the masculinity of the cat was biologically correct (which it was) and, feeling quite relieved, reassured the owner that the cat was indeed male. 'But it can't be,' replied the owner, 'it's called Tinker-belle.'

The terms used for these routine operations are also great fun when modified by clients. Female cats are brought in to be splayed or sprayed; males to be incarcerated or castigated, while either sex can be brought in to the surgery to be neutralized or nurtured. One proud owner presented a superb little kitten and exclaimed, 'I want to know whether it is a boy or a girl and if it is a girl I want it incarcerated.' She was obviously terribly confused!

These operations are perfectly routine and side-effects are virtually nonexistent. In the case of dogs, bitches occasionally put on weight when spayed but only if fed too much of the wrong food. Cats, however, seem to regulate their body weight by correct feeding and exercise. Very few cats become highly overweight. An exception is a neuter male I am at present treating for a bladder complaint. He weighs 36 lbs. When one considers that 10lbs is a fairly healthy weight for a normal male, this one is obviously grossly overweight. He somewhat resembles a miniature seal and is so wide that, when he sits lengthways along a wall, one front leg hangs down on each side of the wall. How he manages to climb the wall I have no idea! Apart from his present problem, which is not associated with his obesity, he remains active and healthy and loving with his owners. He does, however, resent my presence and interference for some reason and tries to make life difficult. Because of the amount of fat under his skin, he has no scruff, as this is obliterated by the fat. The scruff of the neck in cats was designed purely and simply for veterinary surgeons to hold onto while examining the cat and, when it is nonexistent, restraint of the cat becomes a major problem.

Some cats, however, appear to like and respect us. A colleague tells me of a blue-point Siamese cat called Buttons, brought to his surgery by his owners who live only a few doors away. Buttons had an injury to one ear, causing a large blood blister which had to be drained under an anaesthetic and then sutured to prevent its filling up again. The sutures are passed through the ear flap and knotted through a button to prevent the nylon suture pulling through the skin. Thereafter, Buttons used to arrive on his own at the surgery about every third day to have his buttons checked and finally removed. The only time his owners came with him was the first time.

The life we lead is sometimes exhausting but invariably rewarding. It is very satisfying to see patients recovering: to see Ginger running and climbing again after having sustained a broken leg in a road accident; to see Suki and kittens thriving after a Caesarean operation; to see Sandy recover from the slug-bait poisoning or even feline influenza. We do get attached to our patients but, as cats do not live to our life span, we necessarily see most of our patients pass on eventually over the years. It is very sad to see an old patient pass away when one can remember delivering him or her what seems like only yesterday. It is an interesting life, however, and the many bright moments brought about by such incidents as I have mentioned, either by the apparent wit of the cat or often the wit of the owner, send one home chuckling at the end of a hard day.

Gershwin

JUDY GARDINER

L ADDY SILVER sat looking out of the window and thinking that next year he would be seventy. The idea struck him as preposterous. He didn't look old, neither did he feel it except for a tendency towards heartburn when he stooped. Then it occurred to him that it wasn't people who changed so much as the things they did. Once he had been a dance-band leader, Laddy Silver and his Syncopated Rhythm, playing at the Savoy, the Dorchester, the Trocadero and once at Buckingham Palace at a private supper party. And he was still capable of running a band if anyone wanted him to. He was a good tenor sax player, musical arranger and businessman, but nobody wanted dance bands any more because nobody wanted to dance. At least, not properly.

So Laddy lived a life of enforced retirement in a block of flats in North Finchley with his wife Dolly. And Dolly hadn't changed either, except to become a little fatter and a little more disparaging. They had met when she auditioned as a girl vocalist, and they still had the record she made of *Two Dreams Met* in a very young voice with a throb in it. But he hadn't let her sing any more after they were married because it would have been bad for her status as Mrs Laddy Silver.

He looked across at her now, on this long sunny afternoon filled with nothing but thoughts and the prospect of a cup of tea and a slice of chocolate torte at four o'clock. She was lying back in her chair with her shoes off and her mouth slightly open, and one hand was curved protectively round Gershwin, their cat.

'Gershhh . . .' whispered Laddy, forming his lips into a funnel. The cat opened lazy eyes and regarded him speculatively for a moment before going back to sleep.

'Who's Daddy's lovely boy then, eh? Daddy's lovely big boy, are we? . . .' His whispering seemed to float on the air and he watched it tickle at Gershwin's ears with a beady satisfaction. 'Coming for a little walkies, Gersh?'

'Why don't you shut up?' mumbled Dolly without opening her eyes. The hand that was round Gershwin moved upwards and began to rub the area around his neck with a drowsy expertise.

'He oughtn't to sleep so much,' Laddy complained. 'He's a fine strong cat and he ought to get about more.'

He turned his attention to the window, craning down to see into the garden. 'Here comes little Miss Whatsit. She's got a string bag full of shopping – looks like mainly vegetables.'

'Go and put the kettle on.'

'Which could be why she's so thin. Vegetables don't give you an ounce of fat, they just pass straight through.'

He went out to the kitchen, which was as warm and torpid as the lounge. A lone fly buzzed on the window. He made the tea, then stacked the tray with cups and saucers, milk and sugar and two plates each containing a hefty slice of chocolate torte.

Dolly was awake now and pushing her flimsy, silver-pink curls back into position. She gave Laddy a calm, distant look.

'Got his as well?'

Without replying Laddy placed the saucer of milk on the carpet between them, then bent down and stirred half a teaspoonful of sugar into it. Dolly poured the tea, and they drank it in silence while Gershwin strolled over to his saucer and inspected its contents with care.

'There's been a train disaster in Canada,' Dolly said through a mouthful of torte. 'But I don't think it's anywhere near Joe.'

'Canada's a big place,' Laddy said.

'Joe's thirty-five.'

'Thirty-six on the 5th of September.'

'I know when my own son's birthday is.'

'He's my son too.'

'We must remember to send him a card this year . . .'

Gershwin finished his milk and wiped round the saucer with his tongue. He washed his hands and face then went over to Laddy and jumped on his lap.

'Where's Daddy's lovely boy, eh? Go little walkies, shall we?'

'I wonder if Joe's got a girl,' Dolly said. Then added sharply: 'Don't hold him upside down when he's full of milk.'

'He's not upside down. He's just lying on his back in my arms.'

'For an animal to lie on its back *is* being upside down to *it*,' Dolly said, and although Laddy continued to rub Gershwin under the chin for a few moments longer, he restored him to an upright position.

'More tea?'

'No thanks.'

Conversation died.

Between the block of flats and its driveway there was a wide strip of garden which had been planted with grass, roses, and some silver birches. Considering that the North Circular was only round the corner, the sound of traffic was minimal.

Having walked as far as the garages at the back of the flats, Laddy turned and began to pace back again, pausing every now and then for Gershwin to stare at whatever caught his attention.

'It must take a lot of patience to train a cat to a collar and lead,' said a voice, and Laddy recognized little Miss Whatsit who lived somewhere on the fourth floor. Seen close to, she had a fresh-skinned face with a bright, rather artless expression, and her age was probably no more than twenty. He noticed that she had changed her dress for a pair of jeans and that she was carrying a magazine. They had never spoken before, only smiled.

'It depends on the cat,' Laddy said. 'This one's very intelligent.'

She bent down and held out her fingers to Gershwin who sniffed them courteously before turning away.

'If animals can't adapt to an urban society they're doomed.'

'You could say the same for humans,' Laddy said. 'If you

brought Queen Victoria back she'd choke to death on diesel fumes within a couple of hours.'

'Not if she was at Balmoral,' the girl said. Then added: 'What's your cat's name?'

'Gershwin. After my favourite composer.'

'I like Tchaikovsky,' she said, 'but you couldn't call a cat that, could you?'

'Don't see why not,' Laddy replied, and wished she would go away. To discourage her he sat down on one of the garden seats and stared hard at a bed of roses, but she sat down beside him, riffling the pages of her magazine.

'I work at the Maudsley Hospital,' she said, 'and I finish at three every afternoon this week.'

'That's nice,' he murmured, and couldn't be bothered to ask what sort of work she did. Or even to ask what her name was. It struck him that he had grown to prefer Gershwin's company to that of almost everyone else.

'I'm a physiotherapist,' she said.

'Uh-huh . . .'

Having examined the four legs of the seat with scrupulous care, Gershwin sprang lightly on to Laddy's lap and began butting his head gently against his hand. Late sunlight smiled in his eyes.

The girl opened her magazine and began to study a knitting pattern, then her attention wandered and she sat watching Laddy's hand caressing Gershwin's ears with an easy rhythm.

'Have you got any children, Mr, er—?'

'A son called Joe who lives in Canada. And the name's Laddy Silver.'

He didn't expect it to mean anything to her, not at her age. With every year that passed, fewer and fewer people betrayed any sign of recognition when his name was mentioned. Nevertheless, something made him add: 'At one time I had a dance band.'

She closed her magazine and sat looking at him with unashamed curiosity.

'How interesting. My grandad once had a letter from Roy Fox.'

'Did he,' said Laddy on a falling note. Not wishing to hear any more he uncoiled Gershwin's lead, set him on his feet and led him back home. Going up in the lift to the first floor he wondered whether the girl knew that Roy Fox had been dead for quite a while.

'Nice to talk to, is she?' asked Dolly, who was in the kitchen mashing Gershwin's boiled fish with a fork.

'Who?'

'Little Miss Whatsit.'

Several answers came to mind. *About on a level with you*, was one of them, but it seemed that she didn't expect him to reply because she began calling Gershwin to come for his supper.

And that was it: Gershwin never needed calling for supper, especially when the scent of boiled fish tinted the atmosphere. He was always present and correct, weaving a vigilant arabesque in and out of her feet and exhorting her to hurry in his high eunuch miaow.

But not this evening. Without speaking they hurried through the flat – the lounge, the bedroom and the bathroom, but there was no sign of him. Only the ping-pong ball by the coffee table and a round flattened patch on Laddy's bathrobe, where he sometimes liked to sleep for a change.

'Gershwin! . . . Gershie, *Gershie!*—'

Simultaneously they arrived at the open front door, open no more than a couple of inches. They glared at one another with hate.

'You didn't close it when you brought him back—'

'Look—' Laddy said, darting back to the lounge to seize the freshly folded evening paper. 'You opened the door to the newsboy while I was in the john—'

'I didn't – that was last night—'

Frantically they tried to disentangle one uneventful evening from another. Sometimes one of them opened the door to the newsboy and other times he shoved the paper through the letterbox.

'Never mind – it doesn't *matter!*'

Without waiting for the lift Laddy sped downstairs with Dolly scuttling rapidly behind him. They flung themselves through the big swing doors that gave on to the drive, and there was a moment of summer evening sweetness with even a blackbird singing before the squeal of tyres and the slam of a car door. And the silence that followed was total. Even the blackbird stopped in mid-phrase.

The car was a blue Renault and the man had come to a party in flat 63. He got up from his knees in front of the car holding Gershwin in his hands like a little fur rug.

'I didn't stand a chance . . .' Although he was a large man he sounded like a shocked child. 'I'd slowed right down but he ran straight under the front wheels . . .'

Ashen-faced, Laddy took Gershwin on his outstretched arms and stumbled away, conscious that Dolly was gasping and trying to touch the motionless body.

Without saying anything to the man, or to one another, they took him back to the flat and laid him tenderly on the kitchen table. There was no movement, no sound. He looked as if he were asleep except that his eyes – their habitual vivid green— were still half-open.

'Gershie . . . Oh, little Gershie . . .'

'Get the vet – ring the vet—'

'What've they done to you, little baby?'

No movement, no sound. A soft, still-warm body encased in sleek fur. Helplessly, Laddy groped between the front paws for the heart but couldn't find it.

'The kiss of life!—' Dolly tried to insert a trembling, red-nailed finger between the jaws, then bent her head and blew explosively into the neat little pink nostrils. Dazed as he was, it struck Laddy as a ludicrous thing to do.

'Don't,' he rasped. 'Can't you see he's already gone?'

She gave a deep choking sob and they stood shoulder to shoulder, watching the light fade from the green silver of Gershwin's eyes. It was like watching night fall.

'He's really died,' Dolly said in a disbelieving croak and, although the tears were running down their cheeks, it was a terrible effort to move, or even to think.

'Come on,' Laddy managed to say finally, and blunderingly dried Dolly's face with the tea towel that hung on the airer. It was the first physical contact between them since Christmas, when he had kissed her on the ear and given her a bottle of bath oil. Passively she allowed him to lead her back into the lounge, and even attempted to swallow a little brandy when he pressed the glass to her lips.

'He's dead. One minute he was alive and now he's dead,' she intoned like a woman in a trance.

'I can't take it in,' Laddy said brokenly. 'It'll be years before I can really take it in . . .'

They had two brandies each before they were able to go back to the kitchen, steeling themselves to face the horror of Gershwin lying dead on the table. But there he was, and the coldness of death was already overtaking the warm supple beauty around which had been built two private, middle-aged worlds.

Dolly wanted to have him buried under one of the silver birches down in the garden and became furiously indignant when permission was witheld on the pretext that, if everyone in the flats wanted a pet interred in the garden, it would cause a health hazard. Then they learned that, in Golders Green, there was an animal cemetery where Gershwin could be laid to rest in a plot reserved especially for cats, with dogs buried at a discreet distance away and the more non-conformist creatures such as guinea pigs and parrots planted in a corner by the entrance gate.

The foam-quilted box cost them £15 and the little headstone with his name engraved on it another £25 (cheques made payable to Elysian Fields Ltd), but at least it was somewhere peaceful and beautiful, and the thought of it brought them comfort.

Returning home from the funeral they found themselves confronted by Gershwin's basket, his collar and lead and his plate and saucer. The basket they hid away, but the empty space it left was so poignant that they brought it out again, even though they avoided looking at it.

'It's all so empty without him.'

'You've still got me,' Laddy said, attempting a joke. They sat looking at one another dubiously.

At tea-time Laddy went out to the kitchen and prepared the tray, wincing when his hand automatically reached for Gershwin's saucer. He cut two large slices of apple cake.

'They said we can go back there any time we like,' Dolly said. She was sitting in her chair with her shoes kicked off. 'They said they like to feel that people go back there any time they want to be with their – their little . . .' Her eyes filled.

'We'll visit him once a week,' Laddy said. 'Twice, if you like.'

Sniffing, she poured the tea, and they both sat staring at the floor between them where Gershwin's saucer was normally placed. They wondered what they were going to do with the rest of their lives.

'A lot of people from the flats have stopped me and said how sorry they were to hear about him. They all said how much they'll miss seeing him go for his little walk in the garden with me.'

'I used to take him sometimes,' Dolly said. 'I used to love taking him for a little walk whenever you'd let me.'

'I never stopped you. You always said you couldn't walk because of your feet.'

'I've got very high insteps.'

'Drink your tea,' he said. 'And eat your cake.'

She tried to, then pushed them aside. 'I can't. I feel I'd choke.'

During the silence that ensued Laddy turned and looked out of the window. The silver birches were swaying in a soft breeze.

'We've got to pull ourselves together,' he said finally. 'The show's still got to go on.'

'Sounds like the old days,' Dolly said tonelessly. 'Broken-hearted clowns, and all that.'

'Which reminds me of a slow foxtrot,' Laddy said, and began to hum in a quavering, experimental way.

'Eat your cake and drink your tea.'

'I can't,' he said. 'I can't, any more than you can.'

'Well, stop making that stupid noise.'

The next silence lasted for five minutes and was only broken by the creak of Laddy's kneecap as he got up from his chair. He went over to the cocktail cabinet and returned with the bottle of brandy and two glasses.

'What's that for?'

'Us. If we can't face tea, we'd better find a substitute.'

Dolly looked doubtful. 'That's what we had on the day – on the day—'

'He died. Yes, I know.' Laddy poured two tots and passed

one across to her. 'Drink up. It's just to help us over the worst.'

They sat listening to the distant murmur of the North Circular.

'I had a rabbit when I was a little girl,' Dolly said in a calmer voice. 'But the dog next door got it.'

'That was awful,' Laddy studied her with sudden attention. 'Didn't your Dad complain?'

'He couldn't. He was away.'

'He was away a lot, wasn't he?'

That's how it is with commercial travellers.'

'Ah, yes,' said Laddy. 'Mine was a gents' outfitter and he had his busy times, too. Just before Ascot he never slept at all.'

'You're talking as if I never met him. I met him at our wedding and when Joe was christened, only I don't think he liked me.'

'He liked you very much.'

'I sometimes get the feeling that nobody likes me very much.'

'I like you,' Laddy said. Then he gave a heavy sigh when he remembered that this was the time of day when he always took Gershwin for a walk.

As there was no point in going on his own he poured another brandy for them both. The summer light faded and lonely shadows gathered in the corners of the room.

'I wish you'd let me go on singing,' Dolly said. 'I'd only just got started when I had to stop.'

'You got married.'

'I could still have gone on singing.'

'Then you had Joe. What about him?'

'Girls manage careers these days as well as husbands and children, so why couldn't they then?'

'Because everything was different. Men liked looking after their wives in those days.'

'You married beneath you,' Dolly said. 'That's why you kept me in the background.'

'Baloney,' said Laddy. 'There's no social difference between a commercial traveller and a gents' outfitter, is there?'

'No, but you were Laddy Silver, weren't you?'

'Laddy Silver.' Raising his hands he stroked with sudden

bitterness at the little wisps of hair still struggling to maintain a foothold on his cranium. 'Who the hell was Laddy Silver?'

Without replying Dolly got up from her chair and went through to the bedroom. He heard the squeak of the cupboard doors, then she returned with a heavy leather suitcase thickly covered with travel labels. She put it on the floor between them and, puffing slightly, sat down beside it. The locks clicked open and she began to rummage beneath the open lid.

'Don't,' Laddy said.

'That was Laddy Silver,' she said, and laid a photograph on his lap. The man in it had thick black hair that gleamed like a wet roof, a white bow tie poised on an immaculate dress-shirt and a cigarette holder held between delicately manicured fingers.

'When I told my mother we were getting married, she said, what's the catch? What's he marrying you for when he could have a debutante? I said I didn't know, and she said, well, watch your step. A man in his position wouldn't marry a girl like you if he hadn't got some ulterior motive.'

'You were little and thin, with big eyes and a way of putting over a lyric that no other girl ever had except Ella,' Laddy said. Leaning forward he drew out a handful of publicity stills, of old dinner-dance programmes and a photograph of the band waving from the deck of the *Queen Mary*.

'It hurts,' he said, looking through them. 'No use pretending it doesn't.'

'We haven't been through them for years,' Dolly said. 'Not since Joe was in a skiffle group.'

'Little boy Joe,' Laddy said. 'Remember how I used to play him a lullaby?'

'I remember. He was the only person I wasn't jealous of.'

'There was never any need to be jealous. I only ever loved you, and I dressed you in mink to prove it, didn't I? All mink you were, from head to toe.'

'But all those women who wouldn't leave you alone. Society women giving you gold cigarette cases, waiting outside the hotel suite and freezing me with hate when I came out instead of you . . .'

She sat by the suitcase absently rubbing the cramp in her bulbous calves, unaware that he had left the room until the first notes of music crept through the open door. He was hunched on the side of the bed with the tenor sax catching the last gleam of light. He hadn't played for years, and the first experimental scale sounded husky and hesitant, then like the moon sliding from behind a bank of cloud the notes sang clear and silver sweet.

Speechlessly she staggered to her feet and stood leaning against the bedroom doorway with her face tilted blindly towards the sound. He played the lullaby for little Joe, breathing the sounds like a sigh before wandering on through the tunes that still carried the elegant dinner-jacket charm of the Savoy, the Dorchester and the old Trocadero.

She sang with him, but only in her mind, and when the final tune was no more than a bitter-sweet echo in the room she opened her eyes like someone awakening from a long sleep.

'That was Gershwin.'

'I know,' he said, laying the sax carefully back in its velvet-lined case. 'I meant it as a kind of tribute.'

She went over to him and he opened his arms. Sitting on the bed he only came up to her chest, and she found herself kissing with sudden passion the bony cranium with its poor little wisps of hair.

They fell backwards, sideways, crying because of Gershwin and laughing because it was all so crazy and because they weren't sure whether they still could any more.

'Listen, sweetie,' Laddy said next day. 'I've got news.'

'Uh-huh?'

They were having breakfast in their bathrobes, a thing they hadn't done for years. The voice of the blackbird came in through the open window.

'We're going to Canada to see Joe. We'll phone him tonight. We could fix a cheap flight, and now that we're – we've no commitments—'

'Now that Gershwin's dead,' she said, dry-eyed.

'Now that we're free, what's to stop us? After all, Joe's our baby. Our real baby—'

'Suppose he doesn't want us? Maybe he's tied up with some woman—'

'Aahh—' Busily he buttered his toast. 'You women are always on about other women. So maybe Joe's got a woman— after all, he's thirty-five and human – but what's that got to do with his poor old Momma and Poppa going to pay him a visit, huh?'

The years had fallen away; Joe was in the forefront of their thoughts in the same way that Laddy had unwittingly slipped back into the transatlantic slang of the dance-band days. He looked across at Dolly in her white towelling bathrobe and silver-pink curls and called her a cutie.

They discussed the idea of going to Canada with steadily increasing enthusiasm, and after more coffee and toast worked out that it would be silly not to ring Joe with the good news straight away. So they rang him, oblivious of the fact that for him it was three o'clock in the morning.

'Joe – hey, Joey – this is Daddy! This is your old Poppa—'

'Christ, England,' said a blurred voice. 'What's wrong?'

'Nothing's wrong,' roared Laddy, 'except that the old gal and I are coming out to see you! We can come any time, so just give the word . . .'

They talked for fifteen minutes, during which time Joe woke up and said he'd be glad to see them only they mustn't expect things to be the same as they were when he went away. He was a grown man now, and things changed, didn't they?

'Of course they do—' cried Dolly, leaning over Laddy's shoulder and blasting his eardrum. 'Things have changed for us, too, and we'd so love to see you, Joe baby—'

When the line clicked they stood looking at one another with happy tears in their eyes, then Laddy shaved and dressed and set off for the travel agent while Dolly washed the breakfast things and dusted around.

'But I still think it's a risk,' she said, when he returned with a collection of coloured brochures. 'We haven't seen Joe since he was twenty-two—'

'And we're going to be there for his birthday on the 5th of September,' Laddy said.

They sat down and began to plan the details.

'We'll be there to see the Indian summer and you'll have to set to and make him a birthday cake. I bet he's never had a bit of decent cake since he left home.'

'What'll I wear? He'll think I'm so old . . .'

'He'll love you,' Laddy said, very seriously. 'Just as much as I do.'

If only he'll love me like he did when he was little, she thought. She could see him so clearly, even without closing her eyes.

They booked the flight, checked the state of their bank account and laughed incredulously at their old passport photographs. Then Laddy sat down to write a long letter to Joe, telling him, among many, many other things, when to expect them.

The doorbell rang when Dolly was in the bedroom trying on an old evening dress. Through layers of flame-coloured chiffon she heard Laddy answer it, and then the muffled sound of voices. One belonged to a woman, and Dolly's head burst through the gathered neckline in time to hear it say: 'It just seems like fate, somehow.'

Silent in stockinged feet she went through to the lounge, then halted abruptly. Little Miss Whatsit in jeans and T-shirt was standing close to Laddy and gently brushing his cheek with something held in her cupped hands.

'She says someone found it outside the Maudsley Hospital,' he said helplessly, 'and she wants to give it to us.'

Without speaking, Dolly stood watching while the girl placed the kitten on Laddy's shoulder. She watched the way it stood up, arching its tiny back and mewing shrilly.

'But we can't—' she heard Laddy say.

'Oh, Mr Silver, you *must*! The only way to get over losing a pet is to have another one in its memory—' Her bright, silly face beamed at him persuasively. 'And if you don't have him, he'll have to be destroyed.'

'Yes, but—'

'I know you're going to love him just like the way you loved the other one,' she said, then with a brief little wave in Dolly's direction, added: 'Don't worry, I'll see myself out.'

The kitten teetered on Laddy's shoulder, continuing to mew. Carefully he detached its claws from his shirt and stood looking at the way it tried to nestle in the hollow of his hands.

'It wouldn't make any difference,' he said at length. 'We'd still go.'

'Of course it makes a difference,' Dolly said. 'You heard her say it'll be destroyed if we don't keep it.'

'We could put it in a boarding place.'

'No, we couldn't. It'd get fleas and things.'

'But what about Joe?'

'We won't be going,' she said.

He looked up from the kitten and met the accusation in her eyes. The old, old accusation that went back to the days of society women giving him gold cigarette cases and waiting outside the hotel suite.

'Look, it's only a little helpless kitten,' he said. 'And she meant it for both of us.'

'Put it in Gershwin's basket while I warm some milk for it.'

But the kitten had gone trustfully to sleep in his hands, so he sat quietly on the arm of the chair until she returned, looking sleazy and dishevelled in the old evening dress that was far too tight and all the wrong colour.

'Don't hold him like that, he can't breathe.'

'But we don't want another cat!' he cried, suddenly desperate. 'Honest to Christ, we don't want another one!'

She put the milk down on the floor, then removed the kitten from his hands in a brusque, proprietorial fashion.

'That's what we said about Gershwin,' she said. 'Remember?'

The Cherry Tree

DEREK TANGYE

T HE FOG came down again as we were having lunch, and, by the time we had finished, was clinging around the porch where we were sitting. I mentioned a photograph album at this point which contained photographs of my brother's previous visit; and Jeannie said she knew where it was, that it was in her studio, and it would not take a minute for her to fetch it.

She was away several minutes.

'What have you been doing?' asked my brother on her return. 'Feeding the birds?'

'Always doing that!'

I sensed, however, that she was in a state of excitement; and I could not understand why. Whatever the cause she was not going to disclose it in front of my brother.

I had to wait until we were alone.

'When I left you both,' she then told me, 'I went down the path feeling sad that the fog was thick again. Then I saw something which I could not believe was real.'

'What was it?'

'I saw a little black cat looking like the double of Lama and Oliver . . . curled up on the grass at the foot of the cherry tree.'

I reacted in the way that might be expected of me.

'I hope you chased it away,' I said.

'It ran away on its own.'

'Good.'

I sensed, however, that there could be trouble between Jeannie and me. There were danger signs. The following morning, for instance, the morning when my brother Colin was to leave for his Guildford home on the Cornish Riviera from Penzance station, there was the first danger sign. She did not wait for me to make her a cup of tea, but she was out of bed and dressed within five minutes. Then, through the bedroom window, I saw her disappear up the lane with a saucer in her hand.

'She's being unfaithful,' I murmured to Ambrose who was curled on the bed beside me.

I could, of course, understand her interest in the cat. If, when living some distance away from any habitation, one has already had two black cats coming uninvited to the door, it is natural to be intrigued by the appearance of yet a third. It was also specially intriguing that the arrivals were always black. When I was a fervent anti-cat person I always acted in friendly fashion towards a black cat, almost as if I was in awe of a black cat. I had this superstitious corner in my nature. The act of a black cat crossing my path gave me encouragement. Any other coloured cat, in those fervent anti-cat days, seemed to me to be vermin.

There had been, besides Lama and Oliver, two other black cats who had sought a home at Minack, but their efforts had failed because their timing was wrong.

The first of these cats was called Felix. He had been abandoned when the farm where he lived was sold, and the farmhouse was left empty. True, a neighbour had agreed to look after him, but the arrangements as far as Felix was concerned were unsatisfactory. Hence he began looking around for another home, and chose Minack as the most suitable.

His method of approach was persistent, aggressive and, for that matter, heart-rending. We first saw his face eagerly looking through the sitting-room window, and when I opened the door he dashed past me indoors, and came face to face with Lama. He would have pounced on Lama in the manner of a heavyweight boxer on a flyweight if I had not instinctively picked him up and thrown him out.

Since we knew where he came from and the circumstances in which he was being cared for, we decided to return him by driving him there in the car. Ten minutes away by road, five minutes across the fields, we deposited him there at midday. At one o'clock he was back on the window sill, his eager face pressed against the glass.

This situation was repeated several times until we decided we had to act drastically. We discovered the address of the new owner of the farm, contacted him and explained that he had bought a black cat as well as the farm. 'Bring him along to me,' said the man immediately – and that was the last we saw of Felix.

The second black cat began roaming around Minack soon after Oliver had died, and when Ambrose was acclimatizing himself to being on his own. He was a small, compact cat and, in contrast to Felix, timid. For no special reason Jeannie called him Fergus.

I became attached to the sight of him coming prancing up the lane, or passing along the stable meadow, or finding him stalking a mouse in the wood. But he was not domineering like Felix. Fergus seemed content just to stay in the neighbourhood without thrusting his personality upon us. Or perhaps he was

watching us, waiting to see whether a home with us, and Ambrose, was possible.

Then came the day I found him curled up in a corner of the Orlyt greenhouse in front of the cottage; and I was so excited that I behaved very clumsily. I shut the greenhouse door and rushed to tell Jeannie. When we returned Fergus was in such terror that he was trying to throw himself through the glass. After that incident he never appeared at Minack again.

There was, however, a happy ending. Margaret and George, the potters who live at the end of the lane, had just lost their old cat. Her basket was still in place in their kitchen when one morning, a few days after the Orlyt greenhouse incident, Fergus walked in through their front door and straight away settled himself in the basket. A wise cat.

We said goodbye to my brother at Penzance station, then drove back home, and when we reached the turn by the gate which leads to Oliver land, Jeannie asked me to stop.

'The saucer, I suppose,' I said grumpily.

'Yes,' she said, getting out of the car, and fetching the saucer.

It hadn't been touched.

'There,' I said, 'you were wasting your time.'

Stray cats the world over are courted, and so I could not blame Jeannie for doing so. There are thousands of stray cats at this very moment who are wandering in the neighbourhood of potential homes, watching the occupants, studying their habits, making up their minds whether such occupants would cater for their requirements to their satisfaction. Cats appear to be loners and many a time you will hear someone, as I used to do, complain that, unlike a dog, a cat is incapable of love; and that it is a selfish, demanding animal which only a fool would pander to.

There is a certain truth in this viewpoint, but I think it is unfair to compare a cat to a dog. I have been a dog person from a child, always will be, but there are circumstances which can make a cat a more suitable companion.

In my case the circumstances concern the change in my attitude towards wildlife since we first came to Minack. In the first years I behaved as I had always been ready to do since, as a teenager, my father gave me my first gun. In those youthful days nothing gave me more pleasure than early morning wanderings, a dog, an old English Sheepdog, in fact, beside me while I kept my gun at the ready to shoot any game bird or rabbit on sight. Rough shooting, as it is called, had almost a poetic quality in its pleasure for me. I was a hunter. Killing provided no sense of guilt.

Then slowly, like an ivy creeping up a building, I began at Minack to become aware of the wonder of life in the countryside, and of its struggle to survive; and when, one hard winter, I heard on the other side of the valley the frenetic gunshots of men shooting, the barks of dogs being urged on to retrieve the ducks, the plovers, the snipe which had been killed or half-killed, I knew I no longer subscribed to the attitude of my youth.

As often happens when there is such a change in the attitude of a person's beliefs, there is always a chance he might go to the other extreme. I have not done that. I could never condone, for instance, a politically motivated animal rights group; or accept that fox hunting is worse than gin trapping. I just do not intend to kill. Nor do I wish to disturb wildlife in its natural habitation. I want pheasants to roam around our land without fear, and birds to nest without disturbance, and badgers to be free of Ministry of Agriculture persecution. It means, too, that a dog is out of place at Minack. I would never be able to give it the free run, the free chase, the free barking, that I would have done if I had been at Minack in my youth.

A cat, I find therefore, is an easier companion than a dog. A cat's sense of independence also enables oneself to be independent. A cat can amuse itself on its own and, if it feels like a walk, off it will go. A dog, of course, will demonstrate its love to someone much more obviously than a cat, but then a dog will wag its tail at anyone who pays it attention. A cat will not do that. A cat, on most occasions, will remain aloof; and this aloofness, curiously, often maddens those very people who profess to adore cats. Such people, with their baby-language noises as they try to coax a cat to take notice of them, are infuriated with the cat which ignores them.

We have been fortunate in that we have never had a cat which caught birds as a pastime; and yet, if I wish to be fair, I do not condemn cats for being bird catchers. I look upon their cats as another example of nature's way of maintaining the balance of nature. There is, after all, continuous warfare in the world of nature, and cats catching birds is part of it.

Nonetheless, I am thankful that our cats have never shown signs of wishing to catch birds; and this thankfulness has always made me hesitate to welcome any new cat arrival at Minack. I would not be able to tolerate such a cat after the peaceful times of Monty, Lama, Oliver and Ambrose.

There was no sign of the cherry tree cat that day, and no sign of it the following day.

'It's returned to wherever it came from,' I said to Jeannie, 'and a good thing too.'

I had no wish for Ambrose's life to be disturbed.

On the Wednesday, however, I went into the hut where once we used to force, by paraffin heat, daffodil buds into full bloom, and I made a disturbing discovery. The hut, among other uses, had become a cat's kitchen. It was here that Jeannie would painstakingly, on a discarded calor-gas stove, boil the coley for Ambrose. The coley came in 10 lb frozen slabs, and Jeannie, the night before, would lay the slab out to de-freeze.

On the Tuesday evening she had laid out such a slab – but when, on the Wednesday, I had gone into the hut I found a part of the still frozen slab gnawed away. The hut door was shut, but there was a small gap between door and floor level. Something had got through it. What?

I said to Jeannie that it must have been a rat, but we never had previous evidence of a rat. The very mention of such a possibility provoked Jeannie into making an extravagant outburst on behalf of the cherry tree cat.

'It was a starving cat that did that,' she said, with all the conviction of a besotted cat lover. 'Only a starving cat would have clawed at frozen fish!'

'How could it have got there? The door was shut.'

'But there was the gap at the bottom, you silly. The cat is a small one, almost a kitten perhaps, and it could easily have got through such a gap.'

I have never tried to pursue my own point of view when Jeannie is in a cat mood. Wise for me to keep silent.

Thursday was a beautiful sunny day, and we got up leisurely, and I said to Jeannie that we should not waste such a lovely day on work, and that we should relax. It is this pure joy of being free to choose the pattern of a day that makes one a millionaire in real terms. No question of what deal to do next, no question of how to spend money to boost one's ego, just the question of whether to take the donkeys first for a walk, or to take Ambrose.

Then, when such pleasurable duties have been decided upon, then completed, there is the question, keeping a sense of guilt always out of sight, as to what to have for lunch – and where.

On this Thursday, Jeannie, because it was like a summer day in October, decided to have our lunch, consisting of Brie from Paxton and Whitfield, on the bridge. We were sitting there, enjoying ourselves, gossiping, making remarks that strangers to us would not understand, when suddenly I saw the cherry tree cat for the first time.

Surrounding Jeannie's studio, which was several yards below where we were sitting, is a high stone wall, high enough to hide the studio from sight. It was on the top of this high wall that I first saw a little black head, then a thin little black body.

'The cat's back!' I called out loudly, loud enough to scare it and make it disappear.

There had been such excitement in the tone of my voice that Jeannie jumped to the conclusion I was pleased to have seen it.

'A little black cat at Minack again! You are pleased, aren't you?'

'No,' I replied, recovering my composure, 'it's going to be a nuisance hovering around, and anyhow where has it come from? It must have come from somewhere.'

My irritation, I have to admit, was superficial only. I was intrigued. I was not, however, going to give Jeannie any encouragement.

'I wonder where it has been since I saw it on Sunday.'

'It is possible,' I said, 'that it is one of Walter's or it belongs to Tregurnow, and it's just a wandering cat.'

Walter Grose, a Pied Piper of cats, had a collection of them at the farm at the top of the lane. Tregurnow was further away, and also had a number of cats.

'Walter,' said Jeannie, 'has never had a black cat.'

'Anyhow,' I said, and felt relieved as I spoke, 'it shows no sign of wishing to be friendly. It is only a shadow at the moment, and long may it remain so.'

Jeannie was silent. Then she said: 'I have a hunch that Cherry is not always going to be a shadow.'

'So you've christened it already.'

'Cherry is the right name for her, finding her under the cherry tree.'

'So it is a her?'

'I'm sure. Small cats are usually female.'

There was no sign of the cat during the rest of the day, no sign of it the following morning, and Jeannie kept wondering where it could have been hiding. In the afternoon, however, she had a pleasant surprise. She had decided to take to Ambrose a saucer of milk in which she had mixed a raw egg, a favourite concoction of his; and as during the day, when he was not hunting, he was usually curled up in the hay which we kept for the donkeys in the Orlyt, she carried it down to him there. Instead of being curled in the hay, however, he was at the far bottom end of the Orlyt staring intently at something. She walked along to him and found, to her astonishment, the cherry tree cat curled up in a round ball, sound asleep, and only a few feet from him.

'Ambrose was absolutely calm,' she told me later, 'but when she woke up and saw me, she bolted. Ambrose didn't chase her. That's a good sign, isn't it?'

Jeannie knew very well that my main objection to any cat infiltration was the question of Ambrose's reaction to it. My own form of loyalty.

'And where did she go?'

'No idea. Completely disappeared.'

'I refuse to believe that Ambrose would ever enjoy the company of another cat.'

'But he didn't chase her, I tell you.'

I guessed that Jeannie had now decided to carry out a secret wooing campaign; saucers containing an assortment of delicacies would be placed at strategic points around Minack. The game would amuse her. She had done it before. I remember when Oliver was hovering in the neighbourhood she left a saucer containing sliced roast chicken halfway up the lane. I happened to look down that way a little later and saw a fox at the saucer, an astonished fox.

I spent the Saturday morning of that week fiddling with my brush cutter. The brush cutter is like an outdoor vacuum cleaner, just as important, even more so because, although you can manually dust and clean a house, it is quite impossible to keep cliff meadows manually in trim. The brush cutter is an instrument you sling over your shoulders, has a six-foot-long frame with a circular blade at the end of it. At this time of year, early autumn, it is my special companion. I use it to cut away the undergrowth of our numerous small meadows in readiness for the February daffodil season. Unfortunately my brush cutter would not operate properly. I had bought an early model and it was now tired. I would have to get a new one, I realized.

After lunch, when Jeannie told me she was going for a walk with Fred and Merlin on Oliver land, I said I would have a Churchill. This meant a rest. Churchill was always in favour of a rest after lunch.

I lay down on our bed, and ruminated. Such a rumination can cover a multitude of subjects in quick succession. A long-ago memory can merge into a present-day conflict I might be having with someone who had part control of my future. A flash, no logical reason for it, recalls a time when I stayed for a month in 956 Sacramento Street, San Francisco, then suddenly comes the recall of the occasion when, preparing the ground for early potatoes, the rotovator upset and one of the spikes pierced my foot. I was lying on the same bed as on that first night we stayed at Minack, rain dripping through the roof and Monty, companion on the journey in the Land Rover from Mortlake, beside us. Suddenly I was aware of a whisper noise on the carpet beside me. I looked down and there was the cherry tree cat.

The sight of her had an effect on me. It suggested that she was more than just a cat wandering around in the hope of food, and that she was indeed a cat who was looking for a home. Hence, when next I saw Jeannie, my attitude was a different one. I said to her we had a moral duty to perform. Somebody, I said, must have lost the little cat and would be searching for her at this very moment. Instead of amusing ourselves by thinking she might be another Minack cat, we had to take steps to see if we could find out who might have lost her.

After her inspection of the bedroom she kept out of sight for a couple of days, and we thought she had possibly left the neighbourhood. Perhaps she had just been making use of us, a pause in a journey. But the following Monday Jeannie, still leaving saucers around, suddenly saw her at a saucer opposite the water butt at the corner of the cottage. Jeannie had placed the saucer of temptation in the miniature bed of a rockery; and there, to Jeannie's delight around eight in the morning, she saw the cherry tree cat gulping its contents.

Jeannie left her at the saucer, and came back to tell me what she had seen. Then we both went out to have a look.

There was no cat; and there appeared to be no saucer.

'Look,' said Jeannie, who had bent down, 'she's covered it up! She's covered it up with old grass, like a wild animal hiding its prey.'

'Perhaps that's the explanation,' I said. 'Perhaps she is a wild cat, just as Lama was wild when she first appeared.'

We did not see her again that day until evening time when Jeannie caught sight of her on the path, and promptly filled another saucer; she placed it in the same place as the morning saucer. The incident was repeated. The cat soon came to consume its contents, left a little, and covered it up again with old grass. She was very nervous and, when she caught sight of us, she immediately ran away. A pity, because we were harmless. It was Ambrose she had to be scared of.

The first public confrontation with Ambrose came two mornings later. There may have been a previous confrontation, perhaps a meeting during the night, but this we did not know. The public confrontation, however, was horrific.

Ambrose came serenely out of the porch after a breakfast of coley, strolled confidently past the water butt at the corner of the cottage . . . and saw her. He arched his back, growled, spat, then, when the lady saw him and fled, he raced after her. She fled up the path to the clothes line – the clothes line with the most beautiful view in the country, looking across Mount's Bay and with sea breezes drying the clothes – she fled towards it, and seconds later there were such screams that I thought Ambrose was killing her. I followed the two of them and found the lady high up on a privet bush, looking down upon a furious Ambrose.

The incident made me determined to get rid of her.

'Impossible for her to stay around here another day,' I said firmly to Jeannie. 'I just won't tolerate Ambrose being upset.'

'I don't want him upset either.'

'All right then, we are both agreed . . . But don't feed that cat again.'

'I will,' replied Jeannie defiantly.

'Absurd, quarrelling over an unknown cat.'

Our collision of views did not last long. We compromised. The cherry tree cat would continue to be fed.

The search for her origin would immediately begin.

Cat's Cruise

MAZO DE LA ROCHE

C AT was as black as a crow. This very blackness made her presence desired by sailors who were sure it brought them good luck. She was not pretty but she had charm which she had spent her life in exercising to get what she wanted. She was eight years old and she had woven into that eight years more travel and more adventure than most humans achieve in eighty. She had also brought forty-five kittens into the world.

She had been born on board a coaling-vessel, the *Sultara*, in the midst of a terrible storm when the crew thought that every moment would be their last. Her mother was ginger-coloured; and she had, while the vessel floundered in distress, produced three ginger-coloured kittens besides this last one, black as the coal which formed the cargo. The stoker, looking gloomily at their squirming bodies, had growled:

'There'll be no need for us to drown *them*. The bloomin' sea'll do it!'

He picked up the black midget and held it in his hand. He felt an instant's compassion for it. It had come out of darkness and was so soon to return; yet there it lay, curved in his palm, bullet-headed, its intricate mechanism of tiny organs and delicate bones padded with good flesh, the flesh covered by thick silky fur, the whole animated by a spirit so vigorous that already ten little claws made themselves felt on his palm.

'If I could find a bottle the right size,' he said, 'I'd put you into it and chuck you into the sea. I'll bet you'd get to land!'

But there was no need to try the experiment. Miraculously, it seemed, the storm began to abate. The waves subsided; the vessel was got under control. One and all declared that they had been saved by the timely birth of the black kitten. It became the mascot, the idol of the ship.

They could not agree on a name for it. Some wanted a simple one, easy to say and descriptive of its colour, such as Smut, Darkie, Jet or Nigger. Others insisted on some name which would suggest the rescue of their lives by the kitten's timely birth. One offered Nick-o'-Time, with Nick for short. But they could not agree. Then someone called her simply 'Cat', and the others, in spite of themselves, acquiesced, as is often the case with names. From then on she was proudly, affectionately, known as 'Cat' wherever she went.

She had a very round head, with small ears and narrow, clear green eyes. She had exceptionally long, glossy whiskers above a large mouth that displayed needle-sharp teeth in a three-cornered smile or a ferocious grin when her emotions were stirred. Her tail was sleek and sinuous and almost never still. Happy was the sailor round whose neck she wound it. Her attentions were known to bring good luck.

As she grew up she reigned supreme on the vessel. Nothing was too good for her. If what she wanted was not given her at once, she climbed on to the neck of the man who withheld it and put both arms (you could not call them forelegs, because she used them exactly like arms) round his neck and peered into his eyes out of the narrow green slits of her own. If he did not at once surrender, she pressed her stubby nose on first one side of his face then on the other, while with her claws she massaged the weather-beaten back of his neck. If he were still obdurate, or perhaps mischievous enough still to deny her, she reversed her position and put her claws into his thigh. Gladly he gave her then whatever she desired.

She had a loud vibrant purr and when she moved gracefully along whatever deck she was favouring with her presence, purring and swaying her long tail, a feeling of reassurance and tranquillity came to all on board . . . It was a bitter thing to the crew of the coaling-vessel on which she had been born when, at the time of her first litter, she deserted them for a Norwegian schooner. The captain could scarcely persuade the crew to sail. The docks at Liverpool were combed for her without success. The voyage was one of rough weather and general dissatisfaction.

At that time the Norwegians had not heard of her. They had their own cat and did not want another. But she soon won them over and they had the most successful voyage they had ever known. When they next called at Liverpool the mate boasted of Cat in the hearing of one of the crew of the *Sultara*. He boasted of her intelligence, of her blackness, of the luck she brought.

On board the *Sultara* there was joy when they learned that she was safe, rage when they heard that she was living with the Norwegians. They visited the foreigners and saw for themselves that the cat was Cat. They found that she had a litter of ginger-coloured kittens. But the Norwegians would not give her up. They would give up one or all of her ginger-coloured litter but they would not give up 'Katts'.

The crew of the *Sultara* hung about the docks with scraps of kipper in their pockets, because Cat had a weakness for kippers; but the Norwegians guarded Katt with terrible efficiency. When, however, she chose to go ashore, nothing could stop her. A morsel of kipper was proffered her at the right moment. She mounted the shoulder of the giver and was borne in triumph to her birthplace. She gave evidence of the greatest pleasure in her reunion with the crew who were ready to weep with joy at recovering her.

Cat remained with them for two voyages. Then again she disappeared, this time in favour of an oil-tanker bound for the East . . . And so it went on, this life of change and adventure. She chose her ships. She remained on them till her love of variety prompted her to seek another lodging. But wherever she sailed she brought good luck and, at regular intervals, she returned to the *Sultara*. On all the Seven Seas she produced litters of ginger or grey kittens but never one of her own glittering black. She held herself unique. She was Cat.

Now, on a morning in late February, she glided down the gangway of the *Greyhound* which had just limped into port after an Antarctic relief expedition. The voyage had lasted for six months, and had been one of the mistakes of Cat's life, so far as her own pleasure was concerned.

The captain and crew of the *Greyhound* had been delighted when she sauntered aboard. The seal of success, they felt, had been set on the expedition. And they were right. The lost explorers had been discovered, living, though in desperate plight. Cat's reputation was still more enhanced.

But she herself was disgruntled through and through. She had never in all her years of travel experienced such a voyage. She felt disillusioned; she felt ill. She felt like scratching the first hand that was stretched out to pat her.

'Hullo, Cat!' exclaimed a burly dock-hand. 'So you're back from the Pole? And what captain are you going to sign up with next?' He bent to scratch her neck but she eluded him and glided off with waving tail.

'Cat don't look very bright,' observed another dock-hand.

'She's fed up, I expect, with the length of the last voyage,' said the first speaker, staring after her. 'She don't generally go for such long ones. *And* the weather! *And* the grub! She could have done much better for herself and she knows it.'

He turned to one of a crew which was about to sail for Norway.

'Hi, Bob! Here's Cat! Just back from the South Pole. P'raps you can make up to her.'

Bob approached, grinning. He planted himself in Cat's way and held two thick tarry hands down to her.

'Puss, puss!' he wheedled. 'Coom along wi' us. Tha can have whativer tha wants. Tha knows me, Cat.'

She knew Bob well and liked him. She suffered herself to be laid across his breast and she gave him a long look out of her narrow green eyes. He felt her ribs with his blunt fingers.

'She's naught but fur and bone,' he declared.

'Her's been frettin' fer home,' said the first.

'The sea is her home,' said Bob. 'But she's a dainty feeder. S'll I carry thee off, Cat?'

She began softly to purr. She relaxed in every fibre. The tip of her tongue showed between her lips. She closed her eyes.

'She'll go with you,' said the dock-hand and Bob began to pick his way among crates and bales, carrying Cat hopefully in his arms.

She heard the varied sounds of the docks, the shouts, the hoarse whistles of ships, the rattle of chains, smelled the familiar smells. It was music and sweetness to her after her long absence. She surrendered herself to the rhythmic movement of Bob's big chest.

In triumph he deposited her on his own deck. The rest of the crew stopped in their work for a moment to welcome her. The cook brought her a brace of sardines.

For politeness' sake she ate one but left the other on the deck. She arched herself against the legs of the first mate and gave her three-cornered smile. A ray of feeble sunlight struggled through the wintry fog and fell across her. She began to think she might sail with his crew.

'Keep an eye on her,' said the mate to a cabin-boy. 'Don't let her out of your sight till we're away.'

All about was hurry and noise. Cat sat on the deck washing the oil of the sardine from her whiskers. The pale sunshine surrounded her but deep within her there was dissatisfaction growing. This was not what she wanted and soon it would be too late to return to the docks. She would be in for another long, cold voyage.

Her little round black head looked very innocent. Her eyes were tight shut. Methodically she moved her curved paw over her face.

Someone called the boy and, forgetting the earlier order, he ran off. Cat was galvanized into life and movement. She flew along the deck. In another instant she would be on the docks.

But Bob saw her and caught her in his huge hands. She liked him; still she did not weaken. She thrust her claws into his hands and, with a yell of triumph and every hair erect, escaped.

It was some time before she regained her calm. She slunk among legs, among trucks, through scattered straw and trampled mud. The fog thickened again, settling clammily on her fur. It was bitterly cold. What she wanted was solitude. She was sick of the sight and sound of men and their doings.

She entered a warehouse and passed between tiers of wooden boxes and bales, stopping to sniff now and again when some smell attracted her. The cold in this building was very penetrating. Was she never to know warmth again?

In a dim shed she found stalls, all empty except one in which a prize ram was awaiting shipment to America where he was to be used for breeding. She clambered up the partition of the stall and perched there, gazing down at him. She did not remember having seen anything like him before. His yellow gaze was as inscrutable as hers.

With paws tucked under her breast she sat, enjoying the sight of him. She stared at his massive woolly shoulders, his curly horns, his restless pawing hoofs. He lowered his head and butted the manger in front of him with his hard skull. Cat felt that she could watch him for ever.

The gruff whistles of the ships shook the hoary air. The faint sunlight coming in at the cobwebbed window was shut off by a curtain of grey dusk. Cat and the ram were wrapped about by a strange intimacy. The chill increased. The docks became almost silent. The ram gave a bereft *baa* and sank to his knees.

Now he was only a pale mound in the dusk but Cat still stared at him. He was conscious of her too and, like some earth-bound spirit, he raised his yellow gaze to the glimmering stars of her eyes.

Towards midnight the cold became unbearable to her. On the Antarctic expedition she had slept in a bunk with a well-fleshed sailor. Now a thin rime was stiffening every hair of her coat. She rose stiffly and stretched. Her tail hung powerless. Some message, some understanding passed between her and the ram.

She leaped from the partition and landed between his shoulders. She sank into the deep oily warmth of his wool. He remained motionless, silent as the hill where he had pastured.

She stretched herself out on him with a purr of delight. She sought to feel his flesh with the fine points of her claws through the depth of his wool. A smell new to her rose from his body and the beginning of a *baa* stirred in his throat. Their two bodies united in the quiet breathing of sleep. Her sleep was light, of a pale luminous quality, always just on the edge of waking; but his was dark and heavy, as though he were surrounded by shaggy furze and thick heather.

A dense fog rose from the sea at dawn and pressed thickly into the stall. With it crept a long grey cat with a white blaze on his face and his ears torn by fighting. He scrambled up the partition of the stall and peered down at the two below. He dropped to the manger and from there to the straw. He touched Cat tentatively.

She had been conscious of his approach. It had brought into her dreams a vague vision of a tawny striped cat she had met in Rio de Janeiro, where the relief ship had called. But the touch of the paw galvanized her. She gave a shriek and, driving her hind claws into the ram's back, she reared herself and struck at the intruder's face as though she would put her mark on it for ever.

But he was not easily frightened off. He sprang to the ram's back also and through the fog Cat saw his white face grinning at her. He set his teeth in the back of her neck. They both shrieked.

The ram's deep, dark, warm slumber was shattered into fright. He bounded up with a clatter of hoofs, overthrowing the cats. His white eyelashes flickered. He glared in primeval rage and lowered his head to charge.

The cats scrambled agilely over the partition and dropped to the stone floor outside, their tails enormous. They sped in opposite directions into dim corners of the shed. The battering of the ram's head against the door of the stall echoed through the fog.

As Cat reached her corner a mouse flickered out of the gloom, squeaking in an agony of fear, and shot past her. With a graceful flourish of her limber body she turned completely round and captured the mouse with one effective movement. She picked it up delicately in her teeth and crouched in the corner.

After a time the door opened and two men came in. They turned on a light and the interior of the shed was revealed in foggy pallor. The men entered the stall where the ram was. There came strange bumping sounds. The men cursed. Then they appeared leading the ram, roped by the horns. He was led out helpless, his little hoofs pattering on the stone floor. He uttered a plaintive, lamb-like *baa*. The men left the door open behind them.

Cat discovered the body of the mouse. It now meant nothing to her. She glided out on to the docks, wondering what ship she would sail in. She passed among them as they were dimly revealed, cargoes being loaded or unloaded, men working like ants. She felt a dim wonder at their activity, a faint disdain for their heaving bodies.

Towards noon, when a shabby blurred disc showed where the sun was, she came upon a passenger ship just departing on a West India cruise. She had never sailed on a passenger ship. They were an untrustworthy and strange world and she hated the sight of women.

As she stood pessimistically surveying it a kitchen worker tossed a slice of chicken-breast through a porthole to her. She crouched on the pier devouring it while shivers of delight made her separate hairs quiver. She had not known that such food existed. After it was gone she sat beaming towards the porthole but nothing more was thrown out.

Luggage was being loaded on to the ship and a throng of people, of a sort she had never before seen, hastened up the gangway. One of them, a man, bent and gently massaged the muscles in the back of her neck, before he passed on. She beamed after him. She had not known such hands existed, so smooth, so tender. They were like the breast of chicken she had just devoured.

She rose, chilled by the clammy cold, and glided up the gangway on to the ship.

She knew that she was a stranger here and some instinct told her that quite possibly she might not be welcome. She slunk along the innumerable white passages, making herself as nearly invisible as possible. She glanced in at the doors of staterooms as she passed. Generally there were women inside and sometimes the rather disgusting smell of flowers was on the air.

Cat heard the thunder of the whistle. She felt a quiver go through the ship. She had a mind to get off it while there was yet time but she felt powerless to turn herself away from the delicious warmth that was radiated from every corner of the liner. It made her feel yielding, soft. She wanted something cosy to lie down on.

She paused at the door of a cabin that was empty except for the promise of a man's coat and hat thrown on the berth. She went in and walked round it, purring. She held her tail stiffly erect, all but the tip which moved constantly as though it were, in some subtle way, gauging the spiritual atmosphere of the cabin.

Gregg, the swimming-instructor, found her there curled up on his coat. They had left the docks so she could not be put ashore. He recognized her as the cat he had caressed and supposed that she belonged on the liner. He tucked her under his arm and carried her to the kitchen quarters. The boy who had thrown her the morsel of chicken recognized her. He had once been galley-boy on an oil-tanker she had favoured with her presence.

'It's Cat,' he explained. ' 'Aven't yer never 'eard tell of Cat?

W'y, we're in luck, mister! And yer ought to be proud to share your berth wiv 'er!'

But Gregg did not want to share his berth with Cat, even after he had heard her history and virtues. He dumped her down and rather glumly retraced his steps. He felt a shrinking from the long cruise that stretched ahead of him. To be sociable was a part of his job and he hated the thought of sociability.

He had, in fact, seen too much of people. He had had more experience of society than was good for him. He was not yet thirty but he had lost a fair-sized fortune, the woman he loved and, worst of all, his hope and fortitude. He had been at his wits' end to find a job when a friend had got him this post as swimming-instructor. He was in a state bordering on despair but, here he was, bound to seem cheerful and gay, to take a passionate interest in the flounderings of fat passengers in the pool.

No one on board was so out of sympathy with the cruise as was he. Indeed, everyone on board was in sympathy with the cruise but Gregg and Cat, who did not at all understand cruising for pleasure.

She was there in his berth waiting for him when he returned to his cabin that night, having found her way through all the intricacy of glittering passages. He was a little drunk, for he was very attractive and people insisted on treating him. The sight of Cat lying there on his bed angered him. He was about to put her out roughly when she rolled over on her back, turned up her black velvet belly and round little face with the glittering eyes narrowed and the three-cornered smile showing her pink tongue. He bent over her, pleased in spite of himself.

'You're a rogue,' he said. 'But you can't get around me like that.'

For answer she clasped her forepaws round his neck and with her hind paws clawed gently on his shirt front. She pressed her face to his and purred loudly in his ear.

'Cheek to cheek, eh?' said Gregg, and gave himself up to her hypnotic overtures.

Morning found them snuggled close together. He sent the steward for a dish of milk for her. He appeared at the swimming-pool with her on his shoulder. She basked in the heavenly warmth of the place.

From that time she spent her days by the pool. Tolerantly, almost benignly, she watched the skill or awkwardness of the swimmers. When the pool was deserted she crouched by its brink gazing at her reflection, dreaming of lovely fish that might have graced it. At night she slept with Gregg. She thrived immensely.

When they were in sparkling southern waters, Cat disappeared early one evening. She met Gregg at the door of his cabin with a tremulously excited air. She advanced towards him, purring, then turned her back and flaunted her sinuous black tail. She looked back at him over her shoulder. Her head and tail met. She caught the tip of it in her mouth and lay down on her back, rolling coyly from side to side. She looked strangely slender.

'So you've been and gone and done it,' said Gregg. 'Not on the bed, I hope!'

No, not on the bed. In the wardrobe, where Gregg's soft dressing-gown had somehow fallen from its peg. There were three of them, all plump, all tawny like the gentleman in Rio de Janeiro.

Next day Gregg got a nice box with a cushion and put the kittens in it. He carried them to the balmy warmth of the air that surrounded the swimming-pool, and all the bathers gathered to admire and stroke them. They were the pets of the ship. But Cat cared only for Gregg. She fussed over him far more than she did over her kittens. She refused to stay with them by the pool at night, so the box had to be carried to his cabin. There she would sit waiting for him, her glowing eyes fixed on the door, every nerve tuned for his coming.

But on one night he did not come. She waited and waited but he did not come. At last she sprang up from suckling her kittens, and they fell back like three tawny balls. The door was fixed ajar. She glided through the opening and began her search for him.

The smoke-room was closed; the lounge was empty, the decks deserted except for a pacing figure in uniform. At last Cat saw Gregg standing, still as a statue, in a secluded corner where a lifeboat hung. Silent as the shadows cast by moonlight, she drew near to him. But she did not rub herself against his leg as usual. She climbed into the lifeboat and over its edge peered down into his face.

That night Gregg felt alone – lost. In spite of the moonlight, the myriad glittering waves, the world was black to him. The life on this luxurious liner, among these spoiled shallow people, was suffocating him; he could not breathe. He looked back on his own life as a waste, on his future with despair. He had made up his mind to end it all.

Cat watched him intently as he leaned against the rail. If he had been her prey she could not have observed him with more meticulous concentration as he mounted it. Just before he would have leaped over the side she sprang on to his shoulders with a shriek that curdled the blood of those whose staterooms gave on to that deck. She not only shrieked but she drove every claw into Gregg. She turned herself into a black fury whose every hair stood on end, whose eyes glared with hate and fear at that gulf below . . .

'I don't know what the devil is the matter with her,' Gregg said to the officer who hastened up. 'She's as temperamental as a prima donna.' His hand shook as he stroked her.

But she had saved him from his black mood, saved him from his despairing self. When he was undressed, he looked in wonder at the little bloody spots on his shoulders . . . Cat slept on his chest.

He made up his mind that he would never part with her. He owed her a debt which could only be repaid by the certainty of affection and gentle living for the rest of her days. He would find lodgings where she would be welcome.

But Gregg reckoned without Cat. By the time they reached port she was sick to death of the luxury liner. There was not a smell on board that pleased her. She liked Gregg but she could do without him. She liked her three plump kittens, but the quality of real mother love did not exist in her. She loved the sea and the men who spent their days in strenuous work on the sea. She disliked women and scent and all daintiness. She was Cat; she could not change herself.

In the confusion of landing no one saw her slip ashore. She vanished like a puff of black smoke. It was as lovely a morning as any they had seen on the cruise. The air was balmy, the sky above the dock blue as a periwinkle. When Cat reached the places she was accustomed to she purred loudly and rubbed herself against tarry trouser-legs, arched her neck to horny hands. But she was coy. She would not commit herself. For a fortnight she lived on the dock, absorbing the satisfying smells of fresh timber, straw, tar, salt fish, hemp, beer, oil and sweat. She even renewed acquaintance, this time more amiably though with loud screams, with the grey-furred gentleman who had called on her in the ram's stall.

At last she sailed on a cattle ship, and all her past was as nothing to her!

Amours

COLETTE

THE ROBIN had won. Now he celebrated his victory in little dry chirps, safe in the depths of a chestnut tree. He was proud that he had not fled from the cat. He had hovered above her buzzing like an angry bee. His taunts, to anyone who understood his chirping, were fiercesome.

'I, Robin red-breast, will peck out your eyes if you take one more step towards the nest which holds my precious eggs.'

I was watching, ready to intervene, but the cat understands that the robin is not to be touched. She understands so many things. Still, she thinks that in allowing the bird to insult her with impunity, she risks being made to look a fool. So, she thrashes her tail like a lion and arches her back. In the end she leaves the frantic bird and we continue on our walk through the dusk.

It is a slow, pleasurable amble in which we both make discoveries. Well, she is making discoveries to be honest. She stops and stares fixedly at something in the distance which I cannot see. She crouches and leaps at a noise I do not hear. I have to guess what she is finding so fascinating.

Being with a cat is always stimulating but did I set out fifty years ago to seek the company of cats? It never seemed that I had to look for them. They were always there at my feet. They came in so many guises: lost and starving, hunting and being hunted, the library cat embalmed in ink, dairy cats and butcher's cats well-fed but with paws cold from the tiled floor. There are flabby bourgeois cats, self-satisfied cats and despot cats who tyrannize over Paul Morand, Claude Farrere and me. They all come to me with pleasure but without surprise.

One day I noticed a poor thin cat being pushed to and fro by the crowd which pours each evening out of the Autreuil metro. In fact it was she who recognized me. 'There you are at last,' she said. 'You are very late. Where is your home? Do not worry, I will follow you.'

When we got home my house seemed to frighten her, perhaps because I lived there with someone else. She soon settled in, however. She lived with me for four years before dying in an accident.

But I must not forget my dogs, just as loving, just as vulnerable. How could I live without you? I am indispensable to you. You make me realise how truly valuable I am to you. Is there anyone else of whom I can say the same? You comfort me with your devotion though maybe you are almost too loving, your eyes too beseeching. I do not know much about a dog's sex life because, out of my favourite ten breeds, I prefer those unable to breed. For instance, sometimes the bitch of the Brabant terrier, the French type of bulldog – pug-nosed with a huge head – instinctively refuses to mate. It knows that giving birth is dangerous because of its size and shape.

Two bitches I had, used to bite dogs who tried to mate outside 'safe periods'. One poodle was happy to feed a rubber puppy instead of the real thing. Though I have owned many dogs, cats have always been more important to me. From them I have learnt to be reserved, self-disciplined and intolerant of noise.

The cat which has meant most to me and was different from all others was the one I mentioned at the beginning. And yet, because she was so special I cannot say too much about her. Only when she was sexually active did she cease to be mine and rejoined the cat world. I can only guess what she saw in the tomcat who raped and abused her. Sex not love brought forth her terrible wails and birdlike cries, insulting and threatening her mate.

In the country she is flirtatious and promiscuous, delighting in her freedom to be truly catlike and not the human's 'best

friend'. To me she is warm, faithful and sensitive – the opposite of all she is to her cat lovers.

In town, in the narrow walled garden of my Paris house, she played happily, sometimes full of energy, sometimes content to dream. She restrained her natural instincts haughtily rejecting would-be mates. There is the old striped conqueror, thin as a rake, bald in places but highly experienced. He is decisive, respected by his rivals, confident of success.

Then there is a young cat, stupid and self-satisfied, enjoying his own beauty – the beauty of the tiger. Finally, there is the farm cat who appears on the top of the wall as though awakened from a dream by an urgent mating call.

She gives all three a hard time using her paws without mercy to slap their faces when they push too hard. Then she rolls around in front of them but follows that exhibition with freezing contempt. She climbs onto a crumbling pillar from which she can pour scorn on her assailants. When she decides to rejoin her three slaves she does so with hauteur. She allows one of her admirers to kiss her nose but when this goes on too long she puts a stop to it with an imperious cry impossible to describe.

The three tomcats jump back in surprise. My cat, seeming to forget her lovers, goes back to grooming herself. Depressed by their long courtship, the male cats begin to fight amongst themselves to pass the time. My cat leaves them to it, renouncing her flirtatious games, pleased to rejoin the humans.

While I work, my cat lies beside me under the warmth of the reading lamp, silent, watchful, content – my she-cat, my friend.

The Cheshire Cat

LEWIS CARROLL

THE ONLY things in the kitchen that did not sneeze were the cook, and a large cat which was sitting on the hearth and grinning from ear to ear.

'Please, would you tell me,' said Alice a little timidly, for she was not quite sure whether it was good manners for her to speak first, 'why your cat grins like that?'

'It's a Cheshire cat,' said the Duchess, 'and that's why. Pig!'

She said the last word with such sudden violence that Alice quite jumped; but she saw in another moment that it was addressed to the baby, and not to her, so she took courage and went on again:

'I didn't know that Cheshire cats always grinned; in fact, I didn't know that cats *could* grin.'

'They all can,' said the Duchess, 'and most of 'em do.'

'I don't know of any that do,' Alice said very politely, feeling quite pleased to have got into a conversation.

'You don't know much,' said the Duchess, 'and that's a fact.'

Alice did not at all like the tone of this remark, and thought it would be as well to introduce some other subject of conversation. While she was trying to fix on one, the cook took the cauldron of soup off the fire, and at once set to work throwing everything within her reach at the Duchess and the baby – the fire-irons came first; then followed a shower of saucepans, plates and dishes. The Duchess took no notice of them even when they hit her; and the baby was howling so much already that it was quite impossible to say whether the blows hurt it or not.

'Oh, *please* mind what you're doing!' cried Alice, jumping up and down in an agony of terror. 'Oh, there goes his *precious* nose,' as an unusually large saucepan flew close by it, and very nearly carried it off.

'If everybody minded their own business,' the Duchess said in a hoarse growl, 'the world would go round a deal faster than it does.'

'Which would *not* be an advantage,' said Alice, who felt very glad to get an opportunity of showing off a little of her knowledge. 'Just think what work it would make with the day and night! You see the earth takes twenty-four hours to turn round on its axis —'

'Talking of axes,' said the Duchess, 'chop off her head!'

Alice glanced rather anxiously at the cook, to see if she meant to take the hint; but the cook was busily engaged in stirring the soup, and did not seem to be listening, so she ventured to go on again: 'Twenty-four hours, I *think*; or is it twelve? I —'

'Oh, don't bother *me*,' said the Duchess. 'I never could abide figures!' And with that she began nursing her child again, singing a sort of lullaby to it as she did so, and giving it a violent shake at the end of every line:

> Speak roughly to your little boy,
> And beat him when he sneezes:
> He only does it to annoy,
> Because he knows it teases.

Chorus (which the cook and the baby joined):

> Wow! wow! wow!

While the Duchess sang the second verse of the song, she kept tossing the baby violently up and down, and the poor little thing howled so, that Alice could hardly hear the words:

> I speak severely to my boy,
> I beat him when he sneezes;
> For he can thoroughly enjoy
> The pepper when he pleases!

Chorus:

Wow! wow! wow!

'Here! You may nurse it a bit, if you like!' the Duchess said to Alice, flinging the baby at her as she spoke. 'I must go and get ready to play croquet with the Queen,' and she hurried out of the room. The cook threw a frying-pan after her as she went out, but it just missed her.

Alice caught the baby with some difficulty, as it was a queer-shaped little creature and held out its arms and legs in all directions, 'just like a star-fish', thought Alice. The poor little thing was snorting like a steam-engine when she caught it, and kept doubling itself up and straightening itself out again, so that altogether, for the first minute or two, it was as much as she could do to hold it.

As soon as she made out the proper way of nursing it (which was to twist it up into a sort of knot, and then keep tight hold of its right ear and left foot, so as to prevent its undoing itself), she carried it out into the open air. 'If I don't take this child away with me,' thought Alice, 'they're sure to kill it in a day or two; wouldn't it be murder to leave it behind?' She said the last words out loud, and the little thing grunted in reply (it had left off sneezing by this time). 'Don't grunt,' said Alice, 'that's not at all a proper way of expressing yourself.'

The baby grunted again, and Alice looked very anxiously into its face to see what was the matter with it. There could be no doubt that it had a *very* turn-up nose, much more like a snout than a real nose; also its eyes were getting extremely small for a baby. Altogether, Alice did not like the look of the thing at all. 'But perhaps it was only sobbing,' she thought, and looked into its eyes again to see if there were any tears.

No, there were no tears. 'If you're going to turn into a pig, my dear,' said Alice, seriously, 'I'll have nothing more to do with you. Mind now!' The poor little thing sobbed again (or grunted, it was impossible to say which), and they went on for some while in silence.

Alice was just beginning to think to herself, 'Now, what am I to do with this creature when I get it home?' when it grunted again, so violently, that she looked down into its face in some alarm. This time there could be *no* mistake about it: it was neither more nor less than a pig, and she felt that it would be quite absurd for her to carry it any further.

So she set the little creature down, and felt quite relieved to see it trot away quietly into the wood. 'If it had grown up,' she said to herself, 'it would have made a dreadfully ugly child; but it makes rather a handsome pig, I think.' And she began thinking over other children she knew, who might do very well as pigs, and was just saying to herself, 'If one only knew the right way to change them —' when she was a little startled by seeing the Cheshire Cat sitting on a bough of a tree a few yards off.

The Cat only grinned when it saw Alice. It looked good-natured, she thought; still, it had *very* long claws and a great many teeth, so she felt that it ought to be treated with respect.

'Cheshire Puss,' she began, rather timidly, as she did not at all know whether it would like the name; however, it only grinned a little wider. 'Come, it's pleased so far,' thought Alice, and she went on: 'Would you tell me, please, which way I ought to go from here?'

'That depends a good deal on where you want to get to,' said the Cat.

'I don't much care where —' said Alice.

'Then it doesn't matter which way you go,' said the Cat.

'— so long as I get *somewhere*,' Alice added as an explanation.

'Oh, you're sure to do that,' said the Cat, 'if you only walk long enough.'

Alice felt that this could not be denied so, she tried another question: 'What sort of people live about here?'

'In *that* direction,' the Cat said, waving its right paw round, 'lives a Hatter; and in *that* direction,' waving the other paw, 'lives a March Hare. Visit either you like; they're both mad.'

'But I don't want to go among mad people,' Alice remarked.

'Oh, but you can't help that,' said the Cat: 'We're all mad here. I'm mad. You're mad.'

'How do you know I'm mad?' said Alice.

'You must be,' said the Cat, 'or you wouldn't have come here.'

Alice didn't think that proved it at all; however, she went on. 'And how do you know that you're mad?'

'To begin with,' said the Cat, 'a dog's not mad. You grant that?'

'I suppose so,' said Alice.

'Well, then,' the Cat went on, 'you see a dog growls when it's angry, and wags its tail when it's pleased. Now *I* growl when I'm pleased, and wag my tail when I'm angry. Therefore, I'm mad.'

'I call it purring. not growling,' said Alice.

'Call it what you like,' said the Cat. 'Do you play croquet with the Queen today?'

'I should like it very much,' said Alice, 'but I haven't been invited yet.'

'You'll see me there,' said the Cat, and vanished.

Alice was not much surprised at this, she was getting so used to queer things happening. While she was looking at the place where it had been, it suddenly appeared again.

'By the by, what became of the baby?' said the Cat. 'I'd nearly forgotten to ask.'

'It turned into a pig,' Alice quietly said, just as if it had come back in a natural way.

'I thought it would,' said the Cat, and vanished again.

Alice waited a little, half expecting to see it again, but it did not appear, and after a minute or two she walked on in the direction in which the March Hare was said to live. 'I've seen hatters before,' she said to herself; 'the March Hare will be much the most interesting, and perhaps, as this is May, it won't be raving mad – at least not so mad as it was in March.' As she said this, she looked up, and there was the Cat again, sitting on a branch of a tree.

'Did you say pig, or fig?' said the Cat.

'I said pig,' replied Alice, 'and I wish you wouldn't keep appearing and vanishing so suddenly. You make one quite giddy.'

'All right,' said the Cat; and this time it vanished quite slowly, beginning with the end of the tail and ending with the grin, which remained some time after the rest of it had gone.

'Well! I've often seen a cat without a grin,' thought Alice, 'but a grin without a cat! It's the most curious thing I ever saw in all my life!'

Alice began to feel very uneasy; to be sure she had not, as yet, had any dispute with the Queen, but she knew that it might happen any minute, 'and then,' thought she, 'what would become of me? They're dreadfully fond of beheading people here; the great wonder is that there's anyone left alive!'

She was looking about for some way of escape, and wondering whether she could get away without being seen, when she noticed a curious appearance in the air. It puzzled her very much at first, but, after watching it a minute or two, she made it out to be a grin, and she said to herself, 'It's the Cheshire Cat; now I shall have somebody to talk to.'

'How are you getting on?' said the Cat, as soon as there was mouth enough for it to speak with.

Alice waited till the eyes appeared, and then nodded, 'It's no use speaking to it,' she thought, 'till its ears have come, or at least one of them.' In another minute the whole head appeared, and then Alice put down her flamingo and began an account of the game, feeling very glad she had someone to listen to her. The Cat seemed to think that there was enough of it now in sight, and no more of it appeared.

'I don't think they play at all fairly.' Alice began, in rather a complaining tone, 'and they all quarrel so dreadfully one can't hear oneself speak – and they don't seem to have any rules in particular; at least, if there are, nobody attends to them – and you've no idea how confusing it is all the things being alive; for instance, there's the arch I've got to go through next walking about at the other end of the ground – and I should have croqueted the Queen's hedgehog just now, only it ran away when it saw mine coming!'

'How do you like the Queen?' said the Cat in a low voice.

'Not at all,' said Alice; 'she's so extremely —' Just then she noticed that the Queen was close behind her listening, so she went on, ' – likely to win, that it's hardly worth while finishing the game.'

The Queen smiled and passed on.

'Who *are* you talking to?' said the King, coming up to Alice, and looking at the Cat's head with great curiosity.

'It's a friend of mine – a Cheshire Cat,' said Alice, 'allow me to introduce it.'

'I don't like the look of it at all,' said the King; 'however, it may kiss my hand if it likes.'

'I'd rather not,' the Cat remarked.

'Don't be impertinent,' said the King, 'and don't look at me like that!' He got behind Alice as he spoke.

'A cat may look at a king,' said Alice. 'I've read that in some book, but I don't remember where.'

'Well, it must be removed,' said the King very decidedly, and he called to the Queen who was passing at the moment. 'My dear! I wish you would have this cat removed!'

The Queen had only one way of settling all difficulties, great or small. 'Off with his head!' she said, without even looking around.

'I'll fetch the executioner myself,' said the King eagerly, and he hurried off.

Alice thought she might as well go back and see how the game was going on as she heard the Queen's voice in the distance, screaming with passion. She had already heard her sentence three of the players to be executed for having missed their turns, and she did not like the look of things at all, as the game was in such confusion that she never knew whether it was her turn or not. So she went in search of her hedgehog.

The hedgehog was engaged in a fight with another hedgehog, which seemed to Alice an excellent opportunity for croqueting one of them with the other; the only difficulty was that her flamingo was gone across to the other side of the garden where Alice could see it trying in a helpless sort of way to fly up into one of the trees.

By the time she had caught the flamingo and brought it back, the fight was over and both the hedgehogs were out of sight. 'But it doesn't matter much,' thought Alice, 'as all the arches are gone from this side of the ground.' So she tucked it under her arm, that it might not escape again, and went back for a little more conversation with her friend.

When she got back to the Cheshire Cat she was surprised to find quite a large crowd collected around it; there was a dispute going on between the executioner, the King, and the Queen, who were all talking at once, while all the rest were quite silent and looked very uncomfortable.

The moment Alice appeared, she was appealed to by all

three to settle the question, and they repeated their arguments to her, though as they all spoke at once, she found it very hard to make out exactly what they said.

The executioner's argument was, that you couldn't cut off a head unless there was a body to cut it off from; that he had never had to do such a thing before, and he wasn't going to begin at *his* time of life.

The King's argument was, that anything that had a head could be beheaded, and that you weren't to talk nonsense.

The Queen's argument was, that if something wasn't done about it in less than no time, she'd have everybody executed, all round. (It was this last remark that had made the whole party look so grave and anxious.)

Alice could think of nothing else to say but, 'It belongs to the Duchess; you'd better ask *her* about it.'

'She's in prison,' the Queen said to the executioner, 'fetch her here.' And the executioner went off like an arrow.

The Cat's head began fading away the moment he was gone and, by the time he had come back with the Duchess, it had entirely disappeared.

The Yellow Terror

W. L. ALDEN

'S PEAKING OF CATS,' said Captain Foster, 'I'm free to say that I don't like 'em. I don't care to be looked down on by any person, whether he be man or cat. I know I ain't the President of the United States, nor yet a millionaire, nor yet the Boss of New York, but all the same I calculate that I'm a man, and entitled to be treated as such. Now, I never knew a cat yet that didn't look down on me, same as cats do on everybody. A cat considers that men are just dirt under his or her paws, as the case may be. I can't see what it is that makes a cat believe that he is so everlastingly superior to all the men that have ever lived, but there's no denying the fact that such is his belief, and he acts accordingly. There was a Professor here one day, lecturing on all sorts of animals, and I asked him if he could explain this aggravating conduct of cats. He said that it was because cats used to be gods, thousands of years ago in the land of Egypt; but I didn't believe him. Egypt is a Scripture country, and consequently we ought not to believe anything about it that we don't read in the Bible. Show me anywhere in the Bible that Egyptian cats are mentioned as having practised as gods, and I'll believe it. Till you show it to me, I'll take the liberty of disbelieving any worldly statements that Professors or anybody else may make about Egypt.

'The most notorious cat I ever met was old Captain Smedley's Yellow Terror. His real legal name was just plain Tom: but being yellow, and being a holy terror in many respects, it got to be the fashion among his acquaintances to call him "The Yellow Terror". He was a tremendous big cat, and he had been with Captain Smedley for five years before I saw him.

'Smedley was one of the best men I ever knew. I'll admit that he was a middling hard man on his sailors, so that his ship got the reputation of being a slaughter-house, which it didn't really deserve. And there is no denying that he was a very religious man, which was another thing which made him unpopular with the men. I'm a religious man myself, even when I'm at sea, but I never held with serving out religion to a crew, and making them swallow it with belaying pins. That's what old Smedley used to do. He was in command of the barque *Medford*, out of Boston, when I knew him. I mean the city of Boston in Massachusetts, and not the little town that folks over in England call Boston: and I must say that I can't see why they should copy the names of our cities, no matter how celebrated they may be. Well! The *Medford* used to sail from Boston to London with grain, where she discharged her cargo and loaded again for China. On the outward passage we used to stop at Madeira, and the Cape, and generally Bangkok, and so on to Canton, where we filled up with tea, and then sailed for home direct.

'Now thishyer Yellow Terror had been on the ship's books for upwards of five years when I first met him. Smedley had him regularly shipped, and signed his name to the ship articles, and held a pen in his paw while he made a cross, same as if he had been a Dago. You see, in those days the underwriters wouldn't let a ship go to sea without a cat, so as to keep the rats from getting at the cargo. I don't know what a land cat may do, but there ain't a seafaring cat that would look at a rat. What with the steward, and the cook and the men forrard, being always ready to give the ship's cat a bite, the cat is generally full from kelson to deck, and wouldn't take the trouble to speak to a rat, unless one was to bite her tail. But, then, underwriters never know anything about what goes on at sea, and it's a shame that a sailorman should be compelled to give in to their ideas. The Yellow Terror had the general idea that the *Medford* was his private yacht, and that all hands were there to wait on him. And Smedley sort of confirmed him in that idea, by treating him with more respect than he treated his owners, when he was ashore. I don't blame the cat, and after I got to know what sort of a person the cat really was, I can't say as I blamed Smedley to any great extent.

'Tom, which I think I told you was the cat's real name, was far and away the best fighter of all cats in Europe, Asia, Africa, and America. Whenever we sighted land he would get himself up in his best fur, spending hours brushing and polishing it, and biting his claws so as to make sure that they were as sharp as they could be made. As soon as the ship was made fast to the quay, or anchored in the harbour, the Yellow Terror went ashore to look for trouble. He always got it too, though he had such a reputation as a fighter, that whenever he showed himself, every cat that recognised him broke for cover. Why, the gatekeeper at the London Docks – I mean the one at the Shadwell entrance – told me that he always knew when the *Medford* was warping into dock, by the stream of cats that went out of the gate, as if a pack of hounds were after them. You see that as soon as the *Medford* was reported, and word passed among the cats belonging to the ships in dock that the Yellow Terror had arrived, they judged that it was time for them to go ashore, and stop till the *Medford* should sail. Whitechapel used to be regularly overflowed with cats, and the newspapers used to have letters from scientific chaps trying to account for what they called the wave of cats that had spread over East London.

'I remember that once we laid alongside of a Russian brig, down in the basin by Old Gravel Lane. There was a tremendous big black cat sitting on the poop, and as soon as he caught sight of our Tom, he sung out to him, remarking that he was able and ready to wipe the deck up with him at any time. We all understood that the Russian was a new arrival who hadn't ever heard of the Yellow Terror, and we knew that he was, as the good book says, rushing on his fate. Tom was sitting on the rail near the mizzen rigging when the Russian made his remarks, and he didn't seem to hear them. But presently we saw him going slowly aloft till he reached our crossjack yard. He laid out on the yard arm till he was near enough to jump on to the mainyard of the Russian, and the first thing that the Russian cat knew Tom landed square on his back. The fight didn't last more than one round, and at the end of that, the remains of the Russian cat sneaked behind a water cask, and the Yellow

Terror came back by the way of the crossjack yard and went on fur brushing, as if nothing had happened.

'When Tom went ashore in a foreign port he generally stopped ashore till we sailed. A few hours before we cast off hawsers, Tom would come aboard. He always knew when we were going to sail, and he never once got left. I remember one time when we were just getting up anchor in Cape Town harbour, and we all reckoned that this time we should have to sail without Tom, he having evidently stopped ashore just a little too long. But presently alongside comes a boat, with Tom lying back at full length in the sternsheets, for all the world like a drunken sailor who has been delaying the ship, and is proud of it. The boatman said that Tom had come down to the pier and jumped into his boat, knowing that the man would row him off to the ship, and calculating that Smedley would be glad to pay the damage. It's my belief that if Tom hadn't found a boatman, he would have chartered the government launch. He had the cheek to do that or anything else.

'Fighting was really Tom's only vice; and it could hardly be called a vice, seeing as he always licked the other cat, and hardly ever came out of a fight with a torn ear or a black eye. Smedley always said that Tom was religious. I used to think that was rubbish; but after I had been with Tom for a couple of voyages I began to believe what Smedley said about him. Every Sunday when the weather permitted, Smedley used to hold service on the quarter-deck. He was a Methodist, and when it came to ladling out Scripture, or singing a hymn, he could give odds to almost any preacher. All hands, except the man at the wheel, and the lookout, were required to attend service on Sunday morning, which naturally caused considerable grumbling, as the watch below considered they had a right to sleep in peace, instead of being dragged aft for service. But they had to knock under, and what they considered even worse, they had to sing, for the old man kept a bright lookout while the singing was going on, and if he caught any man malingering and not doing his full part of the singing he would have a few words to say to that man with a belaying pin, or a rope's end, after the service was over.

'Now Tom never failed to attend service, and to do his level best to help. He would sit somewhere near the old man and pay attention to what was going on better than I've seen some folks do in first-class churches ashore. When the men sang, Tom would start in and let out a yell here and there, which showed that he meant well even if he had never been to a singing-school, and didn't exactly understand singing according to Gunter. First along, I thought that it was all an accident that the cat came to service, and I calculated that his yelling during the singing meant that he didn't like it. But after a while I had to admit that Tom enjoyed the Sunday service as much as the Captain himself, and I agreed with Smedley that the cat was a thoroughgoing Methodist.

'Now after I'd been with Smedley for about six years, he got married all of a sudden. I didn't blame him, for in the first place it wasn't any of my business; and, in the next place, I hold that a ship's captain ought to have a wife, and the underwriters would be a sight wiser if they insisted that all captains should be married, instead of insisting that all ships should carry cats. You see that if a ship's captain has a wife, he is naturally anxious to get back to her, and have his best clothes mended, and his food cooked to suit him. Consequently he wants to make good passages and he don't want to run the risk of drowning himself, or of getting into trouble with his owners, and losing his berth. You'll find, if you look into it, that married captains live longer, and get on better than unmarried men, as it stands to reason that they ought to do.

'But it happened that the woman Smedley married was an Agonyostic, which is a sort of person that doesn't believe in anything, except the multiplication table, and such-like human vanities. She didn't lose any time in getting Smedley round to her way of thinking, and instead of being the religious man he used to be, he chucked the whole thing, and used to argue with me by the hour at a time, to prove that religion was a waste of time, and that he hadn't any soul, and had never been created, but had just descended from a family of seafaring monkeys. It made me sick to hear a respectable sailorman talking such rubbish, but of course, seeing as he was my commanding officer, I had to be careful about contradicting him. I wouldn't ever yield an inch to his arguments, and I told him as respectfully as I could, that he was making the biggest mistake of his life. "Why, look at the cat," I used to say, "he's got sense enough to be religious, and if you was to tell him that he was descended from a monkey, he'd consider himself insulted." But it wasn't any use. Smedley was full of his new agonyostical theories, and the more I disagreed with him, the more set he was in his way.

'Of course he knocked off holding Sunday morning services; and the men ought to have been delighted, considering how they used to grumble at having to come aft and sing hymns, when they wanted to be below. But there is no accounting for sailors. They were actually disappointed when Sunday came and there wasn't any service. They said that we should have an unlucky voyage, and that the old man, now that he had got a rich wife, didn't consider sailors good enough to come aft on the quarter-deck, and take a hand in singing. Smedley didn't care for their opinion, but he was some considerable worried about the Yellow Terror. Tom missed the Sunday morning service, and he said so as plain as he could. Every Sunday, for three or four weeks, he came on deck, and took his usual seat

THE YELLOW TERROR

near the captain, and waited for the service to begin. When he
found out that there was no use in waiting for it, he showed
that he disapproved of Smedley's conduct in the strongest
way. He gave up being intimate with the old man, and once
when Smedley tried to pat him, and be friendly, he swore at
him, and bit him on the leg – not in an angry way, you
understand, but just to show his disapproval of Smedley's
irreligious conduct.

'When we got to London, Tom never once went ashore, and
he hadn't a single fight. He seemed to have lost all interest in
worldly things. He'd sit on the poop in a melancholy sort of
way, never minding how his fur looked, and never so much as
answering if a strange cat sang out to him. After we left
London he kept below most of the time, and finally, about the
time that we were crossing the line, he took to his bed, as you
might say, and got to be as thin and weak as if he had been
living in the forecastle of a lime-juicer. And he was that melancholy that you couldn't get him to take an interest in anything.
Smedley got to be so anxious about him that he read up in his
medical book to try and find out what was the matter with him;
and finally made up his mind that the cat had a first-class
disease with a big name something like spinal menagerie. That
was some little satisfaction to Smedley, but it didn't benefit the
cat any; for nothing that Smedley could do would induce Tom
to take medicine. He wouldn't so much as sniff at salts, and
when Smedley tried to poultice his neck, he considered himself
insulted, and roused up enough to take a piece out of the old
man's ear.

'About that time we touched at Funchal, and Smedley sent
ashore to lay in another tom-cat, thinking that perhaps a fight
would brace Tom up a little. But when the new cat was put
down alongside of Tom, and swore at him in the most impu-
dent sort of way, Tom just turned over on his other side, and
pretended to go asleep. After that we all felt that the Yellow
Terror was done for. Smedley sent the new cat ashore again,
and told me that Tom was booked for the other world, and that
there wouldn't be any more luck for us on that voyage.

'I went down to see the cat, and though he was thin and
weak, I couldn't see any signs of serious disease about him. So
I says to Smedley that I didn't believe the cat was sick at all.

97

' "Then what's the matter with him?" says the old man. "You saw yourself that he wouldn't fight, and when he's got to that point I consider that he is about done with this world and its joys and sorrows."

' "His nose is all right," said I. "When I felt it just now it was as cool as a teetaller's."

' "That does look as if he hadn't any fever to speak of," says Smedley, "and the book says that if you've got spinal menagerie you're bound to have a fever."

' "The trouble with Tom," says I, "is mental: that's what it is. He's got something on his mind that is wearing him out."

' "What can he have on his mind?" says the captain. "He's got everything to suit him aboard this ship. If he was a millionaire he couldn't be better fixed. He won all his fights while we were in Boston, and hasn't had a fight since, which shows that he can't be low-spirited on account of a licking. No, sir! You'll find that Tom's mind is all right."

' "Then what gives him such a mournful look out of his eyes?" says I. "When you spoke to him this morning he looked at you as if he was on the point of crying over your misfortunes – that is to say, if you've got any. Come to think of it, Tom begun to go into thishyer decline just after you were married. Perhaps that's what's the matter with him."

'But there was no convincing Smedley that Tom's trouble was mental, and he was so sure that the cat was going to die, that he got to be about as low-spirited as Tom himself. "I begin to wish," says Smedley to me one morning, "that I was a Methodist again, and believed in a hereafter. It does seem kind of hard that a first-class cat-fighter like Tom shouldn't have a chance when he dies. He was a good religious cat if ever there was one, and I'd like to think that he was going to a better world."

'Just then an idea struck me. "Captain Smedley," says I, "you remember how Tom enjoyed the meetings that we used to have aboard here on Sunday mornings!"

' "He did so," said Smedley. "I never saw a person who took more pleasure in his Sunday privileges than Tom did."

' "Captain Smedley," says I, putting my hand on the old man's sleeve. "All that's the matter with Tom is seeing you deserting the religion that you was brought up in, and turning agonyostical, or whatever you call it. I call it turning plain infidel. Tom's mourning about your soul, and he's miserable because you don't have any more Sunday morning meetings. I told you the trouble was mental, and now you know it is."

' "Mebbe you're right," says Smedley, taking what I'd said in a peaceable way, instead of flying into a rage, as I expected he would. "To tell you the truth, I ain't so well satisfied in my own mind as I used to be, and I was thinking last night, when I started in to say 'Now I lay me' – just from habit you know— that if I'd stuck to the Methodist persuasion I should be a blamed sight happier than I am now."

' "To-morrow's Sunday," says I, "and if I was you, Captain, I should have the bell rung for service, same as you used to do, and bring Tom up on deck, and let him have the comfort of hearing the rippingest hymns you can lay your hand to. It can't hurt you, and it may do him a heap of good. Anyway, it's worth trying, if you really want the Yellow Terror to get well."

' "I don't mind saying," says Smedley, "that I'd do almost anything to save his life. He's been with me now going on for seven years, and we've never had a hard word. If a Sunday morning meeting will be any comfort to him, he shall have it. Mebbe if it doesn't cure him, it may sort of smooth his hatchway to the tomb."

' "Now the very next day was Sunday, and at six the Captain had the bell rung for service, and the men were told to lay aft. The bell hadn't fairly stopped ringing, when Tom comes up the companion way, one step at a time, looking as if he was on his way to his own funeral. He came up to his usual place alongside of the capstan, and lay down on his side at the old man's feet, and sort of looked up at him with what anybody would have said was a grateful look. I could see that Smedley was feeling pretty serious. He understood what the cat wanted to say, and when he started in to give out a hymn, his voice sort of choked. It was a ripping good hymn, with a regular hurricane chorus, and the men sung it for all they were worth, hoping that it would meet Tom's views. He was too weak to join in with any of his old-time yells, but he sort of flopped the deck with his tail, and you could see he was enjoying it down to the ground.

'Well, the service went on just as it used to do in old times, and Smedley sort of warmed up as it went along, and by and by he'd got the regular old Methodist glow on his face. When it was all through, and the men had gone forrard again, Smedley stooped down, and picked up Tom, and kissed him, and the cat nestled up in the old man's neck and licked his chin. Smedley carried Tom down into the saloon, and sung out to the steward to bring some fresh meat. The cat turned to and ate as good a dinner as he'd ever eaten in his best days, and after he was through, he went into Smedley's own cabin, and curled up in the old man's bunk, and went to sleep purring fit to take the deck off. From that day Tom improved steadily, and by the time we got to Cape Town he was well enough to go ashore, though he was still considerable weak. I went ashore at the same time, and kept an eye on Tom, to see what he would do. I saw him pick out a small measly-looking cat, that couldn't have stood up to a full-grown mouse, and lick him in less than a minute. Then I knew that Tom was all right again, and I admired his judgment in picking out a small cat that was suited to his weak condition. By the time that we got to Canton, Tom was as well in body and mind as he had ever been; and when we sailed, he came aboard with two inches of his tail missing, and his starboard ear carried away, but he had the air of having licked all creation, which I don't doubt he had done, that is to say, so far as all creation could be found in Canton.

'I never heard any more of Smedley's agonyostical nonsense. He went back to the Methodists again, and he always said that Tom had been the blessed means of showing him the error of his ways. I heard that when he got back to Boston, he gave Mrs Smedley notice that he expected her to go to the Methodist meeting with him every Sunday, and that if she didn't, he should consider that it was a breach of wedding articles, and equivalent to mutiny. I don't know how she took it, or what the consequences were, for I left the *Medford* just then, and took command of a barque that traded between Boston and the West Indies. And I never heard of the Yellow Terror after that voyage, though I often thought of him, and always held that for a cat he was the ablest cat, afloat or ashore, that any man ever met.'

C Stands for Cuisine

BEVERLEY NICHOLS

EVERY PUSSY, if given a chance, is an epicure. The pussy who has been brought up with love and understanding never gobbles her food, and though on rising from the table she may not send her compliments to the chef in so many words, she makes it very clear if she has been pleased or not. Even non-Fs will agree that this demeanour is in striking contrast to the behaviour of dogs who gulp their meals in a grossly animal manner, and very seldom complain even if they are offered the sort of fare which used to be provided on British Railways. In which their conduct strikingly resembles that of their masters.

My own cats have always been fortunate in the fact that they have been served by a first-class chef in the form of Gaskin. He takes as much trouble with their meals as with mine, and would be as distressed if their whiting were not *à point* as if my soufflé had failed to rise. I need hardly say that, in the course of twenty-five years, neither of these disasters has yet occurred.

Moreover, Gaskin takes almost as much trouble with what might be called the general arrangements of the table as with the actual preparation of the dishes. Thus, he regards placing as of vital importance. Many of us have probably attended dinner parties in Paris where there have been frightful *froideurs* about procedure, when some obscure but legitimate count has threatened to leave the room because he has been placed in an inferior position to an equally obscure, but bastard, marquis.

Throughout history, members of the French aristocracy have always been so busy fussing about where they sit at table that they usually have failed to notice that the entire country is sinking rapidly into the abyss. Gaskin's seating arrangements for the pussies arise from no such foolish snobbishness; he has merely learned, from long experience, that there are certain places where they like to dine and certain places where they do not, and that is that. Why they have chosen these places, nobody knows, and, as far as I am aware, nobody has ever been so vulgar as to ask them.

Thus, 'Four' insists on breakfasting under the kitchen sink, 'Five' on the kitchen table, and Oscar in a corner by the side of the dresser. Were the plates to be placed in any other position, they would be ignored. There would be pained expressions, lashings of the tail, shruggings of the shoulders and exits into the garden, and no food would be partaken until Gaskin had come to his senses.

This fastidiousness has its drawbacks. There have been a few unhappy occasions when I have been abroad, and when Gaskin has gone away for the night. Needless to say, before doing so, he has engaged a reliable woman as a 'temporary' to attend to the cats' menus. He has inquired into her antecedents, vetted her character and thoroughly coached her in the technique. The fish must be cooked just so long, and no more. The milk must be warmed. There must be a large bowl of fresh water. The times for breakfast and dinner must be strictly observed: 7.45 for breakfast, 4.15 for dinner. Above all, the position of the plates must never vary . . . 'Four' under the sink, 'Five' on the kitchen table, and Oscar by the dresser. 'You understand?' says Gaskin. Yes, says the temporary, she understands. Whereupon Gaskin, with a last beetling glance, hands her the latchkeys keys and departs, not without forebodings.

Alas, the forebodings have sometimes been justified. Even reliable women, with clean aprons and rosy faces, may have a sinister streak of non-Fness in their characters. Such a one was Mrs . . . never mind, we will call her Mrs X. How was Gaskin to know that Mrs X, who had impeccable references, with duchesses raving about her soufflés across pages of coroneted writing paper, could possibly be so wickedly incompetent about feeding the cats? No – it was not incompetence, it was

done with deliberation. For Mrs X, arriving on the following morning in the empty house – admittedly on time – suddenly decided that the cats were 'pampered'. (In subsequent cross-examination she actually *confessed* to this.) And so, having cooked the fish, she set it all on a large plate in the centre of the floor and left the cats to it, under the astonishing impression that they would eat it. She had some odd, barbaric notion that she was 'teaching them a lesson'. I am not suggesting that she was actually a sadist, and I believe that she was quite a good mother to her own three very plain and sniffly children who would probably have eaten with the greatest relish off a communal plate in the middle of the floor. All the same, I really do think it a great pity that there should be such women in the world.

Cats, of course, have exquisite table manners, though their etiquette differs somewhat from the more restricted human variety. I wonder if any of the following customs are shared by the pets of other Fs?

1. *Dabbing*. This is permissible in the best circles. My own principal dabber is 'Five'. He usually decides to dab when offered a small piece of the dish one is eating oneself. He enters the dining-room, sits by one's chair, and subjects one to a steady stare. Needless to say, he would never do anything so impolite as to mew, or to reach up to the table. The stare is duly rewarded by a small portion of chicken or steak or whatever one may be eating. This is cut up, as a *bonne bouche*, and placed before him. Whereupon 'Five' lowers his head and contemplates the *bonne bouche*. This contemplation may last for several minutes. 'Really, "Five", you are a spoilt cat,' one says. 'That is a beautiful piece of chicken. There are many cats, sleeping on the Embankment, who would be most grateful for . . .' But one does not finish the sentence, for if one begins to think of cats sleeping on the Embankment one will have a wretched night and get no sleep oneself. However, the reproof seems to have registered, for 'Five' suddenly emerges from contemplation and gives the piece of chicken a sharp dab with his right paw. It slides to the edge of the plate; then it is dabbed back again with the left paw. For all I know, this may be 'Five's' retort to one's remark about the Embankment; it may be his way of saying that such painful subjects should not be mentioned at meal

times. Whatever the reason, he eventually eats the piece of chicken. Having done so, he sits down and makes his toilet. He never asks for more.

2. *Growling*. This habit may seem to non-Fs to conflict with the claim for 'exquisite table manners'. I do not think so, for two reasons. Firstly, because there is only one dish – at least as far as my own cats are concerned – which gives rise to growling . . . rabbit. Why this should be, I do not pretend to understand. I can only register the fact that, when rabbit is on the menu, growls are in the air. They are very fierce growls, accompanied by dramatic movements of the head over the shoulder, as though seeking some imaginary enemy.

The other reason why I am, as it were, pro-growling, is because I think it would greatly enliven human dinner parties if it were generally adopted. I would not growl over most of the dishes one is offered in British households, but I would certainly growl over caviare. If one is the least important guest, as one usually is, and if one is sitting in Starvation Corner, and if one sees great dollops of this ambrosia being ladled out to fat rich ladies who could well afford to buy it by the bucket, and if one is eventually given a tiny reluctant scraping from the bottom of the jar . . . surely one *should* growl? One should not only growl, but scratch and pounce and hiss. One dies, in spirit, but not in fact, and repression, as we all know, ties the psyche up in knots.

3. *Leaving a small piece uneaten*. All delicately nurtured felines do this. It is the ultimate proof of good breeding. Even if one adopts the scruffiest alley cat, as soon as he has been plumped out and given the blessed assurance that his days of scrummaging in dustbins are over, he will leave a little bit of dinner uneaten. I have never known any exceptions to this rule. It is absolutely *de rigueur* and it suggests that somewhere, in the Feline Archives, there must be some venerated volume of Etiquette for Cats, thumbed by countless paws and sniffed over by hosts of little noses, whose lessons are passed down from generation to generation.

The Coat

MARY WILLIAMS

A T FIRST, I didn't mind. The cat had been Fay's mascot during her theatrical career, and I realized there was a strong bond between them. So when we got married, and Fay Lester 'gave up her career' . . . her own words . . . to live with me in the wilds of Cornwall, where I was mining engineer to a flourishing tin company, it seemed quite natural for her to bring her pet along.

She was ten years my senior, although she didn't look it . . . being a natural blonde: slight, fair, with large hazel eyes glittering gold one moment and green the next between thick dark lashes that owed nothing to artifice.

I *should* have realized, but didn't, that, despite her appearance, her grip on audiences was beginning to wane, owing perhaps to a slightly over-emotional old-fashioned style of acting, and possibly a subtle deterioration of physical vitality that left occasional gaps in communication. But I never thought of it, being far too infatuated to delve into abstruse whys and wherefores. It was sufficient that she cared enough to jump into matrimony so promptly, and with such apparent zest.

I'm not denying that, at thirty-two, women hadn't liked me before . . . they had, in the way the frail type often go for strong men six-footers of the rugged kind. But until Fay came along I'd managed to avoid any long-term commitment.

Anyway, after the wedding which had all the glamorous, corny trappings of a famous stage beauty stepping off into the

106

romantic unknown with, to quote . . . 'the *one* man this time
. . . the love of her life' . . . we went straight back, at her wish,
to Port Erith, and our new home which stood on a hill overlooking the sea, two miles from the little town and four from St
Tude's where I had my job.

The house, originally a large cottage which had been converted recently to modern standards and added on to considerably, cost me a packet, but I didn't mind.

'But darling, it's *heavenly*,' Fay had exclaimed the first time
I'd taken her round. 'How did you *know* so *exactly* what I'd like?
And the garden! Quite, gorgeous. Sheba will love it.
Everything she needs . . . trees, little secret hidey-holes, and
that darling little copse at the end . . .'

Her voice had trailed off dreamily into a 'little girl' vision of
her own which amused me in a mild way . . . *then*.

Sheba, of course, was the cat; a spayed Persian queen . . .
pure white with glinting green eyes, staring enigmatically with
a kind of remote contempt from an abundance of thick fur. No
one could have denied she was quite a beauty, and for the first
few weeks at Moongate – Fay's name for our house – the sight
of her padding proudly around, fine tail erect, added a certain
air of feline luxury to the new premises, although Fay eventually was always her target . . . the object of her passion and
desire.

It didn't worry me in the least, during those early days, to go
off each day leaving the curled-up white form on Fay's lap in a
lounge chair, or wandering by her side in the garden when I
returned. Sheba, after all, was just a pet, and Fay was a very
feminine type of woman; the kind that needed something to
cuddle, in solitary moments. Maybe, I thought . . . just *maybe*
perhaps, there could be a child if we didn't leave it too late.
Women around forty had been known to have children without much trouble.

I was kidding myself, though. Fay didn't want any. And as
the weeks passed it was all too obvious, though she did her
best not to show it.

I didn't blame her really. It would have been wrong, I suppose. But there were other ways of getting over that hurdle
than the one she chose . . . a certain withdrawal of passion, too
subtle at first to be conclusive . . . just . . . 'Oh darling. I've had

a hard day . . . Mrs Thomas was late, and I had to get down to the chores myself . . .' Mrs Thomas was our 'daily' who came three hours each morning to tackle the domestic work. Or, on other occasions . . . 'I'm tired. Really exhausted, Rod. Guess it's all the excitement . . .' and she'd looked at me with the frail imploring gaze that I just couldn't argue with. So I'd accepted it at first. I had to. But eventually, after a month or two, it was just too much.

It happened to be a Saturday and, as it was fine, with the pungent, heady magic of early autumn in the air, I suggested a picnic out, on the moors somewhere.

'What about it?' I asked Fay, early. 'Let's take off like a couple of kids and eat sandwiches in the bracken.' Although of course there was more to it in my mind than that.

I thought for a moment her eyes were wary; they had a kind of sideways glance . . . a bit critical, as though she doubted my masculine motive. Then she said, gaily . . . too gaily, I suppose, though I'd shrugged off the thought at the time, 'All right darling. Just as you say. It'll be fun for Sheba too. She's not had a real sniff of the moors yet.'

'*Sheba*?' I echoed sharply, 'surely, for once, that cat of yours can make shift for herself in the house. She has a box, all our silk cushions, a bed, eiderdown and armchairs to choose from; and a choice of chicken and rabbit to guzzle at. For God's sake darling, let's be *free* for once.'

'*Free*? From Sheba? Don't be *mean*, Rod.' Her voice was suddenly cold. 'The house is still strange to her. And if there was a storm or anything . . . she'd be *terrified* alone. No. If we can't have Sheba, I shan't go either.'

And so, of course, Sheba went along with us. Possibly if I'd been cleverer and more cooperative, the outing might have worked. But from the time we found a suitable place sheltered from the breeze by rocks, and clumps of bushes, making it a kind of bower, Sheba took charge, claiming the first taste of our sandwiches . . . chicken, and, as usual, crouching close to Fay with her green eyes glinting adoringly from her furry face. Once, as I watched the two of them in feline communication, I said irritably to the creature, 'Go on . . . shoo! *Shoo*! . . .' waving a paper napkin at its nose. 'Take a walk, can't you?'

The cat merely blinked, while Fay said defensively, 'How *can* you! Don't be so cruel, Rod. I thought you *liked* animals.'

'I do in their place,' I said shortly.

'Then why . . .?' Her voice trailed off. She shrugged before adding, 'Sheba's place is *here*; with me. It always has been. So please, darling, don't interfere.'

'Interfere?' I thought, savagely, grabbing a sandwich. Fay was my wife, wasn't she? And I bloody well hadn't gone with her on an outing like a couple of scouts with a mascot, to make a friendly threesome.

There was the scent of heather, fallen blackberries, and brine in the air. The bracken beneath us was a bed for lovers. I desired her urgently, with a sudden thrusting need. Always before, I'd managed to be gentle; now restraint was gone and I was suddenly on top of her, my hands about her breasts, locating through the thin blouse she wore. She struggled, screamed . . . at least, I thought it was a scream, or it could have been a cat's cry.

The next moment a smothering ball of soft fur had landed on my head, and streaks of pain were seering my cheek. One fist shot out, as I managed to free myself and jump up. Blood splashed my shirt, trickling down my jaw from jagged, clawed scars.

I didn't speak, just mopped my face, while Fay sat up, arranged her clothes again, and said with a mixture of triumph and contrition, in smug, well-bred tones, 'I'm sorry you're hurt, Rod. Sheba didn't *mean* that . . . did you, my sweet . . .?' Her voice, like her eyes, were liquid with love for the wild brute.

'No?' I said harshly.

'Of course not. She's protective that's all. You shouldn't have . . . have . . . tried to . . . to . . .'

'Seduce my wife?' I finished for her. 'No, I shouldn't. Not in the presence of that damned animal. Well . . . I'm telling you Fay, it'll have to *go*.'

'Sheba will never go, unless I go with her,' Fay said coldly. 'Obviously you resent her. You haven't the first inkling of how to treat animals, and they always *know*. If you were more tolerant . . .'

'Tolerant?' I snapped, 'What, for God's sake, have I been for weeks now? When was it we last made love? Tell me that.

You've been a pretty tired woman where I've been concerned lately, and that's a fact. But Sheba! . . . Oh *no*. Sheba comes first, doesn't she? Love me, love my cat. That's about the size of it. But get this into your head, darling, and I mean it . . . no more of it. In future, when I want you, you'll grin and bear it, whether you like it or not. And no *cat* around. Understand?'

She didn't reply. But I knew I'd made my point.

And that night, following the travesty of the picnic, I proved it.

Fay was lying between the pink sheets, with a book, when I went upstairs and, as usual, Sheba huddled close to her. She glanced at me as I undressed, and maybe there was a hint of fear in her eyes as I went to the bed. But I didn't say anything; just lifted the cat up . . . I'd taken the precaution of wearing gloves . . . and threw her, hissing, out of the room on to the landing.

Then I went to Fay, very deliberately pulled back the sheets, and took the lacy thing from her body, revealing the almost childlike breasts and slender thighs pressed together protectingly.

'Don't,' she whispered. 'Don't you *dare* . . . Rod . . .'

But I did dare. I took her as ruthlessly as I'd have taken a petulant mistress, forgetting temporarily that this was the delicately cherished glamorous woman I'd adored and felt so privileged to marry.

Afterwards, of course, I was ashamed . . . not for showing her once and for all how things were going to be when I felt that way . . . but of my manner of showing it. I tried to apologize but she lay simply staring at the ceiling, moaning a little, though tearlessly. It was as though I didn't exist for her any more, and that one act . . . induced by my resentment of the cat, had alienated and divided us completely.

She was withdrawn and silent the next morning, refusing breakfast which I took up to her on a tray.

'Fay . . .' I said, trying to ignore the malicious gleam of Sheba's eyes . . . the sickening sight of white fur curled against my wife's shoulders . . . 'be sensible, *please*. We've got to adjust a bit . . . both of us. In marriage these things do happen sometimes. It can't always be one or the other. It's *both* of us.

Our life together.' She didn't answer. 'So please do eat something. You'll feel better then.'

'I'll eat when I feel like it,' she answered, coldly remote. 'Mrs Thomas will be here presently. If I want anything, she'll get it.'

Smothering a hot retort, I kissed her forehead lightly and left for St Tude's. When I returned that evening she was nowhere in the house; everywhere seemed strangely quiet and still. The days were closing in now and, though fine, the autumn sky was already yellowing to grey behind the copse bordering the garden. As I stared across the lawn a leaf dropped soundlessly from a nearby chestnut, leaving the networked branches dark and exposed, except for the last remaining foliage grouped in hanging fingered shapes . . . the shapes of dead hands . . . which would soon be gone.

I felt uneasy. Chilled by foreboding. And then I saw them . . . two white shapes, Fay and Sheba, strolling slowly, almost glidingly, from the trees, along the path bordering the lawn. The cat was in her arms when they reached the house.

'Oh hullo, Rod,' she said absently. 'You're early, aren't you?'

'No,' I answered abruptly. 'Late if anything, and hungry.'

'I'll get you something.' Her voice was quiet; very cold and composed. I'd have preferred her to be edgy or sharp.

'Don't let it worry you,' I told her. 'I can fend for myself if necessary. I expect you're tired after your ramble.' My heavy sarcasm seemed to escape her. 'Oh no,' she said, sweetly reasonable. 'Sheba and I have just been gorgeously aimless and at peace . . . haven't we, my pet?'

Churning inwardly with mounting rage and resentment, I managed to say briefly, 'What is it then . . . the meal?'

'Oh . . .' she paused, wiping a strand of pale hair vaguely from her forehead. 'There's cold pie in the fridge . . . or eggs . . . we've had ours. But . . .' Her voice trailed off.

I turned on my heel savagely and went to the kitchen. 'We'! It was then I knew I was going to kill Sheba. And as the days went by my resolve intensified. Possibly if Fay had shown the slightest warmth to me . . . even once let me touch her without wincing, I might have weakened. But she didn't. She remained outwardly poised, cool and remote . . . though what went on in her mind I never knew . . . could only guess at the emotional yearnings over that damned cat.

It was unnatural. I knew I had to end it.

And so one evening when Fay was having her bath and Sheba, as usual, waiting for her in the bedroom, I took a syringe . . . and with all the skill I'd learned in an early brief training as a vet . . . very deliberately put her painlessly to sleep. She was an oldish cat. It didn't take long . . . no more than a minute. And, when it was over, I went downstairs, leaving her there, curled up on the pink eiderdown, waiting for Fay.

Even now, so long afterwards, I consider I was quite justified, arguing that, with Sheba gone, Fay and I would have the chance of a new beginning and a normal life ahead.

But it didn't work out that way.

She didn't fight me. Oh no; it would have been better if she had. She just accepted my explanation that cats did die like that sometimes . . . just curled up and went to sleep . . . 'or maybe she could have picked up something that disagreed with her', I concluded. It made no difference at all. Fay was beyond theorizing or argument. She just fretted and went about in a bemused way, as though nothing mattered any more. I buried Sheba at the bottom of the garden on the edge of the copse, because there had to be a stone, suitably inscribed, according to my wife . . . although I thought it pretty mawkish and morbid. Still, if that was what she wanted, I made no objection, and was thankful when the whole thing was over.

At least I *thought* it was over.

As it happened, it was only the beginning.

With the approach of winter, I made tentative overtures to Fay and, once or twice, made love to her, if you could call it lovemaking. She didn't resist but lay there cold, rigid and unresponsive, while I tried desperately to rouse some emotion . . . even anger, rather than such dead negation of body and spirit.

One evening, when we lay afterwards side by side without warmth or words between us, she turned her head suddenly, gave me a long searching look, and then said, 'Did *you* kill Sheba?'

Though taken aback, I managed to answer calmly enough, 'Don't be silly. If I'd wanted to get rid of her I'd have put her in a sack and chucked her over the cliffs into the sea . . . or at least drowned and buried her. You'd never have known then, would you? You'd have thought she'd just wandered off like cats do and got lost . . . or injured.'

'Not Sheba,' she said firmly.

'Fay! For heaven's sake,' I prevaricated . . . 'do I look like a murderer?' She stared at me reflectively before answering in a queer, contemptuous sort of way, 'Yes, I think you do.'

'Then get your thoughts straight,' I said abruptly, 'and don't mention that bloody animal to me again.'

Nothing more was said that night. But all the next day I couldn't get the incident out of my mind. Work was impossible; I just mooched about, smoked, and toyed unsuccessfully with books of figures that didn't make sense at all. I felt so browned off, in fact, that I gave Fay a ring telling her not to keep a meal for me, I'd be dining out – business appointment.

There was no business, of course. I just went to a place I knew on the harbour where they had slap-up meals to candle-light, with all the expensive trappings that attracted the select few who could afford to pay for it. There weren't many in . . . just half a dozen or so, including a girl I used to know, Cora Ellis. She was an artist and, at one time, I'd toyed with the idea of taking the plunge with her . . . not necessarily marriage, but at least some sort of steady relationship that would have satisfied our wandering libidos. Cora was dark, picturesque, and quite luscious in her own particular way. Clever too. She had a mind of her own that saw things clearly, which probably accounted for her considerable success as an abstract painter.

That night she was wearing an orange cape over some dark green maxi thing . . . kaftans they call them, don't they? . . . Immense silver ear-rings swung below her black hair. Yes, her hair was truly black. Maybe she had gipsy blood in her; she liked to think so, but had told me once, 'It's all an act, darling. Good publicity.'

She was very honest with her friends. This was one of the things I liked about her, and several times I'd thought lately what a fool I'd been not to marry her instead of Fay. But then our chemistries, I suppose, hadn't clicked. There'd been no mystery . . . no subtle conquest of the unknown. Whereas with Fay . . . *Fay!* I pulled myself together, and went to Cora's table.

'Mind if I join you?' I asked.

'Darling Rod, of course not. Thrilled.' She indicated a chair. I took it and glanced at the menu, a fantastic crimson affair embossed with gold. 'What's up?' Cora said after a brief pause. 'You look a bit . . .'

'Browned off,' I finished for her. 'That's putting it mildly.'

'No. I wasn't going to say that,' she remarked. 'Belligerent, I think . . . like someone wanting a fight, who can't find anyone to fight with.'

I couldn't help smiling. She had so completely hit the nail on the head. Well, naturally, after I'd ordered a meal that would have burned a hole in anyone's pocket, I gave her the rough outline of my married history.

'Hm.' Cora commented when the story was finished . . . and I admit it must have sounded a pretty adolescent situation, the way I told it. 'You have got yourself into a state. I wouldn't have believed it, honest I wouldn't . . . a down-to-earth hefty male like you shattered by a cat . . .'

'The cat's dead,' I interrupted.

'It makes no difference. You've got it on your mind still . . . a kind of guilt complex, I suppose. And there's no need. You had to do something; well, you did it. But that's not your problem, is it, Rod?'

'What do you mean?'

'The real trouble's Fay.'

'I don't need telling that.'

'Yes you do, darling, so you can see straight.' She shrugged. 'Or maybe you'd rather go round in circles. But that's not like you.'

'Go on.'

'She's a whole ten years older than you. I know what you're going to say . . . she doesn't look it, she's beautiful, and famous and very, very feminine. True enough. But forty plus doesn't always go for passion. Some women are frigid then. I do know, my father's a doctor. Remember? In any case, I shouldn't have to tell you this.' She stubbed a cigarette on the tray and lit another, stared at me thoughtfully for a moment or two, then concluded, 'You've either got to play things gently, *her* way, or not at all. That is, unless you want a divorce . . .'

'I don't,' I replied.

A wry smile touched her lips. 'I thought not. Some women don't know their luck . . .'

'Cora. I . . .' for a moment I wondered; just played again with the idea of what it would be like to go to bed with her, have something for once that was mutual and unrestricted by fears and frustration! She had a beautiful body, and despite her diamond-bright mind, those limpid eyes of hers, full, perfectly modelled lips indicated an inner sensuality that could be exciting. And yet . . . my thoughts wavered off doubtfully, which she must have sensed, because she remarked apropos of nothing I'd spoken aloud . . . 'Don't, Rod.' Her hand touched mine lightly. 'I know you like me. So let's leave it that way. There could be more if you were that kind. But you're not, Fay's still the only one, I can see that . . .'

'Yes,' I admitted. 'I love her.'

'Then why not go home and tell her so . . . say it the way you've just said it to me, and try your damnedest, darling, to believe things will adjust in time. Maybe they will; I hope so, because I know that's what you want.'

I doubted that her advice would work; still, I decided to give it a try, and half an hour later was on my way back to Moongate.

As I walked up the path to the front door I thought Fay's name for the house had been an apt choice. The moon, indeed, was bright that night, spilling a luminous pattern of light and shade across the landscape, in which the cottage crouched, looking curiously alone and bereft.

At moments, the windows that side were lit to momentary pale clarity . . . then just as quickly became bleak and dark as though an immense hand had washed all vestige of life away.

I went in. Fay was nowhere about; I was puzzled, briefly, and a little frightened, until I went to the lounge windows, opened the curtains, and saw a white shape at the end of the garden, standing perfectly motionless by Sheba's grave. The sight of her back, so grief-stricken somehow, filled me with remorse; yet behind the sympathy jealousy still lingered, because of her concentration . . . her overwhelming passionate devotion to the creature that had for so long shared her life. Can desire, if strong enough, resurrect the dead? Since then I have never really been able to make up my mind. But, at one

point, I could have sworn a ghostly feline shape emerged round the stone, tail waving in the sudden unclouded light, as it moved and curled round Fay's still form. Her head was slightly bent, her hands, I imagined, clasped in an attitude of prayer. The sight was unnerving; my whole body felt cold suddenly, as though death itself had touched me.

Then the moon slipped behind a veil of cloud, and I jerked myself to reality. It was a cold night. Fay was not robust. She could catch pneumonia out there in only her night things and flimsy wrap. As I went to bring her in I blamed myself for not getting a specialist to see her earlier; obviously she was ill . . . physically and mentally depleted through her unwholesome love and grief for Sheba.

When I reached the copse where the headstone stood like some pagan memorial to an ancient god, Fay turned and looked at me.

I was shocked by her expression . . . the dead, transfixed stare of her eyes, which in the moonlight glinted pure green, with no flicker of movement . . . no recognition, or even surprise. She could have been in a trance. Catalepsy or something, and I thought how apt was the word.

I took her hand. It was ice-cold. 'Fay,' I said, 'come along . . . come back darling. You'll catch your death. You shouldn't . . . you really shouldn't do this sort of thing . . .'

I don't know whether she heard me or understood. She made no response, but allowed herself to be led compliantly back to the house. I guided her upstairs to bed, then got a hot drink for her which she took without demur.

She went to sleep quite soon, and lay there breathing deeply and evenly like a child, apparently at peace. I wondered, then, how I could ever have desired her so remorselessly and with such savage physical urgency. There was nothing of her at that moment I wanted, or could imagine I would want again. Before I switched off the light I noticed the tiny lines networking the corner of her closed eyes . . . the faintly sunken upper lip, and too thin neck already faintly creased. Cora's words echoed through my mind . . . 'She's a whole ten years older than you . . .' and for the first time I recognized their truth.

I was swamped by pity that held no passion or need, except the need in myself to expiate what I'd done. I would get her

another pet, I thought, as I lay wakeful and ill at ease . . . a kitten, or puppy perhaps . . . something she could lavish her affection on, leaving me free of the burden of guilt and loving.

Or . . . had I ever really loved her?

A man does not like to doubt himself or his motives. But that night I faced a whole lot of them; and, when at last I went to sleep, it was not of Fay I dreamed but of a vibrant, clear-eyed young woman of warmth and generosity. Cora . . . who wanted me, and had sent me back to my own sterile illusion, and . . . though she did not know it . . . to so much else that was unspeakable and degrading.

By a strange quirk of fate, Fay's mood was subtly different the next morning. Although still quiet and remote, her eyes held awareness, as though for the first time since our early married days she was seeing me as a person . . . or even as a man. There was something discomforting about it. I usually took up her breakfast first, and had mine on my own, but that day she came down herself, made tea and toast, sat opposite me at the breakfast table, pouring from the pot, with all the grace displayed so effectively in the past on the stage. She was, I remembered, looking more than usually glamourous . . . and I was quite aware that she knew it and had laid it on for my benefit. It was all rather creepy; I couldn't help wondering if I'd talked in my sleep, or if, with some sixth sense, she guessed about Cora. The guilt complex flooded back in me. I could feel her watching me all the time even when my eyes were turned away.

'Oh damn!' I thought. 'Why *now*? Why for God's sake has she to soften at this point and make me feel a real heel . . .?'

I couldn't fathom it; couldn't make out myself either . . . why, when such a short time ago one warm glance from her could have made me cock-a-hoop . . . all it gave me now was a smothering sense of irritation and longing to be out of the house.

I did my best to appear appreciative, of course, an attempt which encouraged her even to go to the door when I left, with her face tilted slightly upwards, obviously expecting me to kiss her . . . a habit which for weeks she'd discouraged.

I did so very briefly and lightly on the cheek. She smiled, and said, 'Bye darling. Try not to be late tonight.'

As I walked down the lane to the shed where I kept the car I tried to puzzle things out; tried to fathom the reason for my sudden change of heart from Fay to Cora. In the restaurant the previous evening, Cora had registered primarily as a good friend, an attractive confidante of my woes who hadn't counted in any way as a rival to my wife. Now, suddenly, everything was different and, as I traced events retrospectively, I knew the crucial moment had been when Fay and I had stood in the moonlight, face to face by Sheba's grave.

For those few momentous seconds, an empty shell had confronted me. Then, afterwards . . . I recollected the tired, aged look of her in sleep . . . followed, only an hour ago, by an inexplicable decision to make breakfast . . . the look of almost coy supplication when she stood at the door, waiting. I didn't like it. And, at the same time, I didn't know why. After all, it could be she was making an effort at last; had decided to end the 'war' between us, and really try.

But it wasn't that. And deep down I knew it. Fay was not Fay any more. She'd gone, replaced by . . . what? I pulled myself together with an effort. The idea was monstrous, absurd. But at the back of my mind the fantastic idea still niggled and tormented me. And when I returned in the evening she was waiting for me; luxuriously dressed in one of those cream and satiny looking affairs bought at an expensive store for dining and wining in secret . . . a kind of dual-purpose outfit that could be respectably worn in company, or seductively displayed on private occasions. Ours, of course, was intended to be *very* private that evening and, as she bent over the table putting the plate before me, the dress, gown, or whatever they called it, slipped provocatively below the curved breasts, revealing one pink nipple . . . as pink and probing as a . . . a loving cat's tongue.

I pretended not to notice. But I was revolted. Unduly so. And when she didn't zip up properly, I said sharply, 'Fay, your dress is undone.'

She gave a little moue of surprise, arched her eyebrows and replied in a soft, silky voice, 'Darling . . . I'm so *sorry*. But you don't mind, do you? Not as it's just us?'

She returned to a place right behind my chair, and twined

118

her arms round my neck. I could feel her soft hair brush my face by the ear, and I lifted one hand irritably.

'For heaven's sake, Fay. Let me eat. I'm hungry.'

She moved away, and took her place at the table, facing me.

'So am I,' she said, with a meaningful, repelling glance. 'Terribly, *terribly* hungry, darling.'

And that night her hunger consumed me. Not in the normal way of a woman in love with a man, but with sickening possessive lust that made me loathe her soft white limbs, the pressure of her body against mine . . . close, so close, I nearly suffocated.

It was not until early morning that I had any sleep at all and, when I got up, I found Fay was already downstairs with an excellent breakfast prepared and, as before, looking quite glamorous in a nauseating way.

After that things intensified. When I was at home she could not leave me alone, but was forever fawning and purring over me, pressing her lips against my face, and her thighs against mine. As the days passed though, those thighs weren't so slender any more. She was putting on weight, and gradually becoming more luscious and overbearing.

One evening I met Cora by chance as I was about to get into the car. In contrast to Fay she now looked almost coltish in her youthful safari trouser-suit showing blue beneath her green anorak.

'Hullo,' she said, half timidly. 'How are things, Rod?'

I paused before replying . . . 'They're . . . different.'

'Oh.' I thought she looked briefly disappointed, then she said, quite gaily, though the gaiety was probably forced. 'I'm glad.'

'You needn't be,' I retorted curtly.

'How come?'

Looking her straight in the eyes, I answered:

'Because I made one hell of a mistake, Cora.'

'You mean . . . she doesn't want you? But you've just said . . .'

'Oh she *wants* me,' I retorted bitterly. 'She wants me too much. The trouble is, I don't want *her* any more. I . . . loathe her, Cora . . .'

She stared at me blankly, uncomprehendingly for a moment, then she said, 'What do you propose to do about it?'

'Nothing. Not for the moment,' I told her. 'Except just get into this car, drive straight back so I'm there in time for our tasty little meal together.'

'Rod . . . you're not well,' she protested. 'What is it? Do explain . . . just a little. I've no right to ask, I know; but . . .'

'You have, Cora. You've every right. The snag is, it's too late now. I'm hooked. For good. By a *cat*. A feline sickening cat of a woman who won't let me alone . . . even at work, she's *there*, in my mind. And I don't know how long I can stand it.'

As I drove away I glanced back once and saw Cora standing motionless watching me, most probably thinking I'd gone quite off my chump. Recalling a little of our conversation I thought so myself.

Shortly before Christmas when I returned in the evening I saw a furry pale shape poking about a holly bush in the garden. My heart lurched, and almost stopped for a moment, then bounded on again as the form straightened and came towards me. The half light was already quickly fading into darkness, but when she straightened, lifting her head, I saw it was Fay, wearing a coat I'd not seen before . . . a long-haired, very thick and soft affair, with a hood in purest white.

'How do you like it?' she cooed under the light when we went in, turning this way and that . . . prancing and preening herself like any prize feline animal on show. From the hood her hazel eyes had a green covetous look, and it seemed to me for a sickening second that the fur on her head was slightly pointed above each ear, reminding me of the one thing I wanted to forget. 'I bought it for a song . . .' she went on, 'honestly. Don't you think it's the most gorgeous creation on earth?'

'Take it off,' I shouted, unable to control myself. 'Take it off, do you hear? And never let me see you wearing it again.'

She looked temporarily stupefied but, after a brief pause, did what I said, muttering almost under her breath, 'I don't understand you, darling. I believe you're jealous.' She sidled up to me, touching my arm fawningly. '*Is* that it, Rod? Are you really jealous of a coat?'

I did then what I'd not done before, pushed her quite roughly away, so that she fell against a chair. She straightened herself, one hand to her side, while I found grace enough to say, 'I'm sorry, I didn't mean to do that.'

She came towards me stealthily, and very maliciously, her eyes narrowed and fiery-cold . . . 'Then don't ever do it again, darling,' she said through her teeth, with a hissing sound. 'I have very sharp claws, you know.'

Yes, I knew. I think I'd known it for quite a time.

The question was . . . how to clip them.

At Christmas, mercifully, I went down with a touch of flu which meant that Fay's amours, to a certain extent, were curtailed, though at nights I was aware of her sexual and emotional yearnings as she lay beside me, plump and white limbed, with her hair occasionally tickling my face. I had a slight temperature which probably accounted for the illusion that she was growing down round her mouth and contours of her chin. Even her arms sometimes seemed to have the sheen of silky hair on them, and occasionally, when she went out at night, 'for a little wander', in her own words, because she couldn't sleep, I would watch her from the window cross the lawn to the copse where she would stand briefly by Sheba's grave, looking for all the world like a great cat herself, in her white coat, before passing on down a path through the trees which led eventually to a picturesque but dangerous place . . . an abandoned quarry of precipitious depth where sheep in the past had fallen and died.

It was thinking of the quarry that gave me the idea, although I would not at first acknowledge it, even to myself. However, when I came round to facing things squarely, the idea seemed reasonable and a very practical solution to a situation that had become intolerable.

If I could have tackled Fay honestly, and said frankly, 'Look Fay . . . our marriage isn't a success. We're not suited to each other . . . I don't love you as I thought I did; will you, for both our sakes, consider a divorce? I'll be generous . . . fit in with any arrangements you want, financially speaking, and we could remain good friends . . .'

But I couldn't. Several times I tried, with the words on the tip of my tongue. Then my courage faltered. She was so intimidating, facing me in the way she'd had lately, of devouring me with her eyes, hands half extended towards me, palms upwards, with fingers slightly curved, pearly pointed nails held inwards . . . though graspingly, waiting for what she could have of me. Yes, it was *me* she wanted . . . and only me. Money, security . . . friendship . . . these had no meaning for Fay any more. I was her 'thing' . . . her possession, or, as some would say, her 'familiar'.

And so I coldly and calculatingly formulated my plan.

As time passed Fay's nightly jaunts through the copse became more frequent . . . a procedure which did not escape the vigilant eyes of the scattered local population. I was well aware that she was becoming known as an eccentric who, whatever the weather, went about always smothered in white fur, poor thing, and mostly at night when ordinary folk were asleep in bed. This opinion suited me perfectly, and when a farmer's wife suggested to me one day that, although it wasn't her business and she didn't like interfering, it had occurred to her that my wife perhaps ought to see a doctor, I agreed, with a show of worried concern.

'I wouldn't have said a *word*,' the woman emphasized, 'except that my husband saw her wandering about by that quarry place the other night . . . quite clear it was, moonlight . . . anyway, he thought it a bit dangerous. So he went up to her and she was acting kind of strange . . . making funny little sort of mewing noises, and didn't seem to recognize him. So I thought . . .' her voice wavered off uncertainly.

'Thank you for telling me, Mrs Carver,' I answered. 'I'm most grateful, and I'm afraid you're right. My wife isn't at all well.'

'I expect it's only temporary,' she said encouragingly. 'Sometimes at her age . . . forgive me . . . she *is* older than you, isn't she, sir? . . . Well, women have funny ideas, if you know what I mean. Just a phase. We all go through it one way or another.'

But not in Fay's way, I thought, with savage irony, when the woman had gone. And there was nothing temporary about it. That's why it had to be ended, once and for all . . . the whole morbid uncanny business of Fay and Sheba.

I chose a night that was not too clear or dark . . . just a film of cloud passing intermittently over a ringed moon.

THE COAT

Fay had been amorous in bed, entwining me by her white, now fleshy thighs, pushing her face suffocatingly against my own, so the down on it, almost whiskers now, tickled and half stifled me. I had tried once to push her off, but she was on top of me, and around me, luscious, soft, and demanding, and there was nothing I could do but let her have her way. When it was over, she stretched, sighed, and presently, thinking I was asleep, got up, went to the wardrobe for her furry white coat, put it on, slunk downstairs, and let herself out.

I was only a minute behind, having put my dark coat ready with a pair of rubber-soled black shoes that should make no sound above the moaning of the rising wind. Her hooded white shape was quite visible crossing the lawn; but I kept to the side path, well in the shadow of the bushes, and waited as she paused by Sheba's grave. Then, after a moment, she went on and I followed.

Really, what happened after that was incredibly simple.

It was so easy to keep track of her figure ahead, padding almost slidingly along the winding thread of path which led eventually to a sudden clearing of trees, and the precipitous edge of the quarry.

I waited in the darkness of undergrowth and tangled branches until I was certain of her direction . . . of whether or not she intended to prowl around a bit before returning or if, with luck, she would make straight for the quarry which seemed to hold for her such fascination.

My luck was in and I grabbed it. She must have heard me before she fell; I had a glimpse of a pale, cat-like face turned quickly, with baleful terrified eyes staring accusingly from its furry hood. Then my arm shot out, and she was gone, screaming, into the darkness of the pit.

Her body was found in the morning by the farmer owning the adjoining land.

Naturally, Fay's death caused a stir in the district; there was gossip which, despite sympathetic concern for the 'poor husband', held a hint of relish in it. After all, the poor thing had been crazy, hadn't she? Always wandering off like that. It was obvious . . . folk had said for some time . . . that she'd end up, sooner or later, by taking a header over the cliff.

And so it was.

The verdict at the inquest a week later was recorded as 'Death by misadventure' and sympathy accorded, as was customary, to the bereaved husband, myself.

Everything was properly rounded off, I thought, as I walked up the path of Moongate that cold February evening following the inquiry. I was alone now. Free for the first time since my marriage, which, on looking back, seemed an eternity. Now all that remained for me to do was, first, to get rid of every trace of Fay's clothes and possessions, and have that odious stone removed from Sheba's grave, so that no reminder of either lingered. Later, probably, I would sell the cottage too. But that would be when I'd had a holiday to restore health and equilibrium.

It was a cold night; the house felt chill and damp when I went in. Wan light streaked through the windows where the curtains were still open, revealing a landscape bereft of life or colour . . . just dull, quickly fading grey, merging into the yellowing darkness of enveloping twilight. I felt the heaters in hall and lounge. They were full on, but no warmth seemed to penetrate the atmosphere. So I pulled the curtains close, switched on three bars of the electric fire, got a stiff whisky, and settled down to enjoy it as warmth spread through my body again, making me feel once more a human being.

Then I turned on the television.

Everything was silent at first. I waited one minute, two. No picture, no sound; nothing. Then rather faintly, as though from a great distance, the announcer's voice started its ritual of evening news. The screen flickered, shot with dancing lines which suggested there was a technical fault somewhere, then, gradually, the distortion resolved into the dim outlines of the newsreader's face. But the screen was misty and, as the voice droned on, my muscles and senses stiffened with horror, because clouding the male features were those of another, so that the impression given was of a badly taken photograph with one film overlaying a first. I rubbed my eyes with a shaking hand, trying to get the thing . . . whatever it was, either erased completely or properly into focus so that I knew what I was dealing with.

When I looked again though, there was no difference, except that the slant, amber-green eyes staring from the woolly white hood were slightly more defined. *Fay*! . . . or Sheba . . . it didn't matter any more. The features were there, overlapping those of the broadcaster . . . mouth malicious and mocking, moving silently, to the ordinary accompaniment of the programme.

I sat rooted to the chair for a minute, then I struggled to my feet, and smashed my fist against the screen. 'Go away. Damn you,' I shouted, with my heart thumping unevenly against my ribs, and in my ears. 'Leave me alone . . . can't you?' I was breathing heavily, and staggered back to the chair with sweat trickling from my face down the collar of my shirt.

There was a soft kind of feline chuckle; followed by a cessation of all sound. When the giddiness had passed and I could see properly again, everything was perfectly normal. The announcer's face was in proper perspective, as I knew it, and relief flooded me. An hallucination, I told myself, when I'd steadied my nerves with a second whisky; and it was a wonder I'd not shattered the screen with the lunge I'd delivered.

All the same, I switched off presently, taking no chance of a repetition.

I slept badly that night. Once or twice I woke, with the nightmare sensation of Fay's body pressing against mine . . . of her silky hair tickling my face, creeping everywhere, up my nostrils . . . my ears . . . in my throat even, choking me. But when I switched on the light there was nothing. Only the sound of the clock ticking and my own heart pumping. Tomorrow, I decided, I would move into the spare room, or sleep on the divan downstairs. It was obvious that the sooner I got away on a holiday jaunt the better.

I saw Cora in the morning and, although I didn't say anything about the morbid incident, which, in the light of day I convinced myself had been imagination . . . I told her I was taking off that evening for a brief break in the south of France and, if she'd care to come along too, it would do a whole lot for me.

'Dear Rod,' she said regretfully, 'I'd love to. But I'm on an important commission, and I just can't get away at the moment. It isn't only the money, don't think that. But I've *pro-*

mised to deliver the designs by Tuesday, and it means working half the nights anyway. So you see . . .'

'It's OK,' I said, taking her hand and giving it a little squeeze. 'I understand.'

'Anyway,' she went on consolingly, 'maybe you should be on your own for a bit. Just to get things into perspective again. I'm sure I'm right.'

But she wasn't.

No one could have been more chillingly wrong.

I travelled from one place to another . . . from pension to pension, Brittany first, then further south in France where I thought, at last, I'd found a haven free from Fay's haunting presence. It was a small picturesque place on the outskirts of a village in the Bordeaux district, with lush slopes and vineyards behind, and a café place in front, overlooking the river, frequented every evening by holiday-makers and colourful inhabitants who did their best to entertain tourists with wine and song.

I slept well the first night.

But on the second I was restless, and when I got up to look out of the window she was there, a perfectly static shape, standing in the moonlight, all furry-white but with satiny soft limbs desirous, I knew, beneath the obscene thick coat.

I pulled the curtains to, shuddering went back to bed and lay with hands clenched, body rigid and sweating with fear. I dozed a little at last but, when I woke, suddenly alert, I could feel a soft arm stir round my stomach. I sat up, tore myself free wildly, and jumped out of bed, rushing to the window, which I opened wide, for air.

When I looked back there was no one there. Nothing but my own clothes flung over the back of a chair, an indentation in the sheets, where a body, or *two*, had been lying, and the eiderdown, pink silk, rumpled on the floor.

This was too much for me.

I packed up and left the same day, catching the first possible plane flight for home.

The next day I was back at Moongate, and I know now that I shall never leave.

I am, in fact, beginning to adjust to my new way of life. Fay, at least, never troubles me in the daytime now; and although some nights we are together, at others she prefers to wander aimlessly over the moors and through the copse, pausing for a motionless interlude by Sheba's grave for comfort and sustenance. It is, you see, her home. And while I am there, too, she is a comparatively peaceful ghost.

Cora, of course, can't understand why I never go away . . . why our friendship has never matured into the deeper relationship that once, at the time of Fay's death, seemed inevitable. People consider it unnatural living as I do, a confirmed widower. But then they have no linking of the truth . . . that when I lie in my bed I have frequent company . . . the pressure of soft white limbs entwining mine, and the tickle of fine hair against my cheek.

The Achievement of the Cat

SAKI

(Hector Hugo Munro)

THE ANIMAL which the Egyptians worshipped as divine, which the Romans venerated as a symbol of liberty, which Europeans in the ignorant Middle Ages anathematized as an agent of demonology, has displayed to all ages two closely blended characteristics – courage and self-respect. No matter how unfavourable the circumstances, both qualities are always to the fore.

Confront a child, a puppy, and a kitten with a sudden danger; the child will turn instinctively for assistance, the puppy will grovel in abject submission to the impending visitation, the kitten will brace its tiny body for a frantic resistance. And disassociate the luxury-loving cat from the atmosphere of social comfort in which it usually contrives to move, and observe it critically under the adverse conditions of civilization – that civilization which can impel a man to the degradation of clothing himself in tawdry ribald garments and capering mountebank dances in the streets for the earning of the few coins that keep him on the respectable, or non-criminal, side of society. The cat of the slums and alleys, starved, outcast, harried, still keeps amid the prowlings of its adversity the bold, free, panther-tread with which it paced of yore the temple courts of Thebes, still displays the self-reliant watchfulness which man has never taught it to lay aside.

And when its shifts and clever managings have not sufficed to stave off inexorable fate, when its enemies have proved too strong or too many for its defensive powers, it dies fighting to the last, quivering with the choking rage of mastered resistance, and voicing in its death-yell that agony of bitter remonstrance which human animals, too, have flung at the powers that may be; the last protest against a destiny that might have made them happy – and has not.

Incident on East Ninth

JILL DROWER

I LEANED my head against the cool metal of the reinforced door. Something was digging into my temple – the spyhole. I pictured Arnold peeping through from the other side, squinting at me with a cold, cold eye, resentful, gloating, wishing me dead. He loathed me. I realized it the first moment we were introduced. Arnold got me into this. It was all his fault.

It was hot – somewhere in the eighties. This was a smart apartment block in the East Village, but the corridor still looked like it belonged to cell block B at a state pen. It was stifling but I was shaking more than a leaf on a Dutch elm. Was it embarrassment or shock? Every few minutes the elevator would chime and ping out another group of homecomers. They would glance over in my direction and then look away indifferently. What was the matter? Didn't I look weird enough for them? Dishevelled, furtive, I pressed up close to the apartment door in a feeble attempt to conceal myself behind the architrave.

The T-shirt I was wearing was a little tatty, but it was as bright-white as new. It came down just below my navel and it had giant sans serif letters across the chest which spelt out the word 'RELAX'. This was my first night in New York and I was locked out of my friend's apartment. I was telling myself to calm down. Difficult. Apart from the T-shirt, all I was wearing was a pair of gold-hoop earrings.

Arnold's relationship with Laura was entirely platonic. Having shared the apartment for some years they were now as close as brother and sister. Laura was relieved to find a flatmate who accepted her as she was, someone who didn't squabble about petty things like who did the washing-up. Besides, living in New York was a lonely business and Arnold was entertaining company. The problem was, he was jealous of her friends. Maybe he thought that, if she found someone and fell in love, she might want to get married and 'the other man' would boot him out. Whatever it was, Arnold made it his business to frighten away any friends whom she invited in. She had taken to visiting singles bars, and this brought a fairly high number of invitations from her to 'come back to my place for coffee'. Arnold developed what he called his 'spooking-out technique' which, after a couple of evenings, he had down to a fine art. Laura, unsuspecting, would disappear into the kitchen to fix the percolator. Arnold, very friendly, would join the visitor on the sofa and, at a given moment, he would put on this stare and become strangely menacing. When Laura returned with the tray, he was back to being the nice guy and would make a big ceremony of leaving the room tactfully to let them sit alone together on the sofa. After one visit, these poor hopefuls never returned.

I was in New York principally to meet a number of old friends who were now living there but, as this was my first visit to the city, I wanted to see as much of Manhattan as possible in the ten days I had.

'You're welcome to stay at my place, if you like, so long as you don't mind sleeping on the sofa.' I took Laura up on her offer. She lived on East Ninth, somewhere near the bottom of Fifth Avenue and near enough to Washington Square Park for us to go jogging there every morning.

The journey from La Guardia to Laura's apartment had me in a trance. It was all exactly like those cop shows and Scorcese films I'd seen, only much more so. It was all so different from the ribbons of mock Tudor en route from Heathrow or Gatwick. I took it all in: the weatherboard houses, the freeways, the automobiles, the 'last exit to . . .' signs and the bluntness of the yellow cab driver who took me from the bus terminal to Laura's place. Like the uninitiated in any major city,

I saw the place as a series of clichés. All that was missing was the steam coming out of subway gratings, but I suppose I had the wrong time of year for that. This was summer in the city and fire-hydrant-unlocking time. Firecrackers snapped all around, a constant reminder that July the 4th was only a day away.

Laura was a model host. She took me for brunch and a short walk through the Village. Being an architect, she was able to talk interestingly about the brownstone buildings around. She did warn me briefly about Arnold, saying he was a bit fractious, but no more was said about him that afternoon. Anyway, I reckoned I could manage to soften him up easily enough and that, in no time, we'd be getting along fine.

That first evening a whole group of us ate out in Little Italy to celebrate the reunion of an old gang of friends. I had Conchiglie alla Siciliana which seemed to me the most wonderful dish I had ever tried. We toasted the chef and then drank to absent friends. The man who served us was attentive and gave me a special smile which made him look like a member of the Corleone family. 'I haven't said goodbye to the waiter,' I exclaimed as we were leaving the building. 'He'll live,' said the manageress in the kind of Brooklyn accent I'd kill for if I were an actress. We all laughed and linked arms walking briskly back past the down and outs on the Bowery.

'Do come with us,' said Emil. 'You're only here for a few days.' He wanted me to join them for a late-night showing of *Kiss Me Kate* in 3D. 'No, I'm really too tired, I haven't slept for nineteen hours,' I made my excuses, trying to draw some sympathy. 'I'll see you all tomorrow when the jet lag's worn off.' They accompanied me as far as the junction of Astor Place and Broadway. Laura explained once more how the spare key worked. 'If you get stuck, ask the super.' I looked blank. 'The janitor,' she translated. 'What's a janitor?' I joked in my most pompous English accent.

I let myself in without difficulty and walked over to the window. It was wide open. Just level with the bottom of the frame was a large expanse of flat roofing. At the far end was the ironwork of a fire escape. 'Fire escapes,' I thought. 'Now I *know* I'm in New York. Cookie, elevator, faucet, super, janitor, I wonder if they have their own word for fire escape too.'

On the sofa was a neat pile of sheets. I managed to assemble it all into some sort of order and struggle into my T-shirt ready for bed. As I lay there half-asleep, I wondered mildly why Laura was so lax about security, but I was too sleepy to get up and close the window. I sank under the cover and within a few seconds I had drifted into sleep.

I woke with a start and lay there for several minutes listening to the whoop-whoop-whoop of police patrol cars and watching the thin curtains billow in the grimy night air.

At some point, I realized I was not alone. The intruder was there somewhere in the room. I stumbled through the darkness towards the door, upsetting a table as I went. I felt something sharp slash my flesh as I groped madly around the wall for a light switch and found it. Then we were looking straight at each other in the lighted room. My attacker, with his vicious penetrating eyes, was standing a few feet away, holding my gaze with his, pinning me to the spot with nothing more than his burning, piercing, hating eyes.

I knew that, if I moved, my assailant would try another slash. We stayed frozen like that for a few moments – musical statues without the music – blood dripping down from the deep gashes in my legs. I had to protect my body from the next attack. Beside me on the floor was a pile of old copies of *Rolling Stone* magazine. Moving quickly, I tried to whip the newsprint in front of me as a shield, but he was far quicker on the draw and cut through the backs of my hands in a trice. He was now taking systematic swipes at any exposed part of me that he could reach. I was no match.

I grappled with the front-door latch and shot through to the hallway. This time Arnold was not quite quick enough. I pulled the door until I heard a gentle click as the latch locked home.

I don't know how long I stood there in that Greenwich Village hallway, half-naked, in a state of trembling indecision.

At last, I crept down to the basement by the back stairs and followed the sound of an early hours news channel reporting preparations for the Independence Day celebration fireworks on the West Side. The janitor looked me slowly up and down, but more down than up.

'Do you happen to have a first-aid box?' I asked meekly. 'And something for me to wear?' He shuffled about and produced a large paint-spattered sheet which I wrapped around me like a toga. After further searching he came up with an old rag, stiff with dried metal polish. After dabbing at the gashes with it for a few moments, I managed to work out that it had once been some kind of undergarment.

'I've been attacked by a cat,' I explained. 'Lady,' he replied, 'you got problems.' He wasn't planning to solve them for me, just commenting. He went back to listening to the broadcast. 'I've also been locked out of apartment number 208. I don't suppose you've got a spare key, have you?'

He dug a credit card out of his wallet and I followed him back up to the flat. He started to work away with the plastic. He seemed amazingly skilled at breaking in and I began to wonder what he did for a living before he was a janitor. Still, this was not the moment to doubt the man whose help I badly needed. My assistant was the silent type, so I did all the talking. 'As soon as the door opens, I'll throw this in.' I waved the polishing-rag undies. 'Don't leave until I've got past him into the bedroom.' I rolled them up tight into a ball and got ready to throw.

The door swung wide open. Arnold was across the other side, eyeing me, quivering in readiness. Ignoring the janitor, he waited for me to make my move. I bowled the brasso ball, medium speed, with a bit of spin. While he was savaging it, I slipped past into Laura's bedroom and shut the door, calling out my thanks to the indifferent janitor. Wasting no time, I took a ladderback chair and tucked it smartly under the door handle.

I switched on the TV. It was tuned to a Spanish language programme. 'Adónde vas? A que no te atreves a besarme?' I flicked the button to the next channel number. Behind me the bedroom-door handle was rattling and jerking. I checked the chair back was still tightly wedged in position, and then settled down to the programme. It was a threesome gameshow. The secretary was called Barbara. She knew far more about husband Bob than wife Connie did. Still, Connie was being very sporting about it; even when it emerged that it was Barbara, not Bob, who had chosen her tenth anniversary present, she

laughed ecstatically and applauded her humiliation along with the studio audience.

All this time, Arnold was still pounding on the handle, trying to hurry up the metal fatigue. I turned the volume up to maximum and set my face to the screen. Then suddenly, nothing. Silence outside.

I heard the front latch turn and heard Laura's voice. 'Hi, Arnold, how yer been?' She walked in to greet me wearing cardboard glasses, one red side, one green. She stopped in her tracks. 'Looks like you've been having some 3D effects in here.' She looked round at all the furniture in disarray.

Over the next few days Laura did what she could to try to make Arnold see me in a more positive light. These efforts included getting me to give him a bowl of Nine Lives Formula, a plan which went disastrously wrong. Simple tasks like walking to the bathroom or making a cup of coffee were now a nerve-wracking ordeal. 'Try and relax,' Laura would encourage me as I started my journey across the room. 'Are you sure this is a good idea? Couldn't we lock Arnold away just till I go out?' I pleaded. Then I'd hear him scurrying along after me and feel his claws as they found their way through the denim to my tender flesh.

Laura eventually brought in a cat psychiatrist because she was seriously worried about his worsening behaviour. A neighbour had already threatened litigation after Arnold took a swipe one afternoon. 'I'd better do something or, sooner or later, someone is going to take me to court. Suing someone you know is our most popular national pastime. People take classes in it at night school.'

A series of appointments were set up with a very nice Argentinian therapist called Graciela. 'She says I am Arnold's emotional blanket,' Laura confided after one of these consultations. 'And she thinks he's suffering from an abandonment complex.' I felt this was all a very pricey way to find out the obvious, but I kept these thoughts to myself.

The therapist explained what single-cat syndrome was, and suggested that Laura buy Arnold his own little kitten to play with. He was also put on a course of Valium. With half a tablet he was still attacking me. On one whole pill he couldn't quite coordinate enough, so he would just stare at me. In fact, Arnold did a lot of staring over the next few days. At primary school, I can remember a huge portrait of the Queen which hung in the dining-room. I noticed that it didn't matter which table I sat at, her eyes would always be looking directly at me. Having Arnold around was a bit like that, only it wasn't a case of wherever I looked from but whenever I looked. From time to time, it might be two minutes or twenty, I would glance up from my guide book or Manhattan street plan, and there he'd be, eyeballing me. I never saw him blink.

Laura followed all the advice she was given except the bit about buying Arnold his own little kitten. Somehow, she never got around to visiting that pet store on Hudson Street. It would, on reflection, have been a bad idea. Picture Arnold patting and putting the fluffy little thing around the room like an outsize mouse.

This story does have a happy ending (for Arnold at any rate) because, after a few days, I gave up and moved to a hotel. He celebrated his victory by becoming docile and lovable once more. He continued to preside over Laura's spinsterhood, but now with increased confidence.

As for Laura, she carried on her social life outside the flat and rarely invited people back. The offers of a bed to visiting tourist friends ceased after my trip which, for someone living in such a sought-after spot on the globe, must have come as something of a relief. It certainly gave her more time to concentrate on her work and later that year she was promoted, so I suppose there was a happy ending for her too.

'I've landed this incredible job,' she phoned me about a year later. 'It's a complete renovation of an art gallery in SoHo.'

'How's Arnold these days?' I asked.

'Oh, he couldn't be better. He's right by my side, can't you hear him purring?'

Ye Marvelous Legend of Tom Connor's Cat

SAMUEL LOVER

THERE WAS a man in these parts, sir, you must know, called Tom Connor, and he had a cat that was equal to any dozen of rat traps, and he was proud of the baste, and with rayson; for she was worth her weight in goold to him in saving his sacks of meal from the thievery of the rats and mice; for Tom was an extensive dealer in corn, and influenced the rise and fall of that article in the market, to the extent of a full dozen of sacks at a time, which he either kept or sold, as the spirit of free trade or monopoly came over him. Indeed, at one time, Tom had serious thoughts of applying to the government for a military force to protect his granary when there was a threatened famine in the country.

'Pooh, pooh, sir!' said the matter-of-fact little man. 'As if a dozen sacks could be of the smallest consequence in a whole country – pooh, pooh!'

'Well, sir,' said Murtough, 'I can't help you if you don't believe; but it's truth what I'm telling you, and pray don't interrupt me, though you may not believe; by the time the story's done you'll have heard more wonderful things than *that* – and besides, remember you're a stranger in these parts, and have no notion of the extraordinary things, physical, metaphysical and magical, which constitute the idiosyncrasy of rural destiny.'

The little man did not know the meaning of Murtough's last

sentence – nor Murtough either; but, having stopped the little man's throat with big words, he proceeded:

'This cat, sir, you must know, was a great pet, and was so up to everything, that Tom swore she was a'most like a Christian, only she couldn't speak, and had so sensible a look in her eyes, that he was sartin sure the cat knew every word that was said to her. Well, she used to set by him at breakfast every morning, and the eloquent cock of her tail, as she used to rub against his leg, said. "Give me some milk, Tom Connor," as plain as print, and the plentitude of her purr afterwards spoke a gratitude beyond language. Well, one morning, Tom was going to the neighbouring town to market, and he had promised the wife to bring home shoes to the childre' out o' the price of the corn; and sure enough before he sat down to breakfast, there was Tom taking the measure of the children's feet, by cutting notches on a bit of stick; and the wife gave him so many cautions about getting a "nate fit" for "Billy's purty feet," that Tom, in his anxiety to nick the closest possible measure, cut off the child's toe. This disturbed the harmony of the party and Tom was obliged to breakfast alone, while the mother was endeavouring to cure Billy; in short, trying to make a *heal* of his *toe*. Well, sir, all the time Tom was taking measure for the shoes, the cat was observing him with that luminous peculiarity of eye for which her tribe is remarkable; and when Tom sat down to breakfast the cat rubbed up against him more vigorously than usual; but Tom being bewildered, between his expected gain in corn and the positive loss of his child's toe, kept never minding her, until the cat, with a sort of caterwauling growl, gave Tom a dab of her claws, that went clean through his leathers, and a little further. 'Wow!' says Tom, with a jump, clapping his hand on the part, and rubbing it. 'By this and that, you drew the blood out o' me,' says Tom. 'You wicked divil – tish! – go along!' says he, making a kick at her. With that the cat gave a reproachful look at him, and her eyes glared just like a pair of mail-coach lamps in a fog. With that, sir, the cat, with a mysterious "meow", fixed a most penetrating glance on Tom and distinctly uttered his name.

'Tom felt every hair on his head as stiff as a pump handle; and scarcely crediting his ears, he returned a searching look at the cat, who very quietly proceeded in a sort of nasal twang:

' "Tom Connor," says she.

' "The Lord be good to me!" says Tom. "If it isn't spakin' she is!"

' "Tom Connor," says she again.

' "Yes, ma'am," says Tom.

' "Come here," says she. "Whisper – I want to talk to you, Tom," says she, "the laste taste in private," says she – rising on her hams and beckoning him with her paw out o' the door, with a wink and a toss o' the head aiqual to a milliner.

'Well, as you may suppose, Tom didn't know whether he was on his head or his heels, but he followed the cat, and off she went and squatted herself under the hedge of a little paddock at the back of Tom's house; and as he came round the corner, she held up her paw again, and laid it on her mouth, as much as to say "Be cautious, Tom." Well, divil a word Tom could say at all, with the fright, so up he goes to the cat, and says she:

' "Tom," says she, "I have a great respect for you, and there's something I must tell you, because you're losing charac-ter with your neighbours," says she, "by your goin's on," says she, "and it's out o' the respect that I have for you, that I must tell you," says she.

' "Thank you, ma'am," says Tom.

' "You're going off to the town," says she, "to buy shoes for the childre'," says she, "and never thought o' getting me a pair."

' "You!" says Tom.

' "Yis, me, Tom Connor," says she, "and the neighbours wondhers that a respectable man like you allows your cat to go about the counthry barefutted," says she.

' "Is it a cat to ware shoes?" says Tom.

' "Why not?" says she. "Doesn't horses ware shoes? And I have a prettier foot than a horse, I hope," says she with a toss of her head.

' "Faix, she spakes like a woman; so proud of her feet," says Tom to himself, astonished, as you may suppose, but pretend-ing never to think it remarkable all the time; and so he went on discoursin'; and says he: "It's thrue for you, ma'am," says he, "that horses ware shoes – but that stands to rayson, ma'am, you see – seeing the hardship their feet has to go through on the hard roads."

' "And how do you know what hardship my feet has to go through?" says the cat, mighty sharp.

' "But, ma'am," says Tom, "I don't well see how you could fasten a shoe on you," says he.

' "Lave that to me," says the cat.

' "Did anyone ever stick walnut shells on you, pussy?" says Tom, with a grin.

' "Don't be disrespectful, Tom Connor," says the cat, with a frown.

' "I ax your pard'n, ma'am," says he, ". . . as for the horses you wor spakin' about warin' shoes, you know their shoes is fastened on with nails, and how would your shoes be fastened on?"

' "Ah, you stupid thief!" says she, "haven't I illigant nails o' my own?" and with that she gave him a dab of her claw, that made him roar.

' "Ow! murdher!" says he.

' "Now no more of your palaver, Misther Connor," says the cat. "Just be off and get me the shoes."

' "Tare and ouns!" says Tom. "What'll become o' me if I'm to get shoes for my cats?" says he. "For you increase your family four times a year, and you have six or seven every time," says he; "and then you must all have two pair apiece – wirra! wirra! – I'll be ruined in shoeleather," says Tom.

' "No more o' your stuff," says the cat, "don't be standin' here undher the hedge talkin' or we'll lose our characters – for I've remarked your wife is jealous, Tom."

' "'Pon my sowl, that's thrue," says Tom, with a smirk.

' "More fool she," says the cat, "for 'pon my conscience, Tom, you're as ugly as if you wor bespoke."

'Off ran the cat with these words, leaving Tom in amazement. He said nothing to the family, for fear of fright'ning them, and off he went to the town, as he pretended – for he saw the cat watching him through a hole in the hedge; but when he came to a turn at the end of the road, the dickings a mind he minded the market, good or bad, but went off to Squire Botherum's, the magisthrit, to swear examinations agen the cat.'

'Pooh, pooh – nonsense!' broke in the little man, who had listened thus far to Murtough with an expression of mingled wonder and contempt, while the rest of the party willingly gave up the reins to nonsense, and enjoyed Murtough's legend and their companion's more absurd common-sense.

'Don't interrupt him, Coggins,' said Mr Wiggins.

'How can you listen to such nonsense!' returned Coggins. 'Swear examinations against a cat, indeed! Pooh pooh!'

'My dear sir,' said Murtough, 'remember this is a fairy story, and that the country all round here is full of enchantment. As I was telling you, Tom went off to swear examinations.'

'Ay, ay!' shouted all but Coggins. 'Go on with the story.'

'And when Tom was asked to relate the events of the morning, which brought him before Squire Botherum, his brain was so bewildered between his corn, and his cat, his child's toe, that he made a very confused account of it.

' "Begin your story from the beginning," said the magistrate to Tom.

' "Well, your honour," says Tom, "I was goin' to market this mornin', to sell the child's corn – I beg your pard'n – my own toes, I mane, sir.'

' "Sell your toes!" said the Squire.

' "No, sir, takin' the cat to market, I mane —"

' "Take a cat to market!" said the Squire. "You're drunk, man."

' "No, your honour, only confused a little; for when the toes began to spake to me – the cat, I mane – I was bothered clane —"

' "The cat speak to you!" said the Squire. "Phew! Worse than before. You're drunk, Tom."

' "No, your honour; it's on the strength of the cat I come to spake to you —"

' "I think it's on the strength of a pint of whiskey, Tom."

' "By the vartue o' my oath, your honour, it's nothin' but the cat." And so Tom then told him all about the affair, and the Squire was regularly astonished. Just then the bishop of the diocese and the priest of the parish happened to call in, and heard the story; and the bishop and the priest had a tough argument for two hours on the subject: the former swearing she must be a witch; but the priest denying *that*, and maintaining she was *only* enchanted, and that part of the argument was afterwards referred to the primate, and subsequently to the conclave at Rome; but the Pope declined interfering about cats, saying he had quite enough to do minding his own bulls.

' "In the meantime, what are we to do with the cat?" says Botherum.

' "Burn her," says the bishop. "She's a witch."

' "*Only* enchanted," says the priest, "and the ecclesiastical court maintains that —"

' "Bother the ecclesiastical court!" says the magistrate; "I can only proceed on the statutes;" and with that he pulls down all the law books in his library and hunts the laws from Queen Elizabeth down, and he finds that they made laws against everything in Ireland, *except a cat*. The divil a thing escaped them but a cat, which did *not* come within the meaning of any Act of Parliament – *the cats only had escaped*.

' "There's the alien act, to be sure," says the magistrate, "and she was missin', I remember, all last Spy Wednesday."

' "That's suspicious," says the Squire, "but conviction might be difficult; and I have a fresh idea," says Botherum.

' "Faith, it won't keep fresh long, this hot weather," says Tom, "so your honour had betther make use of it at wanst."

' "Right," says Botherum. "We'll make her a subject to the game laws; we'll hunt her," says he.

' "Ow! Elegant!" says Tom; "we'll have a brave run out of her."

' "Meet me at the crossroads," says the Squire, "in the morning, and I'll have the hounds ready."

'Well, off Tom went home; and he was racking his brain what excuse he could make to the cat for not bringing the shoes; and at last he hit one off, just as he saw her cantering up to him, half a mile before he got home.

' "Where's the shoes, Tom?" says she.

' "I have not got them today, ma'am," says he.

' "Is that the way you keep your promise, Tom?" says she. "I'll tell you what it is, Tom – I'll tare the eyes out o' the childre' if you don't get me those shoes."

' "Whist, whist!" says Tom, frightened out his life for his children's eyes. "Don't be in a passion, pussy. The shoemaker said he had not a shoe in his shop, nor a last that would make one to fit you; and he says I must bring you into the town for him to take your measure."

' "And when am I to go?" says the cat, looking savage.

' "Tomorrow," says Tom.

143

' "It's well you said that, Tom," says the car, "or the divil an eye I'd leave in your family this night," and off she hopped.

'Tom thrimbled at the wicked look she gave.

' "Remember!" says she, over the hedge, with a bitter caterwaul.

' "Never fear," says Tom.

'Well, sure enough, the next mornin' there was the cat at cockcrow, licking herself as nate as a new pin, to go into the town, and out came Tom with a bag undher his arm and the cat after him.

' "Now git into this, and I'll carry you into the town," says Tom, opening the bag.

' "Sure, I can walk with you," says the cat.

' "Oh, that wouldn't do," says Tom. "The people in the town is curious and slandherous people, and sure it would rise ugly remarks if I was seen with a cat afther me – a dog is a man's companion by nature, but cats does not stand to rayson."

'Well, the cat, seeing there was no use in argument, got into the bag, and off Tom set to the crossroads with the bag over his shoulder, and he came up, quite innocent-like, to the corner, where the Squire, and his huntsman, and the hounds, and a pack of people were waitin'. Out came the Squire on a sudden, just as if it was all by accident.

' "God save you, Tom," says he.

' "God save you kindly, sir," says Tom.

' "What's that bag you have at your back?" says the Squire.

' "Oh, nothin' at all, sir," says Tom, makin' a face all the time, as much as to say, I have her safe.

' "Oh, there's something in that bag, I think," says the Squire. "You must let me see it."

' "If you bethray me, Tom Connor," says the cat, in a low voice, "by this and that I'll never spake to you again!"

' "Pon my honour, sir," says Tom, with a wink and a twitch of his thumb towards the bag, "I haven't anything in it."

' "I have been missing my praties of late," says the Squire, "and I'd just like to examine that bag," says he.

' "Is it doubting my character you'd be, sir?" says Tom, pretending to be in a passion.

' "Tom, your sowl!" says the voice in the sack. "If you let the cat out of the bag, I'll murther you."

' "An honest man would make no objection to be sarched," said the Squire, "and I insist on it," says he, laying hold o' the bag, and Tom purtending to fight all the time; but, my jewel! Before two minutes, they shook the cat out o' the bag, sure enough, and off she went with her tail as big as a sweeping brush, and the Squire, with a thundering view halloo after her, clapped the dogs at her heels, and away they went for the bare life. Never was there seen such running as that day – the cat made for a shaking bog, the loneliest place in the whole country, and there the riders were all thrown out, barrin' the

145

huntsman who had a web-footed horse on purpose for soft places, and the priest whose horse could go anywhere by reason of the priest's blessing; and, sure enough, the huntsman and his riverence stuck to the hunt like wax; and just as the cat got on the border of the bog, they saw her give a twist as the foremost dog closed with her, for he gave her a nip in the flank. Still she went on, however, and headed them well, towards an old mud cabin in the middle of the bog, and there they saw her jump in at the window, and up came the dogs the next minit, and gathered round the house with the most horrid howling ever was heard. The huntsman alighted and went into the house to turn the cat out again, when what should he see but an old hag lying in bed in the corner!

' "Did you see a cat come in here?" says he.

' "Oh, no-o-o-o!" squeals the old hag in a trembling voice. "There's no cat here," says she.

' "Yelp, yelp, yelp!" went the dogs outside.

' "Oh, keep the dogs out of this," says the old hag – "Oh-o-o-o!" and the huntsman saw her eyes glare under the blanket, just like a cat's.

' "Hillo!" says the huntsman, pulling down the blanket – and what should he see but the old hag's flank all in a gore of blood.

' "Ow, ow! you old divil – is it you? You old cat!" says he, opening the door.

'In rushed the dogs. Up jumped the old hag and, changing into a cat before their eyes, out she darted through the window again, and made another run for it; but she couldn't escape, and the dogs gobbled her while you could say "Jack Robinson." But the most remarkable part of this extraordinary story, gentlemen, is that the pack was ruined from that day out; for after having eaten the enchanted cat, *the divil a thing they would ever hunt afterwards but mice.*'

Rufus the Survivor

DORIS LESSING

EVENTS DID cast their shadow, months before. All that spring and summer, as I went past on the pavement, a shabby orange-coloured cat would emerge from under a car or from a front garden, and he stood looking intently up at me, not to be ignored. He wanted something, but what? Cats on pavements, cats on garden walls, or coming towards you from doorways, stretch and wave their tails, they greet you, walk a few steps with you. They want companionship or, if they are shut out by heartless owners, as they often are all day or all night, they appeal for help with the loud insistent demanding miaow that means they are hungry or thirsty or cold. A cat winding around your legs at a street corner might be wondering if he can exchange a poor home for a better one. But this cat did not miaow, he only looked, a thoughtful, hard stare from yellow-grey eyes. Then he began following me along the pavement in a tentative way, looking up at me. He presented himself to me when I came in and when I went out, and he was on my conscience. Was he hungry? I took some food out to him and put it under a car, and he ate a little, but left the rest. Yet he was necessitous, desperate, I knew that. Did he have a home in our street, and was it a bad one? He seemed most often to be near a house some doors down from ours and, once, when an old woman went in, he went in too. So he was not homeless. Yet he took to following me to our gate and once, when the pavement filled with a surge of shouting schoolchildren, he

147

scrambled into our little front garden, terrified, and watched me at the door.

He was thirsty, not hungry. Or so thirsty, hunger was the lesser demand. That was the summer of 1984, with long stretches of warm weather. Cats locked out of their homes all day without water suffered. I put down a basin of water on my front porch one night and in the morning it was empty. Then, as the hot weather went on, I put another basin on my back balcony, reached by way of a lilac tree and a big jump up from a small roof. And this basin, too, was empty every morning. One hot dusty day there was the orange cat on the back balcony crouched over the water basin, drinking, drinking . . . He finished all the water and wanted more. I refilled the basin and again he crouched down and emptied that. This meant there must be something wrong with his kidneys. Now I could take my time looking at him. A scruffy cat, his dirty fur rough over knobbly bones. But he was a wonderful colour, fire colour, like a fox. He was, as they put it, a whole cat, he had his two neat furry balls under his tail. His ears were torn, scarred with fighting. Now, when I came in and out of the house, he was no longer there in the street, he had moved from the fronts of the houses and the precarious life there with the speeding cars and the shouting, running children, to the back scene of long untidy gardens and shrubs and trees, and many birds and cats. He was on our little balcony where there are plants in pots, bounded by a low wall. Over this the lilac tree holds out its boughs, always full of birds. He lay in the strip of shade under the wall, and the water bowl was always empty, and when he saw me he stood up and waited beside it for more.

By now the people in the house had understood we must make a decision. Did we want another cat? We already had two beautiful, large, lazy, neutered toms, who had always had it so good they believed that food, comfort, warmth, safety were what life owed them, for they never had had to fight for anything. No, we did not want another cat, and certainly not a sick one. But now we took out food as well as water to this old derelict, putting it on the balcony so he would know this was a favour and not a right, and that he did not belong to us, and could not come into the house. We joked that he was our outdoor cat.

The hot weather went on.

He ought to be taken to the vet. But that would mean he was our cat, we would have three cats, and our own were being huffy and wary and offended because of this newcomer who seemed to have rights over us, even if limited ones. Besides, what about the old woman whom he did sometimes visit? We watched him go stiffly along a path, turn right to crawl under a fence, cross a garden and then another, his orangeness brilliant against the dulling grass of late summer, and then he vanished and was presumably at the back door of a house where he was welcome.

The hot weather ended and it began to rain. The orange cat stood out in the rain on the balcony, his fur streaked dark with running water, and looked at me. I opened the kitchen door and he came in. I said to him, he could use this chair, but only this chair; this was his chair, and he must not ask for more. He climbed on to the chair and lay down and looked steadily at me. He had the air of one who knows he must make the most of what Fate offers before it is withdrawn.

When it was not raining the door was still open on to the balcony, the trees, the garden. We hate shutting it all out with glass and curtains. And he could still use the lilac tree to get down into the garden for his toilet. He lay all that day on the chair in the kitchen, sometimes getting clumsily off it to drink yet another bowl of water. He was eating a lot now. He could not pass a food or water bowl without eating or drinking something, for he knew he could never take anything for granted.

This was a cat who had had a home, but lost it. He knew

what it was to be a house cat, a pet. He wanted to be caressed. His story was a familiar one. He had had a home, human friends who loved him, or thought they did, but it was not a good home because the people went away a lot and left him to find food and shelter for himself, or who looked after him as long as it suited them and then left the neighbourhood, abandoning him. For some time he had been fed at the old woman's place but, it seemed, not enough, or had not been given water to drink. Now he was looking better. But he was not cleaning himself. He was stiff, of course, but he had been demoralized, hopeless. Perhaps he had believed he would never have a home again? After a few days, when he knew we would not throw him out of the kitchen, he began to purr whenever we came into it. Never have I, or anyone else who visited the house, heard any cat purr as loudly as he did. He lay on the chair and his sides went up and down and his purring rumbled through the house. He wanted us to know he was grateful. It was a calculated purr.

We brushed him. We cleaned his fur for him. We gave him a name. We took him to the vet, thus acknowledging that we had a third cat. His kidneys were bad. He had an ulcer in one ear. Some of his teeth had gone. He had arthritis or rheumatism. His heart could be better. But no, he was not an old cat, probably eight or nine years old, in his prime if he had been looked after, but he had been living as he could, and perhaps for some time. Cats who have to scavenge and cadge and sleep out in bad weather in the big cities do not live long. He would soon have died if we had not rescued him. He took his antibiotics and the vitamins, and soon after his first visit to the vet began the painful process of cleaning himself. But parts of himself he was too stiff to reach, and he had to labour and struggle to be a clean and civilized cat.

All this went on in the kitchen, and mostly on the chair, which he was afraid of leaving. His place. His little place. His toehold on life. And when he went out on to the balcony he watched us all in case we shut the door on him, for he feared being locked out more than anything, and if we made movements that looked as if the door might be shutting he scrambled painfully in and on to his chair.

He liked to sit on my lap and, when this happened, he set

himself in motion, purring, and he looked up with those clever greyish-yellow eyes: Look, I am grateful, and I am telling you so.

One day, when the arbiters of his fate were in the kitchen drinking tea, he hopped off his chair and walked slowly to the door into the rest of the house. There he stopped and turned and most deliberately looked at us. He could not have asked more clearly: Can I go further into the house? Can I be a proper house cat? By now we would have been happy to invite him in, but our other two cats seemed able to tolerate him if he stayed where he was, a kitchen cat. We pointed to his chair and he climbed patiently back on to it, where he lay silent and disappointed for a while, and then set his sides heaving in a purr.

Needless to say, this made us feel terrible.

A few days later, he got carefully off his chair and went to the same door and stopped there, looking back at us for directions. This time we did not say he must come back, so he went on into the house, but not far. He found a sheltered place under a bath and that was where he stayed. The other cats went to check where he was, and enquired of us what we thought of it, but what we thought was, these two young princes could share their good fortune. Outside the house it was autumn, and then winter, and we needed to shut the kitchen door. But what about this new cat's lavatory problems? These days he waited at the kitchen door when he needed to go out, but once there he did not want to jump down on to the little roof, or climb down the lilac tree, for he was too stiff. He used the pots the plants were trying to grow in, so I put down a big box filled with peat, and he understood and used it. A nuisance, having to empty the peat box. There is a cat door right at the bottom of the house into the garden, and our two young cats had never, not once, made a mess inside the house. Come rain or snow or high winds, they go out.

And so that was the situation as winter began. In the evenings people and the two resident cats, the rightful cats, were in the sitting-room, and Rufus was under the bath. And then, one evening, Rufus appeared in the doorway of the sitting-room and it was a dramatic apparition, for here was the embodiment of the dispossessed, the insulted, the injured, making himself felt by the warm, the fed, the privileged. He glanced at the two cats who were his rivals, but kept his intelligent eyes on us. What were we going to say? We said, Very well, he could use the old leather beanbag near the radiator, the warmth would help his aching bones. We made a hollow in the beanbag and he climbed into the hollow and curled up, but carefully, and he purred. He purred, he purred, he purred so loudly and so long we had to beg him to stop, for we could not hear ourselves speak. Literally. We had to turn up the television. But he knew he was lucky and wanted us to know he understood the value of what he was getting. When I was at the top of the house, two floors up, I could hear the rhythmic rumbling that meant Rufus was awake and telling us of his gratitude. Or perhaps he was asleep and purring in his sleep, for once he had started he did not stop but lay there curled up, eyes shut, his sides pumping up and down. There was something inordinate and scandalous about Rufus's purring, because it was so calculated. And we were reminded, as we watched, and listened to this old survivor, who was only alive now because he had used his wits, of the hazards and adventures and hardships he had undergone.

But our other two cats were not pleased. One is called Charles, originally Prince Charlie, not after the present holder of that title, but after earlier romantic princes for he is a dashing and handsome tabby who knows how to present himself. About his character the less said the better – but this chronicle is not about Charles. The other cat, the older brother, with the character of one, has a full ceremonial name, bestowed when he first left kittenhood and his qualities had become evident. We called him General Pinknose the Third, paying tribute and perhaps reminding ourselves that even the best looked-after cat is going to leave you. We had seen that icecream-pink tinge, but on the tips of noses with a less noble curve, on earlier, less imposing cats. Like some people he acquires new names as time makes its revelations, and recently, because of his moral force and his ability to impose silent judgements on a scene, he became for a time a bishop and was known as Bishop Butchkin. Reserving comment, these two cats lay in their respective places, noses on their paws, and watched Rufus. Charles is always under a radiator, but Butchkin likes the top of a tall basket where he can keep an eye on things. He is a magnificent cat. Familiarity had dulled my eyes: I knew he was handsome, but I came back from a trip somewhere to be dazzled by this enormous cat boldly patterned in his shining black and immaculate white, yellow-eyed, with white whiskers, and I thought that this beauty had been bred out of common-or-garden mog-material by good feeding and care. Left unneutered, a cat who had to roam around in all weathers to compete for a mate, he would not look like this, but would be a smaller, or at least gaunt, rangy, war-bitten cat. No, I am not happy about neutering cats, far from it.

But this tale is not about El Magnifico, the name that suits him best.

When he thought we didn't know, Charles would try to get Rufus into a corner and threaten him. But Charles has never had to fight and compete, and Rufus has, all his life. Rufus was so rickety he could be knocked over by the swipe of a determined paw. But he sat back and defended himself with hard experienced stares, with his wary patience, his indomitability. There was no doubt what would happen to Charles if he got within hitting distance. As for El Magnifico, he was above competing on this level.

During all those early weeks, while he was recovering strength, Rufus never went out of the house, except to the peat box on the balcony, and there he did his business, keeping his gaze on us and even now, if it seemed the door might shut him out, he gave a little grunt of panic and then hobbled back indoors. He was so afraid, even now, he might lose this refuge gained after long homelessness, after such torments of thirst. He was afraid to put a paw outside.

The winter slowly went by. Rufus lay in his beanbag and purred every time he thought of it, and he watched us, and watched the two other cats watching him. Then he made a new move. By now we knew he never did anything without very good reason, that first he worked things out, and then acted. The black and white cat, Butchkin, is the boss cat. He was born in this house, one of six kittens. He brought up his siblings as much as his mother did; she was not a bad mother so much as an exhausted one. There was never any question about who was the boss kitten of the litter. Now Rufus decided to make a bid for the position of boss cat. Not by strength, because he did not have that, but by using his position as a sick cat, given so much attention. Every evening The General, El Magnifico Butchkin, came to lie by me on the sofa for a while, to establish his right to this position, before going to his favourite place on top of the basket. This place by me was the best place, because Butchkin thought it was. Charles, for instance, was not allowed it. But now, just as he had walked deliberately to the kitchen door and then looked back to see if we would allow him to the house itself, just as he had stood in the sitting-room door to find out if we would let him in to join the family, so now Rufus deliberately stepped down off the beanbag, came to where I sat, pulled himself up, first front legs, and then, with difficulty, his back legs and sat down beside me. He looked at Butchkin. Then at the humans. Finally, a careless look at Charles. I did not throw him off. I could not. Butchkin only looked at him and then slowly (and magnificently) yawned. I felt it was he who should make Rufus return to the beanbag. But he did nothing, only watched. Was he waiting for me to act? Rufus lay down, carefully, because of his painful joints. And purred. All people who live with animals have moments when they long to share a language. And this was one. What had happened to him, how had he learned to plan and calculate, how had he become such a thinking cat? All right, so he was born intelligent, but then so was Butchkin, and so was Charles. (And there are very stupid cats.) All right, so he was born with such and such a nature. But I have never known a cat so capable of thought, of planning his next move, as Rufus.

Lying beside me, having achieved the best place in the sitting-room after only a few weeks from being an outcast, he purred. 'Shhh Rufus, we can't hear ourselves think.' But we did not share a language, could not explain that we would not throw him out if he stopped purring, saying thank you.

When we made him swallow pills he made little grunts of protest; he probably saw this as the price he had to pay for a refuge. Sometimes, when we swabbed his ear and it hurt, he swore, but not at us; it was a generally directed curse from one who had much occasion to use curses. Then he licked our hands to show he didn't mean us, and set his purr going again. We stroked him and he gave his rusty grunt of acknowledgement.

Meanwhile, Butchkin the Magnificent watched and thought his own thoughts. His character had a lot to do with Rufus's fate. He is too proud to compete. If he is in intimate conversation with me at the top of the house, and Charles comes in, he simply jumps down off the bed or chair and goes off downstairs. He will not only not tolerate competition felt to be unworthy of him, he won't put up with thoughts not centred on him. Holding him, stroking him, I have to keep my thoughts on him. No such thing, with Butchkin, as stroking him while I read. The moment my thoughts have wandered, he knows it and jumps down and is off. But he doesn't bear grudges. When Charles behaves badly, tormenting him, he might give him a swipe, but then bestows a forgiving lick, *noblesse oblige*.

Such a character is not going to lower himself by fighting any cat for first place.

One day I was standing in the middle of the room addressing myself to Butchkin who was curled on his basket top, when Rufus got down off the sofa and came to stand just in front of my legs, looking at Butchkin as if to say, She prefers me. This was done slowly and deliberately, he was not being emotional or rash or impulsive, all qualities that Charles had too much of. He had planned it, was calm and thoughtful. He had decided to make a final bid to be top cat, my favourite, with Butchkin in second place. But I wasn't going to have this. I pointed at the sofa and he looked up at me in a way which, had he been human, would have said, well, it was worth having a go. And he went back to the sofa.

Butchkin had noted my decisiveness in his favour and did not remark on it more than by getting down off his place, coming to wind himself around my legs, and then going back again.

Rufus had made his bid to be first cat, and failed.

He had not put a paw downstairs for months, but now I saw him trying a clumsy jump on to the roof, and there he looked back, still afraid I might not let him back in, then he eyed the lilac tree, working out how to get down it. Spring had come. The tree was freshly green and the flowers, still in bud, hung in whitish-green fronds. He decided against the tree and jumped painfully back up to the balcony. I picked him up, carried him downstairs, showed him the cat door. He was terrified, thinking it was a trap. I gently pushed him through while he swore and struggled. I went out after him, picked him up, and pushed him back. At once he scrambled up the stairs, thinking I wanted to throw him out altogether. This performance was repeated on successive days and Rufus hated it. In between I petted and praised him so he would know I was not trying to get rid of him.

He thought it over. I saw him get up from his place on the sofa and slowly go down the stairs. He went to the cat door. There he stood, his tail twitching in indecision, examining it. He was afraid; fear drove him back. He made himself stop, return . . . several times he did this, then reached the flap itself, and tried to force himself to jump through it, but his instincts rose up in him and forced him away. Again and again this was repeated. And then he made himself do it. Like a person jumping into the deep end, he pushed his head through, then his body, and was in the garden that was full of the scents and sounds of spring, birds jubilating because they had made it through another winter, children reclaiming their playgrounds. The old vagabond stood there, snuffing the air which seemed to fill him with new life, one paw raised, turning his head to catch the smell-messages (what someone in the house calls smellograms) that brought him reminders of former friends, both feline and human, brought him memories. Easy then to see him as a young cat, handsome and full of vigour. Off he went in his deliberate way, limping a little, to the end of the garden. Under the old fruit trees he looked to the right and he looked to the left. Memories tugged him both ways. He went under the fence to the right, in the direction of the old woman's house – or so we supposed. There he stayed for an hour or so, and then I watched him squeezing his way back under the fences into our garden, and he came back down the path and stood at the back door by the cat flap and looked up at me: Please open it, I've had enough for one day. I gave in and opened the door. But next day he made himself go out through the flap, and he came back through the flap, and after that there was no need for a cat box, not even when it rained or snowed or the garden was full of wind and noise. Not, that is, unless he was ill and too weak.

Most often he went visiting to the right, but sometimes off to the left, a longer journey, and I watched him through binoculars, till I lost him in the shrubs. When he returned from either trip he always came at once to be petted, and he set his purring machinery in motion . . . it was then we realized his purring was no longer the very loud, insistent, prolonged noise it had been when he first came. Now he purred adequately, with moderation, as befitted a cat who wanted us to be sure he valued us and his place with us, even though he was not top cat and we would not give him first place. For a long time he had been afraid we would prove capricious and throw him out, or lock him out, but now he felt more secure. But at that stage he never went visiting without coming at once to one of us, and purring, and sitting by our legs, or pushing his forehead against us, which meant he would like his ears rubbed, particularly the sore one which would not heal.

That spring and summer were good for Rufus. He was well, as far as he could be. He was sure of us, even though once I incautiously picked up an old broom handle, which lay on the back porch, and I saw him jump down on to the roof, falling over, and he scrambled down the tree and was at the end of the garden in one wild panicky rush. Someone in the past had thrown sticks at him, had beaten him. I ran down into the garden and found him terrified, hiding in a bush. I picked him up, brought him back, showed him the harmless broom handle, apologized, petted him. He understood it was a mistake.

Rufus made me think about the different kinds of cat intelligence. Before that I had recognized that cats had different temperaments. His is the intelligence of the survivor. Charles has the scientific intelligence, curious about everything, human affairs, the people who come to the house, and, in particular, our gadgets. Tape recorders, a turning gramophone table, the television, a radio, fascinate him. You can see him wondering why a disembodied human voice emerges from a box. When he was a kitten, before he gave up, he used to stop a turning record with a paw . . . release it . . . stop it again . . . look at us, miaow an enquiry. He would walk to the back of the radio set to find out if he could see what he heard, go behind the television set, turn over a tape recorder with his paw, sniff at it, miaow, *What* is this? He is the talkative cat. He talks you down the stairs and out of the house, talks you in again and up the stairs, he comments on everything that happens. When he comes in from the garden you can hear him from the top of the house. 'Here I am at last,' he cries, 'Charles the adorable, and how you must have missed me! Just imagine what has happened to me, you'll never believe it . . .' Into the room you are sitting in he comes, and stands in the doorway, his head slightly on one side, and waits for you to admire him. 'Am I not the prettiest cat in this house?' he demands, vibrating all over. Winsome, that's the word for Charles.

The General has his intuitive intelligence, knowing what you are thinking and what you are going to do next. He is not interested in science, how things work; he does not bother to impress you with his looks. He talks when he has something to say and only when he is alone with you 'Ah,' he says, finding that the other cats are elsewhere, 'so we are alone at last.' And he permits a duet of mutual admiration. When I come back from somewhere he rushes from the end of the garden, crying out, 'There you are, I've missed you! How could you go away and leave me for so long?' He leaps into my arms, licks my face and, unable to contain his joy, rushes all over the house like a kitten. Then he returns to being his grave and dignified self.

By the time autumn began Rufus had been behaving like a strong, well cat for some months, visiting friends, sometimes staying away for a day or two. But then he did not go out, he was a sick cat and lay in a warm place, a sad cat with sores on his paws, shaking his head because of the ulcer in his ear, drinking, drinking . . . Back to the vet. Verdict: not good, very bad, in fact, sores like these a bad sign. More antibiotics, more vitamins, and Rufus should not go out in the cold and wet. For months Rufus made no attempt to go out. He lay near the radiator, and his hair came out in great thick rusty wads. Wherever he lay, even for a few minutes, was a nest of orange hair, and you could see his skin through the thin fur. Slowly, he got better.

By ill luck it happened that another cat, not ours, needed medicating at the same time. It got itself run over, had a serious operation and convalesced in our house being fussed over and our own two cats did not like it, and took themselves off into the garden away from the upsetting sight. And then Butchkin too seemed ill. When I went into the garden or the sitting-room he was stretching out his neck and coughing in a delicate but gloomy way, suffering nobly borne. I took him to the vet, but there was nothing wrong. A mystery. He went on coughing. In the garden I could not pick up a trowel or pull out a weed without hearing hoarse and hollow coughing. Very odd indeed. One day, when I had petted poor Butchkin and enquired after his health, and given up, and come indoors, I was struck by unpleasant suspicion. I went to the top of the house and watched him through the binoculars. Not a sign of coughing, he was stretched out enjoying the early spring sunlight. Down I went into the garden and, when he saw me, he got into a crouching position, his throat extended, coughing and suffering. I returned to the balcony with the spy glass, and there he lay, his beautiful black and white coat a-dazzle in the sun, yawning. Luckily, the second sick cat recovered and went off to his new home and we were again a three-cat family. Butchkin's cough mysteriously disappeared, and he acquired another name: for a time he was known as Sir Laurence Olivier Butchkin.

Now all three cats enjoyed the garden in their various ways, but pursued in it three parallel existences; if their paths crossed they politely ignored each other.

One sunny morning I saw two orange cats on the fresh grass of the next-door lawn. One was Rufus. His fur had grown back, but thinner than before. He sat firmly upright, confronting a very young male cat who was challenging him. This cat was bright orange, like an apricot in sunlight, a plumy, feathery cat who made delicate jabs, first with one paw and then the other, not actually touching Rufus but, or so it looked, aiming at an imaginary or invisible cat just in front to Rufus. This lovely young cat seemed to be dancing as it sat, it wavered and sidled and patted and prodded the air, and the foxfire shine of its fur made Rufus look dingy. They were alike; this was Rufus's son, I was sure, and in him I was seeing the poor old ragbag Rufus as he had been before the unkindness of humans had done him in. The scene went on for minutes, half an hour. As male cats often do, they seemed to be staging a joust or duel as a matter of form, with no intention of actually hurting each other. The young cat did let out a yowl or two, but Rufus remained silent, sitting solidly on his bottom. The young cat went on feinting with his fringed red paws, then stopped and hastily licked his side as if losing interest in the business, but then, reminded by Rufus's stolid presence that he had an obligation to fight Rufus, he sat up again, all style and pose, like an heraldic cat, a feline on a coat of arms, and resumed his feinting dance. Rufus continued to sit, neither fighting nor refusing to fight. The young cat got bored and wandered off down the garden, prancing at shadows, rolling over and lolling on the grass, chasing insects. Rufus waited until he had gone, and then set off in his quiet way in the direction he was going, this spring, not to the right, to the old lady, but to the left where he might stay hours or even overnight. For he was well again and it was spring, mating time. When he came home he was hungry and thirsty, and that meant he was not making human friends. But then, as spring went on, he stayed longer, perhaps two days, three. He had, I was pretty sure, a cat friend.

Tetchy and petulant Grey Cat had been unfriendly with other cats. Before she was spayed she was unloving with her mates and hostile even to cats living a long time in the same house. She did not have cat friends, only human friends. When she became friendly with a cat for the first time she was old, about thirteen. I was living then in a small flat at the top of a house that had no cat doors, only a staircase to the front door. From there she made her way to the garden at the back of the house. She could push the door open to come in, but had to be let out. She began admitting an old grey cat who would ascend the stairs just behind her, then wait at the door to our flat for her to say he could come up further, and waited at the top to be invited into my room: waited for her invitations, not mine. She liked him. For the first time she was liking a cat who had not begun as her kitten. He would advance quietly into my room— her room, as he saw it – and then went towards her. At first she sat facing him with her back to a big old chair for protection; she wasn't going to trust anyone, not she! He stopped a short way from her and softly miaowed. When she gave a hasty, reluctant mew in reply – for she had become like an old woman who is querulous and bad tempered, but does not know it – he crouched down a foot or so away from her, and looked steadily at her. She too crouched down. They might stay like that for an hour, two hours.

Later she became more relaxed about it all, and they sat crouched side by side, close but not touching. They did not converse, except for soft little sounds of greeting. They liked each other, wanted to sit together. Who was he? Where did he live? I never found out. He was old, a cat who had not had an easy life, for he came up in your hands like a shadow, and his fur was lustreless. But he was a whole cat, a gentlemanly old cat, grey with white whiskers, polite, courtly, not expecting special treatment or, indeed anything much from life. He would eat a little of her food, drink some milk if offered some, but did not seem hungry. Often when I came back from some-where he was waiting at the outside door and he miaowed a little, very softly, looking up at me, then came in after me, followed me up the stairs to the door of our flat, miaowed again, and came up the final stairs to the top where he went straight to Grey Cat who let out her cross little miaow when she saw him, but then permitted him a trill of welcome. He spent long evenings with her. She was a changed cat, less prickly and ready to take offence. I used to watch the two of them sitting together like two old people who don't need to talk. Never in my life have I so badly wanted to share a language with an animal. 'Why this cat?' I wanted to ask her. 'Why this cat and no other cat? What is it in this old polite cat that makes you fond of him? For I suppose you will admit you are? All these fine cats in the house, all your life, and you've never liked one of them, but now . . .'

One evening, he did not come. Not the next. Grey Cat waited for him. She sat watching the door all evening. Then she waited downstairs at the door into the house. She searched the garden. But he did not come, not ever again. And she was never again friends with a cat. Another cat, a male cat who visited the cat downstairs, took refuge with us when he became ill, a few weeks before he died, and lived out the end of his life in my room – her room; but she never acknow-ledged his existence. She behaved as if only I and she were there.

I believed that Rufus had such a friend, and that was where he was going off to visit.

One evening in late summer he stayed on the sofa by me, and he was there next morning in exactly the same position. When at last he got down, he walked holding up a limp and dangling back leg. The vet said he had been run over: one could tell by his claws, for cats instinctively extend their claws to grip when the wheel drags at them. His claws were broken and split. He had a bad fracture of a back leg.

The cast went on from his ankle to the top of his thigh, and he was put into a quiet room with food and water and a dirt box. There he was happy to stay overnight, but then wanted to come out. We opened the door and watched him clumsily descend the stairs, flight after flight, to the bottom of the house where he swore and cursed as he manoeuvred that sticking-out leg through the cat door, then hopped and hobbled up the path, and swore a lot more as he edged himself and the leg under a fence. Off to the left, to his friend. He was away for about half an hour; he had been to report to someone, feline or human, about his mishap. When he came back, he was pleased to be put back into his refuge. He was shaken, shocked, and his eyes showed he was in pain. His fur, made healthy by summer and good feeding, looked harsh, and he was again a poor old cat who could not easily clean himself. Poor old ragbag! Poor Calamity Cat! He accumulated names as Butchkin does, but they were sad ones. But he was indomitable. He set himself to the task of removing his cast, succeeded, and was returned to the vet to have another put on, which he could not take off. But he tried. And, everyday he made his trip down the stairs, to the cat door, where he hesitated, his leg stuck out behind him, then went through it cursing, because he always knocked his leg on it, and we watched him hobble up the garden through the puddles and leaves of the autumn. He had to lie almost flat to get under the fence. Every day he went to report, and came back exhausted and went to sleep. When awake, he laboured at the task of getting his cast off. Where he sat was white with bits of cast.

In a month it came off, the leg was stiff but usable, and Rufus became himself, a gallant adventuring cat who used us as a base, but then got ill again. For a couple of years this cycle went on. He got well, and was off, got ill and came home. But his illnesses were getting worse. His ear ulcer would not heal. He would return from somewhere to ask for help. He would put his paw delicately to his suppurating ear, retch delicately at the smell on his paw, and look helplessly at his nurses. He gave little grunts of protest as we washed it out, but he wanted us to, and he took his medicaments, and he lay around and allowed himself to get well. Under our hands his was a tough, muscled body and he was a strong old cat, in spite of his ailments. It was only at the end of his life, his much too short life, when he was ill and could hardly walk, that he stayed home and did not attempt to go out at all. He lay on the sofa and seemed to think, or dream, when he was not asleep. Once, when he was asleep, I stroked him awake to take his medicine, and he came up out of sleep with the confiding, loving trill greeting cats use for the people they love, the cats they love. But when he saw it was me he became his normal polite and grateful self, and I realized that this was the only time I had heard him make this special sound – in a house where it was heard all day. This is how mother cats greet their kittens, kittens greet their mothers. Had he been dreaming of when he was a kitten? Or perhaps even of the human who had owned him as a kitten, or a young cat, but then had gone off and abandoned him? I shocked, and hurt, this ultimate sound, for he had not made it even when he was purring like a machine to show gratitude. During all the time he had known us, nearly four years, several times nursed back to health, or near-health, he had never really believed he could not lose this home and have to fend for himself, become a cat maddened by thirst and aching with cold. His confidence in someone, his love, had once been so badly betrayed that he could not allow himself ever to love again.

Knowing cats, a lifetime of cats, what is left is a sediment of sorrow quite different from that due to humans: compounded of pain for their helplessness, of guilt on behalf of us all.

The Home Life of a Holy Cat

ARTHUR WIEGALL

O NE SUMMER during a heat wave, when the temperature in the shade of my veranda in Luxor was 125° Fahrenheit, I went down to cooler Lower Egypt to pay a visit to an English friend of mine stationed at Zagazig, the native city which stands beside the ruins of ancient Bubastis.

He was about to leave Egypt and asked me whether I would like to have his cat, a dignified, mystical-minded, long-legged, small-headed, green-eyed female, whose orange-yellow hair, marked with greyish-black stripes in tabby pattern, was so short that she gave the impression of being naked – an impression, however, which did not in any way detract from her air of virginal chastity.

Her name was Basta, and though her more recent ancestors had lived wild amongst the ruins, she was so obviously a descendant of the holy cats of ancient times, who were incarnations, of the goddess Basta, that I thought it only right to accept the offer and take her up to Luxor to live with me. To be the expert in charge of Egyptian antiquities and not have an ancient Egyptian cat to give an air of mystery to my headquarters had, indeed, always seemed to me to be somewhat wanting in showmanship on my part.

Thus it came about that, on my departure, I drove off to the railroad station with the usually dignified Basta bumping around and uttering unearthly howls inside a cardboard hat box, in the side of which I had cut a small round hole for

ventilation. The people in the streets and on the station platform seemed to be under the impression that the noises were
digestive and that I was in dire need of a doctor; and it was a
great relief to my embarrassment when the hot and panting
train steamed into Zagazig.

Fortunately, I found myself alone in the compartment, and
the hatbox at my side had begun to cause me less anxiety,
when suddenly Basta was seized with a sort of religious frenzy.
The box rocked about, and presently out through the airhole
came a long, snake-like paw which waved weirdly to and fro in
space for a moment and then was withdrawn, its place being
taken by a pink nose which pushed itself outward with such
frantic force that the sides of the hole gave way, and out burst
the entire sandy, sacred head.

She then began to choke, for the cardboard was pressing
tightly around her neck; and to save her from strangulation I
was obliged to tear the aperture open, whereupon she wriggled out, leaped in divine frenzy up the side of the carriage and
prostrated herself on the network of the baggage-rack, where
her hysteria caused her to lose all control of her internal
arrangements if and I say modestly that she was overcome with
nausea, I shall be telling but a part of the dreadful tale.

The rest of the journey was like a bad dream; but at the Cairo
terminus, where I had to change into the night express for
Luxor, I got the help of a native policeman who secured a large
laundry basket from the sleeping-car department, and after a
prolonged struggle, during which the train was shunted into a
distant siding, we imprisoned the struggling Basta again.

The perspiring policeman and I then carried the basket at a
run along the tracks back to the station in the sweltering heat of
the late afternoon, and I just managed to catch my train; but
during this second part of my journey Basta travelled in the
baggage-van whence, in the hot and silent night, whenever we
were at a standstill, her appalling incantations came drifting to
my ears.

I opened the basket in an unfurnished spare room in my
house, and like a flash Basta was up the bare wall and on to the
curtain pole above the window. There she remained all day, in
a sort of hypnotic trance; but at sunset the saucer of milk and
plate of fish which I had provided for her at last enticed her

down, and in the end she reconciled herself to her new surroundings and indicated by her behaviour that she was willing
to accept my house as her earthly temple.

With Pedro, my pariah dog, there was not the slightest
trouble; he had no strong feelings about cats, and she on her
part graciously deigned to acknowledge his status – as, I believe, is generally the case in native households. She sometimes condescended to visit my horse and donkey in their
stalls; and for Laura, my camel, she quickly developed a real
regard, often sleeping for hours in her stable.

I was not worried as to how she would treat the chickens and
pigeons, because her former owner at Zagazig had insisted
upon her respecting his hen coop and pigeon cote; but I was a
little anxious about the ducks, for she had not previously
known any, and in ancient times her ancestors used to be
trained to hunt wild geese and ducks and were fed with *pâté de
foie gras*, or whatever it was called then, on holy days and
anniversaries.

In a corner of the garden I had made a miniature duck pond
which was sunk rather deeply in the ground and down to
which I had cut a narrow, steeply sloping passage, or gangway. During the day, after the ducks had been up and down
this slope several times, the surface used to become wet and
slippery, and the ducks, having waddled down the first few
inches, were forced to toboggan down the rest of it on their
tails, with their two feet sticking out in front of them and their
heads well up.

Basta was always fascinated by this slide and by the splash at
the bottom, and used to sit and watch it all for hours, which
made me think at first that she would one day spring at one of
them; but she never did. Field mice, and water rats down by
the Nile, were her only prey; and in connection with the former
I may mention a curious occurrence.

One hot night I was sitting smoking my pipe on the veranda
when my attention was attracted by two mice which had crept
into the patch of brilliant moonlight before my feet and were
boldly nibbling some crumbs left over from a cracker thrown to
Pedro earlier in the evening. I watched them silently for a while
and did not notice that Basta had seen them and was preparing
to spring, nor did I observe a large white owl sitting aloft

amongst the overhanging roses and also preparing to pounce.

Suddenly, and precisely at the same moment, the owl shot down on the mice from above and Basta leaped at them from beside me. There was a collision and a wild scuffle; fur and feathers flew; I fell out of my chair; and then the owl made off screeching in one direction and the cat dashed away in the other; while the mice, practically clinging to each other, remained for a moment or so too terrified to move.

During the early days of her residence in Luxor, Basta often used to go down to the edge of the Nile to fish with her paw; but she never caught anything, and in the end she got a fright and gave it up. I was sitting by the river watching her trying to catch one of a little shoal of small fish which were sunning themselves in the shallow water when there came swimming into view a twelve or fourteen-inch fish which I recognized (by its whiskers and the absence of a dorsal fin) as the electric cat fish, pretty common in the Nile – a strange creature able to give you an electric shock like hitting your funny bone.

These fish obtain their food in a curious way: they hang round any shoal of small fry engaged in feeding, and then glide quietly into their midst and throw out this electric shock, whereupon the little fellows are all sick to the stomach, and the big fellow gets their disgorged dinners.

I was just waiting to see this happen with my own eyes – for it had always seemed a bit far-fetched – when Basta made a dart at the intruder with her paw and got a shock. She uttered a yowl as though somebody had trodden on her and leaped high in the air; and never again did she put her foot near the water. She was content after that with our daily offering of a fish brought from the market and fried for her like a burnt sacrifice.

Basta had a most unearthly voice, and when she was feeling emotional would let out a wail which at first was like the crying of a phantom baby and then became the tuneless song of a lunatic, and finally developed into the blood-curdling howl of a soul in torment. And when she spat, the percussion was like that of a spring-gun.

There were some wild cats or, rather, domestic cats who, like Basta's own forebears, had taken to a wild life, living in a grove of trees beside the river just beyond my garden wall; and it was generally the proximity of one of these which started her off;

but sometimes the outburst was caused by her own unfathomable thoughts as she went her mysterious ways in the darkness of the night.

I think she must have been clairvoyant, for she often seemed to be seeing things not visible to me. Sometimes, perhaps when she was cleaning fish or mouse from her face, she would pause with one foot off the ground and stare in front of her, and then back away with bristling hair or go forward with friendly little mewing noises; and sometimes she would leap off a chair or sofa, her tail lashing and her green eyes dilated. But it may have been worms.

Once I saw her standing absolutely rigid and tense on the lawn, staring at the rising moon; and then all of a sudden she did a sort of dance such as cats sometimes do when they are playing with other cats. But there was no other cat and, any way, Basta never played; she never forgot that she was a holy cat.

Her chaste hauteur was so great that she would not move out of the way when people were walking about, and many a time her demoniacal shriek and perhaps a crash of breaking glass informed the household that somebody had tripped over her. It was astonishing, however, how quickly she recovered her dignity and how well she maintained the pretence that whatever happened to her was at her own celestial wish and was not our doing.

If I called her she would pretend not to hear, but would come a few moments later when it could appear that she had thought of doing so first; and if I lifted her off a chair she would jump back on to it and then descend with dignity as though of her own free will. But in this, of course, she was more like a woman than like a divinity.

The Egyptian cat is a domesticated species of the African wild-cat, and no doubt its strange behaviour and its weird voice were the cause of it being regarded as sacred in ancient times; but, although the old gods and their worship have been forgotten these many centuries, the traditional sanctity of the race has survived.

Modern Egyptians think it unlucky to hurt a cat and, in the native quarters of Cairo and other cities, hundreds of cats are daily fed at the expense of benevolent citizens. They say that they do this because cats are so useful to mankind in killing off mice and other pests; but actually it is an unrecognized survival of the old beliefs.

In the days of the Pharaohs, when a cat died the men of the household shaved off their eyebrows and sat around wailing and rocking themselves to and fro in simulated anguish. The body was embalmed and buried with solemn rites in the local cats' cemetery, or was sent down to Bubastis to rest in the shadow of the temple of their patron goddess. I myself have dug up hundreds of mummified cats; and once, when I had a couple of dozen of the best specimens standing on my veranda waiting to be dispatched to the Cairo Museum, Basta was most excited about it, and walked around sniffing at them all day. They certainly smelled awful.

On my lawn there was a square slab of stone which had once been the top of an altar dedicated to the sun god, but was now used as a sort of low garden table; and sometimes when she had caught a mouse she used to deposit the chewed corpse upon this slab – nobody could think why, unless, as I always told people, she was really making an offering to the sun. It was most mysterious of her; but it led once to a very unfortunate episode.

A famous French antiquarian, who was paying a polite call, was sitting with me beside this sacred stone, drinking afternoon tea and eating fresh dates, when Basta appeared on the scene with a small dead mouse in her mouth, which in her usual way she deposited upon the slab – only on this occasion she laid it on my guest's plate, which was standing on the slab.

We were talking at the moment and did not see her do this and, anyhow, the Frenchman was as blind as a bat; and, of course, as luck would have it, he immediately picked up the wet, mole-coloured mouse instead of a ripe brown date, and the thing had almost gone into his mouth before he saw what it was and, with a yell, flung it into the air.

It fell into his upturned sun helmet which was lying on the grass beside him; but he did not see where it had gone and, jumping angrily to his feet in the momentary belief that I had played a schoolboy joke on him, he snatched up his helmet and was in the act of putting it on his head when the mouse tumbled out on to the front of his shirt and slipped down inside his buttoned jacket.

At this he went more or less mad, danced about, shook himself, and finally trod on Basta, who completed his frenzy by uttering a fiendish howl and digging her claws into his leg. The dead mouse, I am glad to say, fell on to the grass during the dance without passing through his roomy trousers, as I had feared it might; and Basta, recovering her dignity, picked it up and walked off with it.

It is a remarkable fact that, during the five or six years she spent with me, she showed no desire to be anything but a spinster all her life, and when I arranged a marriage for her she displayed such dignified but violent antipathy towards the bridegroom that the match was a failure. In the end, however, she fell in love with one of the wild cats who lived among the trees beyond my wall, and nothing could prevent her going off to visit him from time to time, generally at dead of night.

He did not care a hoot about her sanctity, and she was feminine enough to enjoy the novelty of being roughly treated. I never actually saw him, for he did not venture into the garden, but I used to hear him knocking her about outside my gates; and when she came home, scratched and bitten and muttering something about holy cats, it was plain that she was desperately happy. She licked her wounds, indeed, with deep and voluptuous satisfaction.

A dreadful change came over her. She lost her precious dignity and was restless and inclined to be savage; her digestion played embarrassing tricks on her; and once she mortally offended Laura by clawing her nose. There was a new glint in her green eyes as she watched the ducks sliding into the pond; the pigeons interested her for the first time; and for the first time, too, she *ate* the mice she had caught.

Then she began to disappear for a whole day or night at a time, and once when I went in search of her amongst the trees outside and found her sharpening her claws on a branch above my head, she put her ears back and hissed at me until I could see every one of her teeth and halfway down her pink throat. I tried by every method to keep her at home when she came back, but it was all in vain, and at last she left me forever.

Weeks afterwards I caught sight of her once again amongst

the trees, and it was evident that she was soon to become a mother. She gave me a friendly little mew this time, but she would not let me touch her; and presently she slipped away into the undergrowth. I never knew what became of her.

Solomon and Sheba

DOREEN TOVEY

THE DAY Sheba chased a gnat behind the picture over the bureau and left a row of black footprints up the wall Charles said it wasn't fair to blame the cats for everything. It wasn't her fault, he said, that when it flew past she happened to be looking up the chimney and had her paws covered in soot. I must remember that Siamese were not as other cats, and make allowance for their verve and curiosity.

He didn't say that when we put down the new stair-carpet and Solomon, busily showing Sheba how Strong he was, ripped the daylights out of the bottom-tread while we were still hammering down the top. He said Solomon was a damblasted little pest and if he wasn't careful he'd end up in the Cats' Home. Neither did it improve matters when I, to protect the rest of the carpet until Solomon got tired of sharpening his claws on it, made a set of stair-pads out of folded copies of *The Times*. The idea was to put a pad on each stair whenever we were going out. It worked for a few days – then one morning Charles, dashing up at the last moment to fetch his wallet, slipped on the top copy and slid from top to bottom on his neck. Both Solomon and I were in the dog-house then, and although it didn't worry me unduly – Charles, who is six feet tall, falls down the cottage stairs, which are steep and narrow, quite regularly, and I would get the blame even if I were on the top of Everest at the time – Solomon was quite put out about it.

While Sheba comforted Charles in the hall, walking up and

down on his stomach and asking anxiously if he were Dead, Solomon sat at the top of the stairs delivering a long Siamese monologue about the injustice of it all. Sheba Clawed Things, he said, and Nobody Complained About Her. She did too. The underside of the spare room arm chair sagged like a jelly bag where Sheba, when she first woke up in the morning, dragged herself round and round on her back by way of exercise – and all Charles said about that was that we had to make allowance for her high spirits.

She Knocked Things Down and Hit People Too, wailed Solomon. You could tell when he got to that bit by the pitch of his voice. Always powerful, it rose to an ear-shattering roar when he was in the right and knew it. Solomon didn't knock things down and hit people. He couldn't climb high enough to start with. But Sheba, shinning like a mountain goat up the bookshelves either side of the fireplace, was always bombarding unwary visitors with dislodged encyclopaedias or law books. Lately I had begun to wonder whether that, too, was quite the accident she claimed it to be. It had certainly been no accident the night I was just in time to stop her crowning Solomon with a Benares brass pitcher. When I caught her she was standing on the arm of a chair trying as hard as she could to hook it off the mantelpiece with her paw while he, stretched out full length to warm his stomach, lay innocently asleep on the rug below.

Now, craning his neck over the landing to make sure everybody heard him, Solomon continued his tale of woe. Charles was Clumsy, he wailed, staring reproachfully down at the spot where Sheba, relieved to find that Charles was good for a few more years yet, was making the most of the occasion by treading vigorously on his waistcoat and assuring him that *she* was a good girl. Charles would have Fallen Down the Stairs even without the newspapers, yelled Solomon. Charles Fell Over Everything. Charles Fell Off the Ladder only last Saturday. Nobody, said Solomon, with the mournful wail-cum-sniffle which meant that at that moment he was feeling particularly hard done by, could blame him for that. Charles had done it All By Himself.

Charles had indeed. He had been painting the eaves of the cottage, perched on the sloping hall roof, on a ladder that had a cracked leg and was – despite Father Adams's warning that he knew several blokes who had killed themselves like that— suspended by faith and a piece of ancient rope from the chimney-stack. Charles's own version of what happened was that he was just reaching up to put on the last brushful of paint, thinking to himself (he was given to making up tense little dramas to amuse himself while he worked), 'And at that moment, just as he reached out for the final handhold, there was a sharp crack of breaking rope and he fell like a stone into the abyss below' – when the rope did break. Not with a sharp crack. It unravelled slowly and sadistically before his very eyes as he stood helplessly on the top rung. He didn't fall into any abyss either. He landed on the hall roof with a thump that shook the cottage to its poor old foundations. When I rushed out, convinced that I was a widow at last, he was sitting despondently on the roof in a pool of pale-blue paint while, standing side by side on top of the coal-house, craning their necks like a couple of spectators at a Lord Mayor's Show, Solomon and Sheba anxiously inquired what he wanted to do that for.

Charles said I might not believe it, but as he slid down the roof after the crash he had seen – actually *seen* – that pair gallop down the path and scramble up on to the coal-house as if it were a grandstand. I believed it all right. So often in trouble themselves, there was nothing they liked better than sitting smugly by, tails wrapped primly round their front paws and expressions of pained incredulity on their faces, when somebody else was in the soup. I remember once when a dog chased a neighbour's kitten up the electricity post outside our garden wall. Solomon was hardly in a position to talk, after the incident of the fire brigade, while Sheba had lately developed her mother's habit of demanding to be rescued by Charles from every tree she came across. It made no difference. While Charles and I tried to solve the problem of getting a ladder safely balanced against the rounded post they sat side by side at the foot, their necks stuck out like giraffes to emphasize What A Long Way Up She Was, their eyes round as bottle stops, yelling encouragingly up at her that she was Very Silly To Do A Thing Like That and They Didn't Suppose We'd Ever Get Her Down Again. The fact that no sooner had Charles rescued the kitten than he had to go up again to fetch Solomon, who had meanwhile climbed the ladder himself by way of an experiment and was now stuck half way up bellowing his own head off, was quite incidental. It still left Sheba at the bottom nattering away happily about what a long way up *he* was and she didn't suppose we'd ever get *him* down either.

It was inevitable, of course, that their rubber-necking would one day lead them into trouble. It happened at a time when we had new neighbours in the next cottage and Sol and Sheba, consumed with their usual curiosity, were going up every day to see how they were getting on. We warned the people not to encourage them. Disaster, we said, would unfailingly follow. Solomon would wreck their stair-carpet or raid their pantry and Sheba would either go up their chimney or fall down their lavatory. They wouldn't listen. They hadn't met any Siamese before and they were fascinated, they said, by the way our two marched one behind the other down the garden path, greeted them with an airy bellow and proceeded to inspect the place as if they owned it. Which, so far as we could see, made it entirely the Westons' own fault when they tried to fill their water-butt during a drought by means of a hosepipe sneaking illicitly through the delphiniums and lupins to the kitchen tap and Solomon and Sheba promptly gave them away to the entire village by sitting on the outhouse roof, gazing wide-eyed down at the bubbles, and loudly inviting passers by to come and see what they'd found. Father Adams, who was one of the people who did – years ago his grandfather had lived in the Westons' cottage and that, according to country politics, really gave him more right to walk up the front path than the Westons themselves, who were newcomers from town – said old man Weston turned all the colours of a shammylon when he saw he'd been found out. He hadn't been there long enough to know that practically everybody else – certainly Father Adams – filled their water-butts in exactly the same way, and for days he went round hardly daring to look anybody in the face. Which, as Aunt Ethel said the day Solomon ate her guinea pot of beauty cream, just showed the folly of having anything to do with Siamese at all.

We never managed to get the better of them ourselves. Every time we thought we had them weighed off, up they came with something new. Mouse-catching, for instance. No sooner had we got used to the routine of Sheba catching them and Solomon slinging them round our heads for hours than Sheba, feeling that Solomon was getting too much limelight, decided that she'd better tell us when she caught a mouse in future, so there would be no mistaking it was hers. The first time Solomon heard her coming under the new system, moaning like a travelling air-raid siren, he said it was ghosts and hid under the bath and we had an awful job to coax him out; but it wasn't long before he, in turn, thought up an even better gimmick. He ate the mouse. Not quietly, in a corner, but noisily on the hearth-rug, leaving us the head and tail as souvenirs. The next thing was that Sheba ate a mouse too, but her stomach wasn't as strong as Solomon's and she went straight out and sicked it up on the stairs. And so, as Charles said, life went on.

There was a period, just after Sugieh died and the kittens were beginning to feel their feet as individuals, when if we had visitors we just couldn't move for them, sitting solidly in people's laps, licking their iced cakes when they weren't looking, investigating their handbags and chatting to them under the bathroom door. They liked people so much that when we shut them in the hall one night because one of Charles's friends had a dark suit on and wasn't very fond of cats anyway they climbed the curtains, got out through a transom window which we didn't know was open, and appeared suddenly with their small smudgy faces pressed to the window of the sitting-room, gazing wistfully in like orphans of the storm.

A great success that was. Everybody cooed over them and gave them ice-cream and Charles's friend went home with a suit that looked as if it were made of angora. The next time they were shut out on account of visitors Solomon, remembering the ice-cream, promptly jumped out of a window again. This time, however, as all the hall windows were shut, old Bat Brains went upstairs and jumped out of the bedroom window. One visitor fainted on the spot when she saw him coming down, but he landed in a hydrangea and was quite unharmed. The only thing was that now Solomon had discovered that he could open windows by putting his fat little bullet-head under the catches and pushing them up, in addition to spreading twelve copies of *The Times* on the stairs any time we shut them out, we now had to tie up all the window-catches with string as well.

Though the cats drove visitors nearly mad with their attention when they first arrived, however, if anybody stayed after eleven o'clock things were very different. Then, retiring to the most comfortable armchair (if anybody was sitting in it they just squeezed down behind him and kept turning round and round till he got out; it never failed), they curled up and ostentatiously tried to go to sleep. Tried was the operative word. Any time anybody looked across at the chair there would be at least one Siamese regarding them with half-raised head, one eye open and a pained expression that clearly indicated it was time they went home, Some People were tired. If this had no effect, in due course Solomon would sit up, yawn noisily and subside again with a loud sigh on top of Sheba. Few visitors missed that hint. Solomon yawned like fat men belch—long, loudly and with gusto. What was most embarrassing, though, was the way – after lying for hours as if they'd been working all day in a chain gang – they suddenly perked up the moment people did start to go. It wouldn't have been so bad if they'd just politely seen them off at the door, the way Sugieh used to do. These two sat in the hall and bawled to people to hurry up – and as we shepherded people to the front gate they could be seen quite plainly through the window, hilariously chasing one another over the chairs by way of celebration.

To be quite honest, by that time the visitors usually weren't looking with such a kindly eye on the cats either. There was the friend, for instance, who brought an old pair of stockings for playing with the cats and left her best ones in our bedroom for safety. She expected the old ones to be ruined, and she was right. Solomon gave her a friendly nip in the ankle while we were having tea and bang they went. Unfortunately the bedroom door wasn't properly shut and while Sheba was, of her own accord, bringing the new ones down for the lady they went bang too, hitched up in a snag on the stairs.

There was the friend who unthinkingly left her car keys on the hall table. An innocent enough gesture – except that that was the time when Solomon was being an Alsatian dog and carrying things round in his mouth and it took us two hours to find where he had put them. Down the clock-golf hole on the lawn.

There was the cactus which disappeared mysteriously from its pot while its owner, who had just been given it by another friend, was calling on us for a cup of tea. Charles said if that didn't prove Solomon wasn't right in the head nothing did— but as a matter of fact it wasn't Solomon. It was Sheba, as we discovered later when we started raising cactus ourselves and had to lock them in the bathroom every night for safety while she howled under the door for just a little one to play marbles with.

It was Solomon, though, alone and unaided, who killed the fur coat. We laughed at the look of awe on his face the first time he saw it, and the way he immediately put up his back and offered to fight. We didn't give it a thought as the owner, patting him on the head and saying it was only a coat little man, tossed it nonchalantly on to the hall chair. But Solomon did. As soon as he'd had his share of the crab sandwiches he went out and killed it so dead I shudder even now to think how much it cost us to have it repaired.

We kept a strong guard on fur coats after that. Whenever one arrived Charles held Solomon in the kitchen while I personally locked it in the wardrobe and then locked the bedroom door. Even so I had qualms the night someone arrived wearing a particularly fine leopard coat and Solomon, as soon as supper was over, disappeared quietly into the hall. As soon as I could I slipped out too, to check. Everything seemed all right. The bedroom door was still firmly locked and when I spoke to him Solomon, sitting innocently on the hall table and gazing out into the night, said he was only looking for foxes.

It wasn't until the visitor, getting ready to go, started looking round the hall saying it was funny but she could have *sworn* she left it on the chest that I realized I hadn't taken her hat up to the bedroom as well – and by that time it was too late. It had – or rather it had had – a smart black cocksfeather cockade on one side. When we picked it up, from under the same chair that had once concealed Aunt Ethel's famous telegram, all the feathers fell off.

By the time Solomon was six months old he had, despite his unpromising beginnings, grown into one of the most handsome Siamese we had ever seen. True he still had spotted whiskers and big feet and walked like Charlie Chaplin. But he had lost his puppy fat and was as lithe and sleek as a panther. His black, triangular mask – except for one solitary white hair right in the middle which he said he'd got through worrying over Sheba – shone like polished ebony. His eyes, set slantwise above high, Oriental cheekbones, were a brilliant sapphire and remarkable even for a Siamese. When he lay on the garden wall with his long black legs drooping elegantly over the edge he looked, according to Father Adams, exactly like a sheik in one of them Eastern palaces.

Father Adams, who was a great fan of Ethel M. Dell's, would have liked Solomon to be a sheik in the real romantic sense of the word. At that time he was still dreaming of making a fortune from cat-breeding and Solomon was so magnificent that there was nothing he would have liked more than to see him drag Mimi off into the hills by the scruff of her sleek cream neck and there found a race of Siamese that would, as he was always telling us, fetch ten quid apiece as easy as pie.

He was so disgusted when we had Solomon neutered that he wouldn't speak to us for a week – which was all very well; we didn't want to spoil Solomon's life either, but we had to share it with him and even our best friends wouldn't have lasted long in a house with an un-neutered Siamese. The only way we could have kept him – unless we let him wander, in which case a Siamese tom usually develops into a terrible fighter and rarely comes home at all – would have been outside in a stud-house.

When we asked Solomon about it he said he'd rather have beetles than girls. And cream cakes, he added, casting a speculative eye at the tea-trolley. And sleeping in our bed, he said that night, burrowing determinedly under the blankets to find my head.

That settled it. We could as soon imagine Solomon a studtom as pretending to be a lion at the zoo. The following weekend he was neutered, and Sheba along with him, and not a scrap of trouble did we have with either of them except in the matter of Sheba's stitches. Two she had, and the vet who did the operation – a town one this time; not for one moment did we attach any blame to the vet who did Sugieh's operation, but it seemed fairer all round to have Sheba done by someone else – said we could easily take them out ourselves on the tenth day. Just snip here and there, he said, pull smartly – and the job was done.

It might have been with normal cats, but not with Sheba. She wasn't going to have any ham-fisted amateurs handling her, she said. Every time we approached her with the scissors she fled to the top shelf of the bookcase and barricaded herself in. Even Charles couldn't get her to come down. She liked him very much, she assured him from behind the Britannicas – but not her stitches, if he didn't mind. He could practise on Solomon, Mimi or even me. She wanted a real doctor. After the night when the stitches began to itch and she lay on our bed first trying to get them out herself and then letting Solomon have a go until the perpetual snick-snicking nearly drove us mad she got one, too. We could hardly ask the local vet to do the job, as he hadn't done the operation, so the next morning we rang Doctor Tucker, who came over and obliged at once. Sheba didn't run away from him. She told him at great length what we'd tried to do to her and did he think he ought to report it to the Medical Association. Then, while he snipped and pulled with the self-same scissors we had tried to use, she stood quietly on the table, her eyes happily crossed, and purred.

That, we thought, was the end of our troubles. The cats were growing up now. They had their little idiosyncrasies of course. Like Sheba's habit of turning out the vegetable rack every night, followed by complaints from our new help that it wasn't her job in other houses to fish sprouts and squashed tomatoes from under the cooker every morning. Not that it mattered much because she gave us notice quite soon anyway on account of Solomon's habit of walking over floors as soon as she'd scrubbed them.

Sheba was jolly pleased when she went. Now, she said – and how right she was – she'd be able to file sprouts under the stove until they smelled real high before anybody moved them. Solomon was pleased. She kept throwing the floor-cloth at him, he said, and if he hadn't been a gentleman – in the *highest* sense of the word, he said, ignoring Sheba's aside to Charles

that he Wasn't Any More Was He, Not Since His Operation?—
he'd have bitten her. Charles was pleased. If she hadn't gone,
her said, judging by the looks she gave him when he asked her
to empty the ashtrays, she'd have been throwing the floor-
cloth at him next. The only one who wasn't pleased was me –
and I was too busy doing the housework to complain.

There was Solomon's keen interest in things mechanical
which led him to follow the vacuum-cleaner like a bloodhound,
with his nose glued firmly to the carpet, watching the bits
disappear inside. Come to think of it, it was a good thing the
help wasn't around the day he decided to experiment with that
and, while I was moving a chair, poked his ball of silver paper
curiously into the works. I turned round just in time to see a
long black paw disappearing under the front and to hurl myself
at the switch like a bomb.

Mrs Terry wouldn't have done that. She'd have screamed,
thrown her apron over her head and fainted, the way she did
when she removed the guard from the electric fire in the
sitting-room for cleaning and Solomon, with happy memories
of Mum, promptly walked over and stuck his rear against it.
The only result of that incident had been that, for a while,
Solomon's tail, indented in two places by the electric bars, had
looked more like that of a poodle than a Siamese and Sheba had
made him cross by pretending to be frightened every time she
saw it. What might have happened with the vacuum I hardly
dared to think.

These though, as I have said, were idiosyncrasies such as all
Siamese owners experience. So long as we got up at five in the
morning to let them out – otherwise Sheba knocked the lamp
off the dressing-table and Solomon bit us; so long as we only
ate chocolates wrapped in silver paper and let Solomon have
every single piece – he sulked like mad when somebody gave
us a 4lb box for Christmas without an inch of silver paper
among them: Done It On Purpose he said they had, watching
disconsolately every time the box was opened, and couldn't we
eat them faster than that; so long as we kept a box of All Bran
permanently on the kitchen floor to fill the corners when he felt
peckish – if we didn't he was liable to get in the cupboard and
look for it himself with disastrous results; so long as we remembered little things like that we had no trouble at all. Real little

home birds they were. Always running in to see that we hadn't gone for a walk without them – or even more important, that we weren't eating something behind their backs.

Which made it all the more worrying the morning I called the cats and instead of the usual mad stampede to see what was for breakfast only Sheba appeared, looking very small and forlorn and nattering anxiously that Solomon had vanished; she'd looked all over the place for him and she didn't know where he could be.

We didn't know it then but Solomon, tired of the chains of civilization, had gone to be an explorer – and, as explorers sometimes do, he had met with a hazard. When I found him an hour later, after scouring the countryside till I was practically on my knees, he was in a field more than a mile away with a pair of large and angry geese. When I panted up he was crouching in a corner bawling his head off about what he'd do if they came any nearer, but he didn't fool them – or me. He was scared stiff. His ears stuck up like a pair of horrified exclamation marks. His eyes were nearly popping out of his head. When I called him he gave a long, despairing wail which clearly signified that if I didn't hurry up the cannibals would get him, and he wasn't half in a fix.

I got him out of that by wading knee-deep in a bed of stinging-nettles, leaning over a barbed-wire fence and hauling him out by the scruff of his neck. From the look on the faces of those geese it was obvious there wasn't time to go round by the gate. He never learned, of course. No sooner was he safely on my shoulder and the geese out of earshot than the old bounce was back. All the way home I had a monologue right in my ear about what they said to him and what he said back— punctuated halfway by a decision, which I nipped in the bud by grabbing his tail and hanging on to it firmly, to go right back and tell them some more.

By the time we got home Solomon, in his own mind at least, was a budding Marco Polo. And from then on we had hardly a moment's peace. Summoned by a wail that turned my blood cold when I heard it, I rescued him from one emergency after another. Once, under the impression that she was running away from *him*, he chased a cow that was being tormented by flies. That was fine fun while it lasted, tearing across the field with the wind in his tail and his long black legs going like a racehorse – until the cow turned round, saw Buffalo Bill capering cockily at her heels, and chased him instead.

I rescued him that time from a handy wall, doing a fine imitation of the Stag at Bay with the cow's horns about an inch from his trembling black nose. The time he frightened a little lamb, though, he wasn't so lucky. His nearest point of escape then was through a hedge which topped a steep bank above the woods, and by the time he made it the lamb's mother was so close behind he couldn't stop to look for a proper way through. As I toiled wearily up through the woods in answer to his yell for help he appeared dramatically on the skyline, leapt into space, and landed ignominiously in a pool of mud.

That taught him nothing either. The very next day I saw him – in his own inimitable way, which meant laboriously hiding behind every blade of grass he came across and crawling across the open bits on his stomach – tracking a small kitten into the self-same woods. I let him go that time. His dusky face was alight with eagerness, there was such an Excelsior light in his eyes – and he couldn't, I thought, get into trouble with a little kitten like that.

That was where I was wrong. A few minutes later there was a volcanic explosion, a mad crashing of branches, silence – and then, once more, the familiar sound of Solomon yelling for help. Creeping stealthily through the woods he had, it seemed, come across his enemy from the farmyard, doing a bit of mousing. Judging by the way the tom went streaking up the road as I dashed into the woods he was just as alarmed as Solomon by the encounter – and indeed it wasn't that that Columbus was belly-aching about. It was that, just as he had taken refuge up a tree, so had the kitten. Up the same tree, Solomon had made it first and was clinging for dear life six feet up while the kitten, unable to pass him, was directly under his tail. Solomon, in all his glory, a magnificent, intimidating specimen of a male Siamese, was howling because a tiny kitten no bigger than a flea wouldn't let him get down.

After that Solomon kept away from the woods for a while. He took to sitting on the garden wall instead, pretending, when we asked him why he hadn't gone exploring, that he was Waiting for a Friend. That, unfortunately, was how he came to

get interested in horses. Unfortunately – because when
Solomon got interested in anything he invariably wanted a
closer look. Unfortunately – because it wasn't long before the
owner of the local riding-school was ringing us up to ask
whether we would mind keeping him in while her pupils went
by. He was frightening the horses, she said. Little Patricia had
already fallen into our stinging-nettles twice, and her mother
didn't like it.

When we said, somewhat indignantly, that cats didn't frighten horses, she said ours did. She said he lurked in the grass
until the first one had gone by, then dashed out into the road
and pranced along behind him. It looked, she said, almost as if
he was imitating the horse – though that of course was ridicu-
lous. The first horse was all right because he couldn't see the
cat; the ones behind, she said – and we could quite see her
point – nearly had hysterics.

We saw to it that, after that, Solomon did his imitations from
the hall window when the riding-school went by. Unfortunately, while it was easy enough to tell when they were coming
– what with the trampling of hoofs and instructions to people
to watch their knees or keep their eyes on their elbows they
made, according to Father Adams, more noise than the ruddy
Campbells – solitary riders were different. Sometimes we were
in time to stop Trigger the Second following his latest idol
down the lane. More often the first we knew that a horse had
passed that way was when once again Solomon was missing.

It was very worrying. Sometimes it would be a couple of
hours or more before he came plodding back on his long thin
legs, looking rather sheepish and trying to slip through the
gate so that he could pretend he'd been there all the time. We
tried everything we could think of, short of a cage, to curb this
latest craze. We even bought some goldfish, seeing it was
things that moved he liked, and set up a special tank for him in
the sitting-room.

Sheba and Charles thought they were wonderful. They sat in
front of the tank for ages goggling like a couple of tennis fans as
the fish flipped and glided lazily through the water. Solomon,
however, when he found there was no way in at the top or
sides and that they didn't run away when he looked at them,
lost interest and slipped silently out. Charles was too intent on

the fish to see him go, or to notice the lone, red-coated rider clopping up the lane; and I was in the kitchen. The first I knew of his latest escapade was when the phone rang and a farmer from the other end of the valley said he didn't know whether I knew it but that black-faced cat of ours had just gone by following one of the huntsmen. He was going it well, he said, stepping it out like a proper little Arab. But the horse was a kicker with a red ribbon on its tail and he didn't . . .

I didn't wait to hear any more. I dropped the phone and ran. When I caught up with them Solomon was still, unknown to the rider, following doggedly along behind that pair of wicked-looking hoofs. The huntsman stared in admiration as I picked him up. Plucky little devil, he said, to have followed all that way. Ought to have been a horse himself.

He didn't know me, of course, or Solomon, from Adam. He looked a little alarmed when, holding old Bat Ears firmly by the scruff of his neck, I said it was a remark like that which started all this horse business in the first place.

Pangur Bán

IRISH MONK
8th century

I and Pangur Bán, my cat,
'Tis a like task we are at;
Hunting mice is his delight,
Hunting words I sit all night.

Better far than praise of men
'Tis to sit with book and pen;
Pangur bears me no ill-will,
He too plies his simple skill.

'Tis a merry thing to see
At our tasks how glad are we,
When at home we sit and find
Entertainment to our mind.

Oftentimes a mouse will stray
In the hero Pangur's way;
Oftentimes my keen thought set
Takes a meaning in its net.

'Gainst the wall he sets his eye
Full and fierce and sharp and sly;
'Gainst the wall of knowledge I
All my little wisdom try.

When a mouse darts from its den,
Oh, how glad is Pangur then!
Oh, what gladness do I prove
When I solve the doubts I love!

So in peace our task we ply,
Pangur Bán – my cat – and I;
In our arts we find our bliss,
I have mine and he has his.

Practice every day has made
Pangur perfect in his trade;
I get wisdom day and night
Turning darkness into light.

Calvin, the Cat

CHARLES DUDLEY WARNER

CALVIN is dead. His life, long to him, but short for the rest of us, was not marked by startling adventures, but his character was so uncommon and his qualities were so worthy of imitation that I have been asked by those who personally knew him to set down my recollections of his career.

His origin and ancestry were shrouded in mystery; even his age was a matter of pure conjecture. Although he was of the Maltese race, I have reason to suppose that he was American by birth as he certainly was in sympathy. Calvin was given to me eight years ago by Mrs Stowe, but she knew nothing of his age or origin. He walked into her house one day out of the great unknown and became at once at home, as if he had been always a friend of the family. He appeared to have artistic and literary tastes, and it was as if he had enquired at the door if that was the residence of the author of *Uncle Tom's Cabin* and, upon being assured that it was, had decided to dwell there. This is, of course, fanciful, for his antecedents were wholly unknown, but in his time he could hardly have been in any household where he would not have heard *Uncle Tom's Cabin* talked about.

When he came to Mrs Stowe, he was as large as he ever was, and apparently as old as he ever became. Yet there was in him no appearance of age; he was in the happy maturity of all his powers and you would rather have said, in that maturity, he had found the secret of perpetual youth. And it was as difficult to believe that he would ever be aged as it was to imagine that he had ever been in immature youth. There was in him a mysterious perpetuity.

After some years, when Mrs Stowe made her winter home in Florida, Calvin came to live with us. From the first moment, he fell into the ways of the house and assumed a recognized position in the family – I say recognized, because after he became known he was always enquired for by visitors, and in the letters from other members of the family he always received a message. Although the least obtrusive of beings, his individuality always made itself felt.

His personal appearance had much to do with this, for he was of royal mould and had an air of high breeding. He was large, but he had nothing of the fat grossness of the celebrated Angora family; though powerful, he was exquisitely proportioned and as graceful in every movement as a young leopard. When he stood up to open a door – he opened all the doors with old-fashioned latches – he was portentously tall, and when he stretched on the rug before the fire he seemed too long for this world – as indeed he was. His coat was the finest and softest I have ever seen, a shade of quiet Maltese; and from his throat downwards, underneath, to the white tips of his feet, he wore the whitest and most delicate ermine; and no person was ever more fastidiously neat. In his finely formed head you saw something of his aristocratic character; the ears were small and cleanly cut, there was a tinge of pink in the nostrils, his face was handsome and the expression of his countenance exceedingly intelligent – I should call it even a sweet expression if the term were not inconsistent with his look of alertness and sagacity.

It is difficult to convey a just idea of his gaiety in connection with his dignity and gravity, which his name expressed. As we know nothing of his family, of course it will be understood that Calvin was his Christian name. He had times of relaxation into utter playfulness, delighting in a ball of yarn, catching sportively at stray ribbons when his mistress was at her toilet, and pursuing his own tail, with hilarity, for lack of anything better. He could amuse himself by the hour, and he did not care for children; perhaps something in his past was present to his memory. He had absolutely no bad habits, and his disposition was perfect I never saw him exactly angry, though I have seen his tail grow to an enormous size when a strange cat appeared upon his lawn. He disliked cats, evidently regarding them as feline and treacherous, and he had no association with them. Occasionally there would be heard a night concert in the shrubbery. Calvin would ask to have the door opened, and then you would hear a rush and a 'pestzt', and the concert would explode, and Calvin would quietly come in and resume his seat on the hearth. There was no trace of anger in his manner, but he wouldn't have any of that about the house.

He had the rare virtue of magnanimity. Although he had fixed notions about his own rights, and extraordinary persistency in getting them, he never showed temper at a repulse; he simply and firmly persisted till he had what he wanted. His diet was one point; his idea was that of the scholars about dictionaries – to 'get the best'. He knew as well as anyone what was in the house, and would refuse beef if turkey was to be had; and if there were oysters, he would wait over the turkey to see if the oysters would not be forthcoming. And yet he was not a gross gourmand; he would eat bread if he saw me eating it, and thought he was not being imposed on. His habits of feeding, also, were refined; he never used a knife, and he would put up his hand and draw the fork down to his mouth as gracefully as a grown person. Unless necessity compelled, he would not eat in the kitchen, but insisted upon his meals in the dining-room, and would wait patiently, unless a stranger were present; and then he was sure to importune the visitor, hoping that the latter was ignorant of the rule of the house, and would give him something. They used to say that he preferred as his tablecloth on the floor a certain well-known Church journal; but this was said by an Episcopalian.

So far as I know, he had no religious prejudices, except that he did not like the association with Romanists. He tolerated the servants, because they belonged to the house, and would sometimes linger by the kitchen stove; but the moment visitors came in he arose, opened the door and marched into the drawing-room. Yet he enjoyed the company of his equals, and never withdrew, no matter how many callers – whom he recognized as of his society – might come into the drawing-room. Calvin was fond of company, but he wanted to choose it;

and I have no doubt that his was an aristocratic fastidiousness rather than one of faith. It is so with most people.

The intelligence of Calvin was something phenomenal, in his rank of life. He established a method of communicating his wants, and even some of his sentiments; and he could help himself in many things. There was a furnace register in a retired room, where he used to go when he wished to be alone, that he always opened when he desired more heat; but never shut it, any more than he shut the door after himself. He could do almost everything but speak; and you would declare sometimes that you could see a pathetic longing to do that in his intelligent face. I have no desire to overdraw his qualities but, if there was one thing in him more noticeable than another, it was his fondness for nature. He could content himself for hours at a low window, looking into the ravine and at the great trees, noting the smallest stir there; he delighted, above all things, to accompany me walking about the garden, hearing the birds, getting the smell of the fresh earth, and rejoicing in the sunshine. He followed me and gambolled like a dog, rolling over on the turf and exhibiting his delight in a hundred ways. If I worked, he sat and watched me, or looked off over the bank and kept his ear open to the twitter in the cherry trees. When it stormed, he was sure to sit at the windows, keenly watching the rain or the snow, glancing up and down at its falling; and a winter tempest always delighted him.

I think he was genuinely fond of birds but, so far as I know, he usually confined himself to one a day; he never killed, as some sportsmen do, for the sake of killing, but only as civilized people do – from necessity. He was intimate with the flying-squirrels who dwelt in the chestnut tree – too intimate, for almost every day in the summer he would bring in one, until he nearly discouraged them. He was, indeed, a superb hunter, and would have been a devastating one if his bump of destructiveness had not been offset by a bump of moderation. There was very little of the brutality of the lower animals about him; I don't think he enjoyed rats for themselves, but he knew his business and, for the first few months of his residence with us, waged an awful campaign against the horde and, after that, his simple presence was sufficient to deter them from coming on the premises. Mice amused him, but he usually considered them too small game to be taken seriously; I have seen him play for an hour with a mouse and then let him go with a royal condescension. In this whole matter of 'getting a living', Calvin was a great contrast to the rapacity of the age in which he lived.

I hesitate to speak of his capacity for friendship and the affectionateness of his nature, for I know from his own reserve that he would not care to have it much talked about. We understood each other perfectly, but we never made any fuss about it; when I spoke his name and snapped my fingers, he came to me; when I returned home at night, he was pretty sure to be waiting for me near the gate, and would rise and saunter along the walk, as if his being there were purely accidental – so shy was he commonly of showing feeling; and when I opened the door he never rushed in, like a cat, but loitered and lounged, as if he had had no intention of going in, but would condescend to. And yet, the fact was, he knew dinner was ready, and he was bound to be there. He kept the run of dinner-time. It happened sometimes, during our absence in the summer, that dinner would be early, and Calvin, walking about the grounds, missed it and came in late. But he never made a mistake the second day. There was one thing he never did – he never rushed through an open doorway. He never forgot his dignity. If he had asked to have the door opened, and was eager to go out, he always went deliberately; I can see him now, standing on the sill, looking about at the sky as if he was thinking whether it were worth while to take an umbrella, until he was near having his tail shut in.

His friendship was rather constant than demonstrative. When we returned from an absence of nearly two years Calvin welcomed us with evident pleasure, but showed his satisfaction rather by tranquil happiness than by fuming about. He had the faculty of making us glad to get home. It was his constancy that was so attractive. He liked companionship, but he wouldn't be petted, or fussed over, or sit in anyone's lap a moment; he always extricated himself from such familiarity with dignity and with no show of temper. If there was any petting to be done, however, he chose to do it. Often he would sit looking at me and then, moved by a delicate affection, come and pull at my coat and sleeve until he could touch my face with his nose, and then go away contented. He had a habit of coming to my study in the morning sitting quietly by my side or on the table for hours, watching the pen run over the paper, occasionally swinging his tail round for a blotter and then going to sleep among the papers by the inkstand. Or, more rarely, he would watch the writing from a perch on my shoulder. Writing always interested him and, until he understood it, he wanted to hold the pen.

He always held himself in a kind of reserve with his friend, as if he had said, 'Let us respect our personality and not make a "mess" of friendship.' He saw, with Emerson, the risk of degrading it to trivial conveniency. 'Why insist on rash personal relations with your friends. Leave this touching and clawing.' Yet I would not give an unfair notion of his aloofness, his fine sense of the sacredness of the me and the not-me. And, at the risk of not being believed, I will relate an incident which was often repeated. Calvin had the practice of passing a portion of the night in the contemplation of its beauties and would come into our chamber over the roof of the conservatory through the open window, summer and winter, and go to sleep at the foot of my bed. He would do this always exactly in this way; he never was content to stay in the chamber if we compelled him to go upstairs and through the door. He had the obstinacy of General Grant. But this is by the way. In the morning, he performed his toilet and went down to breakfast with the rest of the family. Now, when the mistress was absent from home, and at no other time, Calvin would come in the morning, when the bell rang, to the head of the bed, put up his feet and look into my face, follow me about when I rose, 'assist' at the dressing, and in many purring ways show his fondness, as if he had plainly said, 'I know that she has gone away, but I am here.' Such was Calvin in rare moments.

He had his limitations. Whatever passion he had for nature, he had no conception of art. There was sent to him once a fine and very expressive cat's head in bronze, by Frémiet. I placed it on the floor. He regarded it intently, approached it cautiously and crouchingly, touched it with his nose, perceived the fraud, turned away abruptly and never would notice it afterwards.

On the whole, his life was not only a successful one, but a

happy one. He never had but one fear, so far as I know; he had a mortal and a reasonable terror of plumbers. He would never stay in the house when they were here. No coaxing could quiet him. Of course, he didn't share our fear about their charges, but he must have had some dreadful experience with them in that portion of his life which is unknown to us. A plumber was to him the devil, and I have no doubt that, in his scheme, plumbers were foreordained to do him mischief.

In speaking of his worth, it has never occurred to me to estimate Calvin by the worldly standard. I know that it is customary now, when anyone dies, to ask how much he was worth, and that no obituary in the newspapers is considered complete without such an estimate. The plumbers in our house were one day overheard to say that, 'They say that *she* says that *he* says that he wouldn't take $100 for him.' It is unnecessary to say that I never made such a remark, and that, so far as Calvin was concerned, there was no purchase in money.

As I look back upon it, Calvin's life seems to me a fortunate one, for it was natural and unforced. He ate when he was hungry, slept when he was sleepy, and enjoyed existence to the very tips of his toes and the end of his expressive and slow-moving tail. He delighted to roam about the garden, and stroll among the trees, and to lie on the green grass and luxuriate in all the sweet influences of summer. You could never accuse him of idleness, and yet he knew the secret of repose. The poet who wrote so prettily of him that his little life was rounded with a sleep, understated his felicity; it was rounded with a good many. His conscience never seemed to interfere with his slumbers. In fact, he had good habits and a contented mind. I can see him now walk in at the study door, sit down by my chair, bring his tail artistically about his feet, and look up at me with unspeakable happiness in his handsome face.

I often thought that he felt the dumb limitation which denied him the power of language. But since he was denied speech, he scorned the inarticulate mouthings of the lower animals. The vulgar mewing and yowling of the cat species was beneath him; he sometimes uttered a sort of articulate and well-bred ejaculation, when he wished to call attention to something that he considered remarkable, or to some want of his, but he never went whining about. He would sit for hours at a closed window, when he desired to enter, without a murmur, and when it was opened he never admitted that he had been impatient by 'bolting' in. Though speech he had not, and the unpleasant kind of utterance given to his race he would not use, he had a mighty power of purr to express his measureless content with congenial society. There was in him a musical organ with stops of varied power and expression, upon which I have no doubt he could have performed Scarlatti's celebrated cat's fugue.

Whether Calvin died of old age, or was carried off by one of the diseases incident to youth, it is impossible to say; for his departure was as quiet as his advent was mysterious. I only know that he appeared to us in the world in his perfect stature and beauty, and that after a time, like Lohengrin, he withdrew. In his illness there was nothing more to be regretted than in all his blameless life. I suppose there never was an illness that had more dignity and sweetness and resignation in it. It came on gradually, in a kind of listlessness and want of appetite. An alarming symptom was his preference for the warmth of a furnace register to the lively sparkle of the open wood fire. Whatever pain he suffered, he bore it in silence, and seemed only anxious not to obtrude his malady. We tempted him with the delicacies of the season, but it soon became impossible for him to eat, and for two weeks he ate or drank scarcely anything. Sometimes he made an effort to take something, but it was evident that he made the effort to please us. The neighbours – and I am convinced that the advice of neighbours is never good for anything – suggested catnip. He wouldn't even smell it. We had the attendance of an amateur practitioner of medicine, whose real office was the cure of souls, but nothing touched his case. He took what was offered, but it was with the air of one to whom the time for pellets was passed. He sat or lay day after day almost motionless, never once making a display of those vulgar convulsions or contortions of pain which are so disagreeable to society. His favourite place was on the brightest spot of a Smyrna rug by the conservatory, where the sunlight fell and he could hear the fountain play. If we went to him and exhibited our interest in his condition, he always purred in recognition of our sympathy. And when

I spoke his name, he looked up with an expression that said, 'I understand it, old fellow, but it's no use.' He was to all who came to visit him a model of calmness and patience in affliction.

I was absent from home at the last, but heard by daily postal card of his failing condition; and never again saw him alive. One sunny morning he rose from his rug, went into the conservatory (he was very thin then), walked around it deliberately, looking at all the plants he knew, and then went to the bay-window in the dining-room and stood a long time looking out upon the little field, now brown and sere, and towards the garden where perhaps the happiest hours of his life had been spent. It was a last look. He turned and walked away, laid himself down upon the bright spot in the rug, and quietly died.

It is not too much to say that a little shock went through the neighbourhood when it was known that Calvin was dead, so marked was his individuality; and his friends, one after another, came in to see him. There was no sentimental non-sense about his obsequies; it was felt that any parade would have been distasteful to him. John, who acted as undertaker, prepared a candle-box for him, and I believe assumed a professional decorum; but there may have been the usual levity underneath, for I heard that he remarked in the kitchen that it was the 'driest wake he ever attended'. Everybody, however, felt a fondness for Calvin and regarded him with a certain respect. Between him and Bertha there existed a great friend-ship, and she apprehended his nature; she used to say that sometimes she was afraid of him, he looked at her so intelli-gently; she was never certain that he was what he appeared to be.

When I returned, they had laid Calvin on a table in an upper chamber by an open window. It was February. He reposed in a candle-box, lined about the edge with evergreen, and at his head stood a little wine glass with flowers. He lay with his head tucked down in his arms – a favourite position of his before the fire – as if asleep in the comfort of his soft and exquisite fur. It was the involuntary exclamation of those who saw him, 'How natural he looks!' As for myself, I said nothing. John buried him under the twin hawthorn trees – one white and the other pink – in a spot where Calvin was fond of lying and listening to the hum of summer insects and the twitter of birds.

Perhaps I have failed to make appear the individuality of character that was so evident to those who knew him. At any rate, I have set down nothing concerning him but the literal truth. He was always a mystery. I did not know whence he came; I do not know whither he has gone. I would not weave one spray of falsehood in the wreath I lay upon his grave.

Puss in Boots

CHARLES PERRAULT

THERE WAS a miller, who had left no more estate to the three sons he had, than his mill, his ass and his cat. The partition was soon made. Neither the scrivener nor attorney were sent for. They would soon have eaten up all the patrimony. The eldest had the mill, the second the ass, and the youngest nothing but the cat.

The poor young fellow was quite comfortless at having so poor a lot. 'My brothers (said he) may get their living handsomely enough, by joining their stocks together; but for my part, when I have eaten up my cat, and made me a muff of his skin, I must die with hunger.' The cat, who heard all this, but made as if he did not, said to him with a grave and serious air, 'Do not thus afflict yourself, my good master; you have nothing else to do but to give me a bag, and get a pair of boots made for me, that I may scamper through the dirt and brambles, and you shall see that you have not so bad a portion of me as you imagine.'

Though the cat's master did not build very much upon what he said, he had, however, often seen him play a great many cunning tricks to catch rats and mice; as when he used to hang by the heels, or hide himself in the meal, and make as if he were dead; so that he did not altogether despair of his affording him some help in his miserable condition. When the cat had what he asked for, he booted himself very gallantly; and, putting his bag about his neck, he held the strings of it in his forepaws, and went into a warren where was great abundance of rabbits. He put bran and sow thistle into his bag and, stretching himself out at length, as if he had been dead, he waited for some young rabbits, not yet acquainted with the deceits of the world, to come and rummage his bag for what he had put into it.

Scarce was he laid down, but he had what he wanted; a rash and foolish young rabbit jumped into his bag and Monsieur Puss, immediately drawing close the strings, took and killed him without pity. Proud of his prey, he went with it to the palace, and asked to speak with his Majesty. He was shown upstairs into the King's apartments and, making a low reverence, said to him, 'I have brought you, Sir, a rabbit of the warren, which my noble Lord, the Marquis of Carabas (for that was the title which Puss was pleased to give his master) has commanded me to present to your Majesty from him.'

'Tell thy master (said the King) that I thank him, and that he does me a great deal of pleasure.'

Another time he went and hid himself among some standing corn, holding still his bag open; and when a brace of partridges ran into it, he drew the strings, and so caught them both. He went and made a present of them to the King, as he had done before of the rabbits which he took in the warren. The King, in like manner, received the partridges with great pleasure, and ordered him some money to drink.

The cat continued for two or three months thus to carry his Majesty, from time to time, game of his master's taking. One day in particular, when he knew for certain that he was to take the air, along the riverside, with his daughter, the most beautiful princess in the world, he said to his master, 'If you will follow my advice, your fortune is made; you have nothing else to do, but go and wash yourself in the river, in that part I shall show you, and leave the rest to me.' The Marquis of Carabas did what the cat advised him to, without knowing why or wherefore.

While he was washing, the King passed by, and the cat began to cry out as loud as he could, 'Help, help, my Lord Marquis of Carabas is going to be drowned.' At this noise the King put his head out of the coach window and, finding it was the cat who had often brought him such good game, he commanded his guards to run immediately to the assistance of his Lordship the Marquis of Carabas.

While they were drawing the poor Marquis out of the river, the cat came up to the coach, and told the King that, 'While his master was washing there came by some rogues who went off with his clothes, though he had cried out, "Thieves! Thieves!" several times, as loud as he could.' This cunning cat had hidden them under a great stone. The King immediately commanded the officers of his wardrobe to run and fetch one of his best suits for the Lord Marquis of Carabas.

The King caressed him after a very extraordinary manner; and, as the fine clothes he had given him extremely set off his good mien (for he was well made and very handsome in his person), the King's daughter took a secret inclination to him, and the Marquis of Carabas had no sooner cast two or three respectful and somewhat tender glances, but she fell in love with him to distraction. The King would needs have him come into the coach, and partake of the airing. The cat, quite overjoyed to see his project begin to succeed, marched on before and, meeting some countrymen who were mowing a meadow, he said to them, 'Good people, you who are mowing, if you do not tell the King that the meadow you mow belongs to my Lord Marquis of Carabas, you shall be chopped as small as herbs for the pot.'

The King did not fail of asking of the mowers, to whom the meadow they were mowing belonged. 'To my Lord Marquis of Carabas,' answered they all together; for the cat's threats had made them terribly afraid. 'You see, Sir (said the Marquis), this is a meadow which never fails to yield a plentiful harvest every year.' The master cat, who went still on before, met some reapers, and said to them, 'Good people, you who are reaping, if you do not tell the King that all this corn belongs to the Marquis of Carabas, you shall be chopped as small as herbs for the pot.'

The King, who passed by a moment after, would needs know to whom all that corn, which he then saw, did belong. 'To my Lord Marquis of Carabas,' replied the reapers; and the King was very well pleased with it, as well as the Marquis, whom he congratulated thereupon. The master cat, who went always before, said the same words to all he met; and the King was astonished at the vast estates of my Lord Marquis of Carabas.

Monsieur Puss came at last to a stately castle, the master of which was an ogre, the richest that had ever been known; for all the lands which the King had then gone over belonged, with this castle, to him. The cat, who had taken care to inform himself who this ogre was, and what he could do, asked to speak to him, saying, 'he could not pass so near the castle without having the honour of paying his respects to him.'

The ogre received him as civilly as an ogre could do, and made him sit down. 'I have been assured (said the cat) that you have the gift of being able to change yourself into all sorts of creatures you have a mind to; you can, for example, transform yourself into a lion, or elephant, and the like.' 'This is true (answered the ogre very briskly), and to convince you, you shall see me now become a lion.' Puss was so sadly terrified at the sight of a lion so near him, that he immediately got into the gutter, not without abundance of trouble and danger because of his boots, which were of no use at all to him in walking upon the tiles. A little while after, when Puss saw that the ogre had resumed his natural form, he came down and owned he had been very much frightened.

'I have been moreover informed (said the cat), but I know not how to believe it, that you have also the power to take upon you the shape of the smallest animals; for example, to change yourself into a rat or a mouse; but I must own to you, I take this to be impossible.'

'Impossible! (cried the Ogre). You shall see that presently,' and at the same time changed himself into a mouse and began to run about the floor. Puss no sooner perceived this, but he fell upon him and ate him up.

Meanwhile the King who saw, as he passed, this fine castle of the ogre, had a mind to go into it. Puss, who heard the noise of his Majesty's coach running over the drawbridge, ran out and said to the King, 'Your Majesty is welcome to the castle of my Lord Marquis of Carabas.'

'What! My Lord Marquis (cried the King), and does this castle also belong to you? There can be nothing finer than this court, and all the stately buildings which surround it; let us go into it, if you please.' The Marquis gave his hand to the

Princess, and followed the King, who went up first. They passed into a spacious hall where they found a magnificent collation, which the ogre had prepared for his friends, who were that very day to visit him, but dared not enter, knowing the King was there.

His Majesty was perfectly charmed with the good qualities of my Lord Marquis of Carabas, as was his daughter who was fallen violently in love with him; and, seeing the vast estate he possessed, said to him, after having drunk five or six glasses, 'It will be owing to yourself only, my Lord Marquis, if you are not my son-in-law.' The Marquis, making several low bows, accepted the honour which his Majesty conferred upon him, and forthwith, that very same day, married the Princess.

Puss became a great lord and never ran after mice any more, only for his diversion.

The Totem of Amarillo

EMMA-LINDSAY
SQUIER

PERHAPS you have heard me speak of Amarillo before. He was a yellow cat who came to us from out of the woods when Brother and I still lived in the little log cabin on the shores of Puget Sound. And he was, in those days, our very special friend. His coming to our home was most spectacular, and his departure was equally dramatic. As for the grand finale of his story, as I learned it from those who cared for him in his last years, it is so curious and hints so much of melodrama that I am afraid that some will doubt it. I offer in explanation of my belief that it is true, only the fact that Amarillo was always a most unusual cat. And the proof of it is that he is perpetuated for ever in the village of Old Man House in a totem pole, carved and painted. Only the truly great are thus honoured by the tribe of Skokomish.

Amarillo, the yellow one, was born, I think, in the woods. And I further believe that complete savagery was only a short generation behind him. For his ears were tufted as are the ears of a bobcat, and his eyes were slanted and amber so that, in moments of complete repose, he resembled a Chinese mandarin pleasantly absorbed in thought.

He had grown up in a region where the law was that only the strongest survived. He had fought many battles and won them, and so had grown to a size unbelievable in an ordinary cat, another fact which hinted strongly at a parentage having nothing to do with domesticity and quiet firesides.

Still, he had within him the instinct of association with man. For when he first came to us, his lovely fur all draggled and covered with blood, he was sorely hurt and dragged a torn and wounded leg. He mewed pitifully and crawled to us, yet was afraid to let us touch him, and sprang back spitting venomously. But the instinct that had brought him down from the woods to the little cabin, where he knew he would find succour for his hurt, finally made him accept us. He let us examine the wounded leg, suffered us to bathe it and anoint it with salve. Then, being completely unable to hunt or care for himself, he allowed us to extend to him the hospitality of our home. He came to love us, and adopted us, and when he was well he stayed with us and became our friend.

Now Brother and I were so fond of Amarillo, the yellow cat, that we saw none of his faults; and when they were called to our attention by the grown-ups, we made excuses for them and pretended that they did not matter. For he was our constant companion during the day and, when I slept out of doors on the camp bed, I would, sometimes during the night, hear his soft 'Prr-t,' which signified that he was about to jump up beside me, and then feel the thud of his soft, heavy body, as he leaped. But the grown-ups did not share our unqualified approval of Amarillo and his ways. For he, never having had any knowledge of civilization, did not know, and could not be taught, that chickens were to be respected, and not stalked and devoured whenever he happened to be hungry. Neither was it permissible that he should molest the pigeons, climb up to the nests and kill their young. So, after all persuasion had failed and many attempts at discipline, it was decreed that Amarillo must go. And Brother and I were very sad because of it.

It was not hard to find a new home for him. He was admired by all who saw him and many places were open to our choosing. But it was deemed best that he be given into the kindly care of a fisherman friend of ours. A huge, dark man with kindly smiling eyes, a man whose descent was traced from Indian and Spanish blood, and whose wife and kinsfolk were of the tribe of Skokomish. They lived in the far-off village of Old Man House, called by the Indians, Suquamish.

They would, we knew, be kind to Amarillo. They had no chickens or pigeons for him to kill unlawfully, and there were rats and much small game in the woods to satisfy his hunting instincts.

So, on the day set for his departure, we took our friend, the Yellow One, down to the fishing launch which anchored at our float, and it was with heavy hearts that we set a dish of milk for him upon the deck. We hoped that eating would occupy his attention and that he would not realize until too late that he was going away from us. The Indian fisherman shoved off very gently from the wharf and did not start the engine until the launch had drifted for a hundred feet or more. But when the whirring of the fly wheel startled Amarillo, and the churning of the propeller whirled the water into eddies of white and green – then he knew that he was being taken away without his will or knowledge.

He sprang to the gunwale and stood, for an instant, gazing out at us, his slanted, amber eyes wide with alarm. The Indian fisherman spoke to him soothingly and moved towards him with friendly hand outstretched. But it was too late. For Amarillo, without an instant's hesitation, had leaped. We saw the flash of his yellow body as he sprang and the splash as he sank from sight. We cried out, because we thought he would drown. But he had no idea of coming to such an inglorious end. For the next instant he was swimming towards us, easily, powerfully, his tufted ears flattened back on his head, his body a lithe, yellow streak in the blueness of the water. When he reached the float, he climbed upon it, sat down with perfect composure, and commenced to wash himself with great earnestness and poise. He appeared to think nothing whatsoever of the swim he had taken. And that day, because of our entreaties, he was allowed to remain with us.

But it was, we knew, only a stay of sentence. On the next day we bade our friend goodbye once more. This time the Yellow One was fastened in a sack and, when the launch started its chugging way out into the blueness of the bay, we saw the frenzied contortions of the burlap bag and dimly heard protesting yowls above the throbbing of the engine. We watched sadly from the float until the fishing launch was but a speck of black athwart the jutting greenery of the Point. Then it was lost to sight and we knew that Amarillo had gone from us for ever.

In the years that followed, we heard of our yellow friend

from time to time. Once the Indian fisherman chugged around the Point and into our tiny cove specially to give us news of him. And once the old fisherman, who made his home with us, put into the village of Suquamish to learn at first hand of Amarillo's welfare. We were assured, each time, that the Yellow One was well and happy, and that he had established a kingship among the lesser cats of the village so that there was none to dispute his authority. But the details of his tempestuous life I did not fully learn until, grown out of childhood and many years away from the country of grey waters and singing pine trees, I came back to the woods and waters of Puget Sound; found at Suquamish our beloved old fisherman, with no trace of time upon the pinkness of his cheeks or within the clear twinkling of his eyes; found, too, the Indian fisherman and his wife who had given Amarillo shelter; and learned from him, and from the blind boy who was their son, the story of the Yellow One's tragic, triumphant career.

Now, the blind boy was a carver of totems. And in the great darkness, where there was no light, he found solace in bringing to remembrance the strange, almost forgotten tales of the Indians of the Sound. He made them live again, cunningly carved into symbols upon pine poles, and he painted them carefully, under the watchful eye of those who could see. There is today, in the open square of the village, a totem pole that the blind boy made. Upon it is depicted the story of how Teet' Motl, with his sweetheart, Hoo Han Hoo, rode upon a dolphin's back towards a far country where the Great Spirit promised them rest and prosperity. Their progress was barred by a school of blackfish, those tigers of the water called by the Indians 'killers'. But the brave dolphin, with a word of encouragement to those upon his back, dived into the depths of the sea, scraping up pebbles in his mouth. Then there came a great storm, and Teet' Motl and Hoo Han Hoo crept into the dolphin's mouth for safety. Inside they found the shining pebbles scraped up by the giant fish. And when at last the storm abated, the dolphin had indeed brought them safely to a pleasant country, green with trees and fruitful with berries. The Indians who inhabited the country used for currency shining pebbles. And Teet' Motl and Hoo Han Hoo, having many of them, were rich and for ever prosperous. Even to this day, said the blind boy, when the killers come from the south, then a storm will rise. So he portrayed upon the totem Teet' Motl and his sweetheart safe in the belly of the dolphin.

It was while the blind boy still carved the story upon the totem pole that Amarillo was brought into the household. And curiously enough, it was to the child who lived in darkness that the Yellow One gave his love and never-ending loyalty. He liked very well indeed the Indian fisherman and his wife, who was of the tribe of Skokomish. He obligingly caught the rats that had formerly made merry under the cabin, and once in the dead of night he gave alarm of fire that had started from a chance spark, by mewing and rubbing his cold nose against the Indian fisherman's face. He repaid the hospitality they offered him with a friendship that was staunch and true. But it was only the blind boy that he loved – and I believe, and would have you believe, that it was because he knew of the darkness in which the blind boy lived, and because he knew that in some ways his friend was helpless.

But because he loved the little blind boy so well, Amarillo was jealous of everything to which he gave his attention. During the long evenings, when the blind boy carved the totem pole, the Yellow One would sit on the table beside him, watching with slanted amber eyes, while the childish, sensitive fingers crept over the long pine pole, feeling out with a sharp knife the contours of the dolphin, the killer blackfish, and the rude figures of Teet' Motl and his sweetheart. When Amarillo thought his friend given too much attention to the work of carving, he would reach out a padded, yellow paw and pat the blind boy's hand. If there was no response, he would yawn prodigiously, get up and stretch, and rub his broad back against the blind boy's face, deliberately walking on the pole, so that he could not carve. Then, if his friend persisted in his work, Amarillo would mew sharply, a little angry sound that ended in a snarl. He would switch his tail violently, jump down from the table with a loud thump, and sulk under the stove, refusing to come out for commands or cajoling words.

Now, Amarillo was not the only four-footed guest in the household of the Indian fisherman and his wife. The hospitality of their little cabin was offered freely to any living thing that needed shelter or aid, and there was rarely a time when they were not caring for some boarder from the wood who had come to grief. Once they found a pheasant's nest with the mother's dead body beside it, bullet-riddled, and the tiny, brown chicks scarcely out of their shells. They took the tiny things to their cabin and fed them so carefully that all of them lived, and would have grown eventually to adult pheasant-hood – had it not been for Amarillo.

At first, it was not difficult to keep the wee brown pheasant chicks secluded. They learned very soon to run briskly to the door of their wire coop when they heard a footstep approaching, and they were as friendly as if their parents had never lived in the wilds. Amarillo watched them with sullen, amber eyes, his tail twitching ever so little, his shoulder muscles moving slightly whenever he saw the baby pheasants running about in the safety of the wire enclosure. But he never attempted to molest them. And even when they grew so large that the coop was deemed too small to hold them comfortably, and so were permitted to roam at liberty, he did not try to pounce upon them – having perhaps in mind the punishment meted out to him at our cabin the day when he tried to kill the chickens.

But upon the day when the little blind boy made his way out to the wire enclosure and called to the pheasants, who came running to peck at the crumbs he held in his hand – upon that day did Amarillo declare war upon the brown invaders. Never did the Indian fisherman or his wife actually catch him doing violence to the pheasant boarders, but one by one they disappeared with only a bunch of feathers left to tell of their passing. And once the Yellow One came into the cabin with one tiny feather still hanging from his whiskers – he had forgotten to remove the evidence. It was the last feather of the last pheasant. So they spanked him soundly, and he snarled and spat, and ran away into the woods, and did not come back for two days, during which time the blind boy missed him sorely. When he returned, it was with sullen, padding steps, and his amber eyes were rather furtive as if he doubted whether he would be welcomed. But the family forgave him the pheasants, and made much of him, and the blind boy cried, holding the yellow cat close against his cheek. So Amarillo purred deeply, like an organ, and dug his toes comfortably into his friend's shoulders, and that night slept upon the blind boy's bed, unrebuked. For a week he would not let the child go out of his sight, but followed him like a dog, and every evening sat near him when he carved upon the totem pole.

It was soon after the incident of the pheasants that another woods friend was brought into the kindly care of the Indian fisherman and his wife. One day the Indian fisherman saw in the woods, near the village of Suquamish, a little lady racoon who had been caught in a trap such as they set for racoons in the Puget Sound country. A hole had been bored in a small log, and honeycomb had been put deep inside it. Then nails had been set in such a way that a racoon hand, reaching inside for the honeycomb, could not pull itself out without tearing the skin completely away. So the Indian fisherman found the racoon lady with one arm inside the hole, her bright eyes blinking worriedly through the black marking that ran completely across her face like a highwayman's mask. She was really very foolish to have kept her clutch on the honeycomb, for by releasing it and squeezing her little black hand together, she could have brought it through the nail barricade without mishap. But she wanted the honeycomb and so she kept her hold of it, thus keeping herself prisoner – as, indeed, those who set the trap knew she would do.

But the Indian fisherman could not bear to see the little lady racoon thus a captive. For she was soon to have babies. He drew out the nails, very carefully, while she stood rigidly alert to all he was doing, but stubbornly refusing to let go her hold on the sweetness that was in the hole. He slipped his hat over her; then, in her sudden alarm, she withdrew her hand, all sticky with honeycomb, and the Indian fisherman brought her to the cabin, wriggling and squeaking in protest.

He saw to it that she had a comfortable pen to live in, and all the family made much of her. By the time her tiny children were born, she was quite at home in her new environment, and accepted philosophically all the kindly attentions bestowed upon her.

They named her Betty, and her children were born in a box behind the kitchen stove. Soon afterwards she was put into a comfortable cage in the woodshed. But one day she escaped from the pen and came into the house, with her three babies following her in single file, their tails curled up high over their backs as if they had been taught just the correct way of holding them thus, and on every tiny face was a black mask through which bright eyes blinked in friendly curiosity at the new world in which they found themselves.

Now, Amarillo saw this strange procession with astonishment not unmixed with alarm. He had been away hunting in the woods when Betty was brought to the cabin and the Indian fisherman had taken care that he had had no access to her cage or to her box behind the kitchen stove. Certainly he had never seen a racoon baby, with a black mask on its face and its tail curling up neatly over its head. He leaped upon a chair and spat vigorously as the little procession trundled across the kitchen floor to a saucer of milk behind the stove. Betty took no notice of him and pursued her even course, her three babies following in a line, one directly behind the other.

Amarillo leaned over the edge of the chair and growled terrifically. Betty looked up at him from behind her highwayman's mask, and her eyes glittered at him. She showed a line of white, menacing teeth. The Yellow One continued to snarl deep in his throat, but made no move, except to settle down on his haunches and watch and speculate. If Betty and her babies had been out in the open, he would have set upon them without delay. But their presence in the kitchen disturbed him, made him vaguely uncertain as to their standing. For he had been punished many times for interfering with domestic friends. He licked his chops and continued to growl.

Then, suddenly, his temper getting the better of him – he sprang. The Indian Fisherman moved to protect the racoon lady, whose life he thought in peril. But Betty was quite capable of defending herself and her family. Although she had apparently given no heed to the yellow cat, yet she was ready for his pounce. She gave a shrill squeal and darted to one side so quickly that even Amarillo's swiftness was not equalled by it. Before the yellow cat could realize what had happened, she was upon him, her black little hands clutching at his neck, her sharp teeth digging through his thick fur and into the flesh beneath. Amarillo snarled and yowled with pain. He rolled over and over, seeking vainly to fasten his claws on the alert, darting body of the lady racoon. The racoon babies scuttled under the stove where they sat and peeped with bright, inquisitive eyes at the rolling, scrambling whirlwind of fur— yellow fur and brown. It was Amarillo who finally cried 'enough' in the unequal battle. His authority had been undisputed for such a long time that it made his surrender the more complete. He bolted for the open door, yowling in wholehearted terror, with Betty astride him like a jockey, her hands deep in his fur, her eyes viciously sardonic through the black highwayman's mask.

Amarillo finally rid himself of his unwelcome rider by rolling with despairing energy. Having freed himself, he climbed a tree, spitting at every step, and found shelter on a limb, very high above the ground, where he snarled and spat, and licked his wounds, and had many harsh and bitter thoughts towards racoons and the world in general.

Betty, on the other hand, took her victory with modest simplicity. She curled her tail high over her head and marched sedately back to the kitchen and her babies. And after taking a refreshing drink of milk from the saucer, she proceeded to give her children their lunch, while she tidied her disordered coat, pulling from it the bits of twigs and tufts of yellow fur that had clung to it in the battle.

Amarillo went away into the woods, as was his custom when insulted, and he stayed so long that the family feared that his nose had been put permanently out of joint. But he came back at last, very sulky and bad-tempered until he found that he was really welcomed, especially by the blind boy who had missed him greatly. So he purred and rolled on the floor like a kitten, and slept at night on the little boy's bed. The racoon family— who now lived under the house – he did not molest. Betty and her children came at will into the kitchen and the room adjoining, they even received food from the hand of the blind boy— and Amarillo did not seek to prevent them. Sometimes he would growl and spit softly, but when Betty glanced at him sharply from behind her menacing mask, he would blink and look away, and pretend that he had not said a word.

The racoons were very cleanly folk. There was a big pan of water for them always upon the black porch, and into it they would dip every morsel of food before they ate it. They would bathe regularly, too, sitting up around the pan like little, furry toys, dipping their black hands in the water and washing their faces and necks very daintily and properly. They knew where the Indian fisherman beached the flat-bottomed boat in which he carried fish to sell. It was his custom to leave a few small fish in it after the day's work, just for the pleasure of seeing Betty lead her children down through the woods to the gravelled shore, the four of them in single file with their tails curled over their heads, and all of them humming a curious little monotone of a song, such as racoons sing when they are journeying and are contented with life.

When the fall came the racoon babies, quite well grown by that time, went away, into the woods, and later Betty, too, slipped away, to be gone for the whole winter. They expected that she would return in the spring. But she did not, and they never knew what became of the intrepid little lady.

Her absence, as you can readily imagine, was no grief at all to Amarillo. His kingship was once more undisputed, and he was happy in the friendship of the Indian fisherman and his wife, and in the affection that the blind boy gave him. The two were more inseparable than ever. It was rarely now that the Yellow One went away to hunt in the woods. He preferred, instead, to remain with the little boy he loved, to follow when the child walked about in the yard with the halting, uncertain steps of those who cannot see, and to sleep on his bed at night.

In due course of time he found a lady cat to his liking, and he brought her to live at the cabin of the Indian fisherman. Only one kitten did the lady cat give birth to, a kitten who was almost as golden in colour as Amarillo himself. And Amarillo as a father, I am glad to say, emulated his savage ancestors rather than his immediate domestic forebears. He cared for the kitten much more tenderly than the mother cat did, for she proved after all to be a careless jade, totally unworthy of Amarillo's affections. Soon after her daughter was weaned she went away into the woods and the kitten, to whom the Indian fisherman gave the outrageous name of 'Whiskey Susan', grew up entirely under her father's supervision.

Whiskey Susan was the only one beside himself whom Amarillo would suffer the family to pet. He was not jealous of the affection they gave her, and even the blind boy could hold the snuggling, yellow kitten in his lap while he carved upon the totem pole, and Amarillo would sit on the table beside him, purring deep in his throat, his eyes closed to mere slits of contentment.

But one day, many months later, there came another, and this time a final, disturbing factor in the life of the Yellow One. The Indian fisherman had found a small mallard duck caught in the meshes of his nets, and one leg had been broken so that he floundered there, helpless, beating the water with his wings. The Indian fisherman released him gently and brought him to the cabin where his wife took kindly charge of the invalid, set the hurt leg in splints, and tended to his wants. It was upon the first evening of his stay that Amarillo, coming in from out-of-doors, spied the newcomer. The blind boy, who could not see the Yellow One's approach, was bending over the wounded duck, stroking him gently. And at the sight Amarillo hissed sharply – and sprang. His leap did no more than knock the astonished duck over on the floor, but the Fisherman's wife was impatient that her invalid should be so treated. She cuffed Amarillo sharply and he stared at her with furious, amber eyes, then laid his ears back on his head and trotted out of the house, his fur in thick, outraged ruffles, and headed straight for the woods.

He did not come back for one week, nor for the two weeks. And the blind boy grew daily more worried and more lonely. He took to wandering about the yard, calling for Amarillo, and when his mother was busy, so that he could not prevent him, he would feel his way through the gate and set off up the trail that led into the deep woods, walking very slowly with his hands outstretched before him, calling Amarillo's name, hoping that the yellow cat would hear and come to him.

Now, it was not safe to go alone or unarmed into the thickness of those forests, for many dangers lurked in the shadowed depths of them and many were the tales told of bold attacks made by cougars and bobcats driven down from the high mountains by hunger or forest fires. Yet always the blind boy came back safely, for he ventured only a little way and returned before his absence could be noticed.

But one day he slipped away, having acquired some confidence in his knowledge of the trail. He went farther and farther, calling to Amarillo with louder tones as he felt himself out of hearing distance from the cabin. The trail became rougher and was unfamiliar to his feet. But still he went on and, at last, he realized that there was a chill in the air that spoke of coming night. The woods were very still, with only the light dropping of pine needles to dot the silence, or the distant call of a heron flying to a tall pine-tree nest. A little frightened, the blind boy turned towards home. But his feet had lost their confidence. He turned into a ragged, wandering trail that led away from the true path. And as the night grew colder, and his feet stumbled over sprawling roots, and low-hanging branches struck his face, he knew that he was lost, lost and helpless.

Then he ceased to call for Amarillo, but sent up his voice in a thin, wavering cry such as the Indians use. It is a sound which carries clearly across great spaces, and the Indians know it for a signal of distress.

Down in the cabin it was nearly sunset before the absence ofthe blind boy had been discovered, for both the Indian fisherman and his wife were at work mending nets upon the beach. When evening came, and they returned home, they looked at each other with startled eyes, and a great fear was in their hearts. For they knew the menace of the dark woods behind them.

The Indian fisherman called the others of the tribe of Skokomish and, with that cunning that Indians possess, they found the child's light, halting footprints in the softness of the earth, and followed them into the forest, until it was too dark for them to see further.

They listened, and presently, from far away, a thin, wavering cry came to their ears. They responded mightily and plunged along the trail, the glimmering of their lanterns throwing dark, grotesque shadows on the path before them.

But suddenly they heard another cry, and they stood breathless for a moment, tingling cold with horror. For it was the savage, hunting cry of the bobcat – the cry he gives as he springs upon his prey.

Firing their guns and shouting fiercely, they set off at a run towards the direction from which the two cries – the call for help and the call of death – had come. It was easy to guide themselves so, for the woods were alive with the savage sounds of fighting – eerie screams that set the birds to twittering nervously and made the men grit their teeth with fear at what they should find.

When they turned down the ragged, wandering trail, they heard above the snarls and shrieks a child's voice sobbing in fear. And the gleam of the lanterns caught a wild tangle of blazing eyes, white, snapping teeth, and rolling, twisting, furry bodies upon the ground. The blind boy crouched in the ferns at the side of the trail and crawled towards them, his arms lifted to his unseen rescuers. His father caught him up with a fierce sobbing of breath. And there came a fusillade of shots barking viciously into the whirl of writhing bodies. There was a sharp, sudden silence. The bodies dropped down loosely, twitched for a moment, then lay still.

Then the child screamed sharply. 'Don't shoot,' he cried, 'don't shoot – you'll hurt Amarillo!'

The men stared. And for once the Indian fisherman was glad that his child could not see. For there before them, in the trail, lay the tawny, dead body of a bobcat its cruel claws clenched about the yellow body of a cat – the gallant body of Amarillo. The body of the Yellow One was torn almost to shreds, and he lay in a pool of blood. But the wildcat had suffered too, for Amarillo's teeth were buried in his throat and even death had not sufficed to loosen the hold.

They carried the poor, torn body very tenderly back to the cabin, and the blind boy sobbed on his father's shoulder. He told them later how, in that cold darkness, he had heard a light swishing of leaves, and then a well-known 'Prr-t,' which told him that Amarillo had heard him at last and was coming to him. But even as he had knelt, his arms outstretched to welcome the Yellow One to his heart, there had come a stirring in the branches over his head – and the wild, savage shriek of a bobcat. Then had come the leap that had knocked him upon his face. But before the bloodthirsty creature could spring again, Amarillo was upon him, fighting savagely, and the bobcat, surprised at the sudden attack, had fought back, for the moment forgetting the human prey whom he had stalked.

So it was that many years later, when I came to the village of Old Man House, known by the Indians as Suquamish, I found the old fisherman, and the Indian fisherman, and his wife who was of the tribe of Skokomish. I met the blind boy, grown now almost to manhood, and I saw in the open square of the village the totem telling the story of how Teet' Motl and Hoo Han Hoo found the promised land.

There, in the cabin yard, is a little grave. It bears no headstone, such as a white man would erect to a well-remembered friend. It has a nobler, more fitting monument of gratitude and love – a carved and painted totem pole. At the bottom of the totem is the fierce, snarling face of a wildcat with white, cruel fangs displayed. Over the snarling face sits the stolid figure of a mallard duck, with one leg stiffly wrapped in splints. Above this are two closed eyes – eyes that cannot see the light. And at the very top, in the place of honour, is the carved portrait of Amarillo himself – his yellow face benign and almost smiling— his tufted ears erect and alert . . .

If he could know this, I am sure he would be proud. For only the truly great are thus honoured by the tribe of Skokomish.

My Boss the Cat

PAUL GALLICO

I F YOU are thinking of acquiring a cat at your house and
would care for a quick sketch of what your life will be like
under *Felis domesticus*, you have come to the right party.
I have figured out that, to date, I have worked for – and I mean
worked for – thirty-nine of these four-legged characters, including one memorable period when I was doing the bidding of
some twenty-three assorted resident felines all at the same
time.

Cats are, of course, no good. They're chisellers and pan-
handlers, sharpers and shameless flatterers. They're as full of
schemes and plans, plots and counterplots, wiles and guiles as
any confidence man. They can read your character better than a
$50-an-hour psychiatrist. They know to a milligram how much
of the old oil to pour on to break you down. They are definitely
smarter than I am, which is one reason why I love 'em.

Cat-haters will try to floor you with the old argument, 'If cats
are so smart, why can't they do tricks, the way dogs do?' It isn't
that cats can't do tricks; it's that they *won't*. They're far too hep
to stand up and beg for food when they know in advance you'll
give it to them anyway. And as for rolling over, or playing
dead, or 'speaking', what's in it for pussy that isn't already
hers?

Cats, incidentally, are a great warm-up for a successful
marriage – they teach you your place in the household. The
first thing Kitty does is to organize your home on a comfortable

218

basis – *her* basis. She'll eat when she wants to; she'll go out at her pleasure. She'll come in when she gets good and ready, if at all.

She wants attention when she wants it and darned well means to be let alone when she has other things on her mind. She is jealous; she won't have you showering attentions or caresses on any other minxes, whether two or four-footed.

She gets upset when you come home late and when you go away on a business trip. But when *she* decides to stay out a couple of nights, it is none of your darned business where she's been or what she's been up to. Either you trust her or you don't.

She hates dirt, bad smells, poor food, loud noises and people you bring home unexpectedly to dinner.

Kitty also has her share of small-child obstinacy. She enjoys seeing you flustered, fussed, red in the face and losing your temper. Sometimes, as she hangs about watching, you get the feeling that it is all she can do to keep from busting out laughing. And she's got the darndest knack for putting the entire responsibility for everything on *you*.

For instance, Kitty pretends that she can neither talk nor understand you, and that she is therefore nothing but a poor helpless dumb animal. What a laugh! Any self-respecting racket-working cat can make you understand at all times exactly what she wants. She has one voice for 'Let's eat,' another for wanting out, still a third for 'You don't happen to have seen my toy mouse around here, the one with the tail chewed off?' and a host of other easily identifiable speeches. She can also understand you perfectly, if she thinks there's profit in it.

I once had a cat I suspected of being able to read. This was a gent named Morris, a big tabby with topaz eyes who lived with me when I was batching it in a New York apartment. One day I had just finished writing to a lady who at that time was the object of my devotion. Naturally I brought considerable of the writer's art into telling her this. I was called to the telephone for a few minutes. When I returned, Morris was sitting on my desk reading the letter. At least, he was staring down at it, looking a little ill. He gave me that long, baffled look of which cats are capable, and immediately meowed to be let out. He didn't come back for three days. Thereafter I kept my private correspondence locked up.

The incident reminds me of another highly discriminating cat I had down on the farm by the name of Tante Hedwig. One Sunday a guest asked me whether I could make a cocktail called a Mexican. I said I thought I could, and proceeded to blend a horror of gin, pineapple juice, vermouth, bitters, and other ill-assorted ingredients. Pouring out a trial glass, I spilled it on the grass. Tante Hedwig came over, sniffed and, with a look of shameful embarrassment, solicitously covered it over. Everybody agreed later that she had something there.

Let me warn you not to put too much stock in the theory that animals do not think and that they act only by instinct. Did you ever try to keep a cat out that wanted to come in, or vice versa? I once locked a cat in the cellar. *He* climbed a straight, smooth cement wall, hung on with his paws (I saw the claw marks to prove it); unfastened the window-hook with his nose and climbed out.

Cats have fabulous memories, I maintain, and also the ability to measure and evaluate what they remember. Take, for instance, our two Ukrainian greys, Chin and Chilla. My wife brought them up on a medicine dropper. We gave them love and care and a good home on a farm in New Jersey.

Eventually we had to travel abroad, so Chin and Chilla went to live with friends in Glenview, Ill., a pretty snazzy place. Back in the United States, we went out to spend Thanksgiving in Glenview. We looked forward, among other things, to seeing our two cats. When we arrived at the house, Chin and Chilla were squatting at the top of a broad flight of stairs. As we called up a tender greeting to them, we saw an expression of horror come over their faces. 'Great heavens! It's those *paupers*! Run!' With that, they vanished and could not be found for five hours. They were frightened to death we had come to take them back to the squalor of a country estate in New Jersey, and deprive them of a room of their own in Illinois, with glassed-in sun porch, screens for their toilets and similar super-luxuries.

After a time they made a grudging appearance and consented to play the old games and talk over old times, guardedly. But when the hour arrived for our departure, they vanished once more. Our hostess wrote us that apparently they got hold of a timetable somewhere and waited until our train was past Elkhart before coming out.

It was this same Chilla who, one day on the farm after our big ginger cat, Wuzzy, had been missing for forty-eight hours, led us to where he was, a half mile away, out of sight and out of hearing, caught in a trap. Every so often Chilla would look back to see if we were coming. Old Wuz was half-dead when we got there, but when he saw Chilla he started to purr.

Two-Timing, or Leading the Double Life, is something you may be called upon to face with your cat. It means simply that Kitty manages to divide her time between two homes sufficiently far apart that each home-owner thinks she is his.

I discovered this when trying to check up on the unaccountable absences of Lulu II, a seal-point Siamese. I finally located her at the other end of the bay, mooching on an amiable spinster. When I said, 'Oh, I hope that my Lulu hasn't been imposing on you,' she replied indignantly, '*Your* Lulu! You mean *our* dear little Pitipoo! We've been wondering where she went when she disappeared occasionally. We do hope she hasn't been annoying *you*.'

The shocking part of this story, of course, is that, for the sake of a hand-out, Lulu, with a pedigree as long as your arm, was willing to submit to being called Pitipoo.

Of all things a smart cat does to whip you into line, the gift of the captured mouse is the cleverest and most touching. There was Limpy, the wild barn cat down on the farm who lived off what she caught in the fields. We were already supporting four cats, but in the winter, when we went to town, we brought her along.

We had not been inside the apartment ten minutes before Limpy caught a mouse, or probably *the* mouse, and at once brought it over and laid it at our feet. Now, as indicated before, Limpy had hunted to survive. To Limpy a dead mouse was Big and Little Casino, a touch-down home run and Grand Slam. Yet this one she gave to us.

How can you mark it up except as rent, or thanks, or 'Here, looka; this is the most important thing I do. You take it because I like you'? You can teach a dog to retrieve and bring you game, but only a cat will voluntarily hand over its kill to you as an unsolicited gift.

How come Kitty acts not like the beast of prey she is but like a better-class human being? I don't know the answer. The point is, she does it – and makes you her slave ever after. Once you have been presented with a mouse by your cat, you will never be the same again. She can use you for a door-mat. And she will, too.

La Ménagerie Intime

THÉOPHILE GAUTIER

IT IS no easy task to win the friendship of a cat. He is a philosopher, sedate, tranquil, a creature of habit, a lover of decency and order. He does not bestow his regard lightly, and, though he may consent to be your companion, he will never be your slave. Even in his most affectionate moods he preserves his freedom, and refuses a servile obedience. But once gain his confidence, and he is a friend for life. He shares your hours of work, of solitude, of melancholy. He spends whole evenings on your knee, purring and dozing, content with your silence, and spurning for your sake the society of his kind.

Minna Minna Mowbray

MICHAEL JOSEPH

AMONG ALL my cats, past and present, Minna Minna Mowbray was an outstanding personality. Except to a connoisseur of cats Minna was not physically impressive. She was a short-haired tortoiseshell tabby, with tiny white paws to match her piquant white face. Her head was small but beautifully shaped. The rather large ears were grey, and streaks of orange fur ran down between her amber eyes and on either side to the under part of her delicate jaw, forming a regularly designed tortoiseshell frame for her white face. A flash of coral pink was visible when she opened her dainty mouth. Her teeth were white and strong. The under part of her body was pure white and even in the soot and grime of London this was nearly always spotlessly clean. At kitten time it was dazzlingly white. This part of her was domestically known as her 'ermine'. When she was feeling particularly sociable, certain favoured members of the household were permitted, sometimes even encouraged, to massage it gently.

Minna was small, as cats go, but exquisitely proportioned. All her movements were graceful. She would sit upright, with her tiny forepaws close together, her long, rather full tail coiled round. Her favourite position for sleep was a crouch, the hind legs drawn up close and head resting on the outstretched forepaws which she converted into cushions by turning them inwards. Sometimes she preferred to lie on her side, legs outstretched luxuriously at queer angles. Various attitudes I learned to recognize as meditative (often assumed, this one), ecstatic, proud (both these when kittens were on view), majestically indignant (accompanied by business with tail), enquiring (as when she wanted to know what I was eating – this was primarily curiosity, for as often as not she rejected after close scrutiny the morsel I offered her) and leave-me-alone-please. This last was indicated by a haughty turning aside of her head; if this failed she would calmly turn her back and if *that* gesture had no effect she would walk off with the air of an offended dowager.

Like her mother, Lady Dudley, she had no voice, her vocal chord being partially paralysed. Oddly enough – for such a physical defect is presumably not hereditary – her kittens seldom cried, except when they were very young. Minna opened her mouth when, for instance, she wanted a door open, but no sound emerged. When she was greatly agitated about something a faint squeak was audible if you listened carefully. She could purr loudly enough but did not purr often. She could also swear, in delicate but determined fashion, but this again was reserved for special occasions.

Minna Minna Mowbray was a gentle cat. She never attempted to scratch a human. Babies and small boys could do what they liked with her. Like all self-respecting cats she disliked rough handling but she never attempted retaliation. If her tail were pulled or her long, sensitive whiskers touched she showed displeasure by asking silently to be allowed to go.

Contrary to expert advice, Minna wore a collar – an elegant green collar with an identity disc and two brass bells. A collar, I have heard, is undesirable because it may catch in the spikes of railings or the branches of a tree, but in my experience this risk is negligible if a cat is trained to a collar when very young. It is possible that a grown cat may so resent the introduction of a collar that he will try to drag it off and thereby injure himself, but I have never heard of an instance.

Minna was proud of her collar and plainly enjoyed wearing it. She put the bells to practical use, whenever she wanted to be admitted to a room, by shaking her head outside the closed door. She never worried if she were late for breakfast, knowing that the tinkle of her bell would cause the door to be opened. Sometimes when she rang outside the door I delayed, for the satisfaction of hearing her tinkle imperiously repeated. And with what an air of affronted majesty she stalked into the room if she had been thus kept waiting! Custom brought her to the dining-room at breakfast time, not hunger, for as often as not she turned up her aristocratic nose at the fish or milk offered her.

Minna also learned to summon her kittens by sounding her bells. When the babies got to the exploring stage and escaped from the maternal eye in house or garden Minna recalled them by an agitated peal. They usually answered the summons promptly but Minna would continue to ring until they did.

Minna could silence her bell as effectively as she could ring it. Not a sound was to be heard when she stalked a bird. What a waste of time it is to 'bell the cat' with the intention of suppressing natural instincts!

The real owner of my house in those days was Minna. She walked about with the manner of a landed proprietor surveying his domain; on the whole proud, but reserving the right to be critical. The day nursery and the kitchen were her favourite rooms. The dining-room and what my family insisted on calling 'the study' were frequently patronized. Her appearances in the other rooms were rare, with the exception of my bedroom in the winter when warm milk was usually to be coaxed from me last thing at night.

When she was younger the bathroom enchanted her. She soon discovered it to be a magic, fascinating and deliciously dangerous place with a queer contraption which was often filled with water. As a kitten, Minna used to insist on stalking round the edge of the bath when there was water in it, balancing precariously at the rounded corners. Running water fascinated her and she would play with a dripping tap for hours. Her mother, and some of Minna's own kittens, shared this fondness for running water; and so did my favourite Siamese, Charles. Micky Jos, one of Minna's most spirited kittens, had a passion for water and thoroughly enjoyed being soaked to the skin. But when she was grown up, with matronly responsibilities, Minna seldom played with water. It was beneath her dignity.

Another forsaken attraction in her middle age was the piano. As a kitten she took a great interest in it. As soon as it was opened she would jump on the keyboard. A series of spirited discords marked her progress from bass to treble and back again. She much preferred the bass, possibly because the deeper volume of sound or the stronger vibration took her fancy. But, as she grew up, Minna tired of the piano and took no notice of it.

Minna had a curious aversion to whistling. If I tried to whistle (it is not one of my accomplishments) Minna was at once agitated and tried to stop it by putting her paw on my lips. So long as I continued she behaved as one would expect an operatic tenor to behave within hearing of a mouth organ. It was not often that I outraged Minna's artistic susceptibilities but, when I did, her agitation was intense.

Flowers had a curious attraction for Minna. She could never resist nibbling at them. Spring flowers particularly; if not prevented she would drag daffodils and tulips to the ground for the aesthetic satisfaction of sampling their flavour at her leisure. It was not that she required vegetable diet for grass, which cats eat regularly when they can get it, was easily accessible. Minna's taste for flowers was not utilitarian.

If there was one thing Minna disliked more than any other it was preparation for a journey. As soon as suitcases were produced she made a prompt and plaintive appearance on the scene. Her agitation always increased when packing began. She would sit mournfully looking on while cupboards and drawers shed their contents, every now and then making a timid and reproachful attempt to interfere with our progress. Even the perfunctory packing of a suitcase for a weekend disturbed her. As for the wholesale removal of the family during the summer, that was a terrible ordeal. On one occasion, when boxes and cases were being brushed as a preliminary to their annual excursion, Minna, shaking her bell in protest, disappeared downstairs, to reappear a few minutes later with Peter, our wire-haired terrier. And then the pair of them sat gazing lugubriously at the signs of departure.

Minna, like most cats, disliked travelling. She had a very commodious basket (I was always annoyed by people who called it a dog basket) and entered it with a poor grace. Poor dear, she knew what was coming. However comfortably the basket was lined, the taxi jolted her up and down and the noise of passing traffic frightened her. The ignominy of being deposited on the platform of a railway station was bad enough, but worse was to follow. The train was the climax of her ordeal.

It was only when Minna was with me in a railway carriage that the sensation of being cooped up in a swiftly moving box oppressed me. To the more sensitive creature, who was my cat, the jolting, swaying movement of the small compartment which carried us so swiftly and mysteriously to an unknown destination must have been a paralysing torture. It was only then that I realized how uncomfortable even the most modern railway carriage is. Poor Minna! She would emerge timidly from her basket, grateful for release, but terrified of the unknown. Even in her fear curiosity compelled her to climb for a view of the rushing landscape. A glimpse was enough, and down on to the floor she would spring, crouching and panting, her little tongue hanging from her mouth like a signal of distress.

Only once do I remember Minna facing a railway journey with equanimity – and that, I am sure, was more apparent than real. On that occasion Minna was the proud mother of five kittens, who had also to be transported. The booking-office clerk stared when I told him I had six cats with me. When I added that they were infants in arms and enquired if there were any reduction on account of either age or quantity, or both, he grinned comprehendingly. I was mad, of course. He gave me one ticket and took my half-crown with cheerful tolerance. I betook myself and my cat basket off hastily before he could change his mind.

Minna, evidently determined to conquer her fears for the sake of her kittens, was remarkably self-possessed. She submitted without anxiety to imprisonment in the basket and made no fuss when it was lifted into the taxi and dumped on the floor. Not until the train was speeding southwards and she was allowed the freedom of the carriage did she betray her usual agitation. And then, I observed, only when she was well clear of the basket and its tiny occupants. On the seat beside me, snatching a furtive look out of the window from time to time, Minna went through the familiar performance of crying silently, appealing to me with a troubled paw to bring the dreadful and mysterious train to a standstill. But she had one eye all the time on the basket below and, at the first whimpering sound, she was back again, comforting her babies with soft maternal purring.

Minna was always an exemplary mother. But cats vary considerably in this respect. I have already mentioned Meestah, an earlier kitten of Lady Dudley's and therefore a half-sister to Minna. Meestah was worse than neglectful. Her nomenclature, by the way, was based on an Arab word meaning 'to hide', for she had a strange habit of hiding away in odd corners.

It was so long before Meestah became a mother that we began to think she would escape the destiny of female cats, but one day the family arrived – two beautiful kittens. Meestah was most resentful. She would have nothing to do with them. All our coaxing was of no avail. Fortunately, this was when I had fourteen cats. About nine of them were females and the kittens problem was rapidly becoming serious. But, luckily for Meestah's kittens, another of my large cat family accommodatingly had kittens just then and, as the litter was small, we were able to add Meestah's offspring to the new nursery. This was met with the complete approval of both mothers. Meestah was enormously relieved. That was her sole venture into motherhood. How Minna must have disapproved of her!

Minna adored having kittens. Indeed, a cynical friend once remarked that it was her life's work. Her kittens were invariably beautiful and never commonplace. Tortoiseshell tabby, orange, and prettily marked black and white were the usual arrivals, and there were often black flecked with bronze, and kittens mottled distinctively which I am at a loss to describe. Sometimes they were long-haired but usually they inherited the smooth, short-haired coat of their mother. Lest it be thought that I was prejudiced in their favour I must add that Minna's kittens excited admiration even in people usually indifferent to cats.

The fame of my Minna's kittens spread far and wide. Her offspring grew into handsome cats in households all over the country. As my work brought me into touch with a large number of authors, several of her kittens were transferred to literary ownership. Other kittens went to more modest family circles. Our milkman was a regular customer. He had been rather unlucky with his kittens and we cheerfully replaced them. The fishmonger begged for one which captivated him; and the little orange tabby which went to the greengrocer's wife was the recipient of so much affection that I am sure he did not begrudge the others the natural advantages of their respective establishments.

Several times we resolved to keep for ourselves a particularly charming kitten. There was Dinah, a fluffy, sentimental and very attractive young lady whom we brought from the country when we went to live in Regent's Park. I was especially fond of Dinah; whenever Minna held herself aloof – and that was often – Dinah could be depended on to stay purring blissfully on my knee. Dinah was as affectionate as she was decorative.

Not long after our arrival in London Dinah was reported missing. The usual frantic search followed, with no result. Dinah's virtues were magnified with the passing days and, when at last I had to admit there was no longer any hope of finding her, my loss seemed irreparable. I can write of my lost Dinah in this lighthearted way on account of what followed.

One Sunday morning, some weeks later, someone looking out of a window said, 'Isn't that Dinah?' I must explain that the back of our house faced the backs of a crescent of other houses, with small gardens abutting on each other. In these gardens were trees and on a low-lying bough there was a cat. It certainly did look like Dinah.

I ran down to the garden and, climbing on to the wall, made my way along until I was close enough to identify the cat. It *was* Dinah. She watched me coming and when I called her name looked down at me with mild interest. I noticed, with relief, that she had evidently been well fed and cared for. If she recognized me she did not show it. Balancing precariously, I tried to coax her down. Dinah took no notice. So, feeling rather foolish, I retired, in the vain hope that she would follow.

Then I had an inspiration. Dinah might have transferred her affections to another human being, but what about her mother? I dashed into the house, picked up Minna and returned to the garden wall. To reach the tree I had to pass along the tops of several garden walls, on some of which my neighbours had erected trelliswork, wire and such-like impediments. With Minna doing her best to escape it was no easy matter to negotiate these obstacles but, apart from blacking my hands and face and tearing my trousers on a nail, I completed the journey safely. I was confident that Dinah would eagerly come down as soon as she saw Minna; and that Minna would be overjoyed to find her lost baby.

I held Minna up in my arms, balancing on tiptoe, so that the two cats could see each other face to face. Dinah looked down on us with surprise, as if to remark what a strange world this was, with human beings performing antics with other cats on the tops of walls. Her innocent eyes looked at Minna with an expression which clearly said, 'I don't know you, madam, and I don't want to know you.' Minna, on the other hand, recognized her offspring at once. Was she overjoyed? Did she utter the crooning call, half purr, half squeak, with which she had always summoned her kittens? Not she. She spat viciously and began to swear under her breath, in a suppressed note of unmistakable feline hate. She kept it up in a steady crescendo until I lowered her on to the wall and let her go; and then she sprang to the ground, lashing her tail with fury.

At the time I was amazed at this unmotherly behaviour. Dinah was still a kitten and only a few weeks before had been the apple of her mother's eye. It was inconceivable that she could have become a stranger in so short a time. I knew that grown cats fail to recognize their parents, and vice versa, but there was Minna behaving in a way most unnatural and offensive.

Later, I became suspicious. It dawned on me that there was something odd about these disappearances of favourite kittens. Whenever we tried to keep one of a litter, it invariably left us before it was many months old. Everyone who has had anything to do with cats knows how distressed the mother cat is when a kitten is lost or taken away, especially if it is the sole survivor of a litter. Now, it struck me as curious that Minna showed no anxiety when these mysterious departures occurred. We all searched high and low, but Minna was quite unconcerned.

It was when Fowey vanished that my suspicions were confirmed. Fowey (named after the Cornish seaport) was a mischievous orange rascal with china-blue eyes, the throatiest purr I have ever heard, an insatiable appetite and absurd fluffy paws which contrasted oddly with the dainty and aristocratic white feet of his mother. He was an intelligent and charming kitten and everyone made a great fuss of him.

When Fowey was about three months old, Minna took him for long walks. On one occasion I discovered them in a field by the railway a long way from the house. No doubt these expeditions were a source of delight to little Fowey, who wanted to see the world, but there seemed to me to be something sinister about them.

One day mother and son left the house together, Fowey as usual prancing with delight at the prospect of yet another expedition into the fascinating unknown. I watched them go, and there was a queer look in Minna's eye, a look which I can only describe as sinister. Maybe it was only my fancy but it was enough to make me ask at once for Fowey when I returned home that evening. My fears were realized; Minna was there, smirking triumphantly, I fancied, but Fowey was missing.

The days went by and Fowey did not return. We searched in vain. When I asked Minna she looked up at me with an expression so blandly innocent that I am sure she understood perfectly well what I was talking about. Now there is no doubt whatever in my mind that what happened was this. Minna took Fowey to some unfamiliar, deserted spot and there turned round and attacked her unsuspecting offspring. Most probably she said something like this to him:

'Look here, young Fowey (*bang*) you understand this (*scratch*). I'm the only cat wanted in Their house (*biff*) and I'm not (*scratch*) going to have you on the premises. (*Bite, scratch, bang.*) You go and find a home of your own. (*Spit.*) You're not wanted, d'you hear me? (*Bang, spit, bite, scratch, and general fireworks.*)'

No wonder poor Fowey beat a retreat like all the others! He reappeared a few weeks later in one of the gardens at the back and I discovered that he was lording it over one of the houses in the neighbouring crescent. He had grown into a magnificent cat with a long coat (carefully brushed, I was glad to note) and a huge plume of a tail which I could see daily fluttering in the trees when I was shaving in my bathroom. He was, to judge by appearances, a happy cat and played joyously in the gardens most of the day. But he never came into ours.

Minna was an expert in the art of getting her own way. I can recall only two occasions when she was defeated and then I think she allowed herself to be. The first occasion was the little matter of Peter's basket.

Peter belonged to my wife before I knew her and, incidentally, there were times when that dog made me feel as a second husband must feel when his wife describes the virtues of his predecessor. Who is this interloper? Peter seemed to say. Well, when Peter became part of the new *ménage* the basket came along too, but in the excitement of meeting Minna Minna Mowbray and the consequent revolution in his habits and ideas of home life, Peter apparently forgot about the basket.

My wife was upset. She said that Peter was so intelligent he wouldn't go to sleep anywhere but in his basket. (That was before she knew the change Minna could produce.) So it came about that Peter slept – I suspect uneasily – on the mat outside her bedroom door. Then one day my wife said, '*Poor* Peter! No wonder he looks unhappy. He hasn't got his basket.' So the basket was dug out of the pile of miscellaneous kit which was awaiting disposal in the new house, and was ceremoniously put outside the door for Peter's accommodation. I rather liked the look of it and reflected aloud, to my wife's indignation, that Minna Minna Mowbray could just do with a basket like that.

Peter wagged his stump, looked intelligent and barked. That night he occupied the basket according to plan. We knew something was wrong (from Peter's point of view) when he scratched at the door the next morning about an hour before his usual time. He came in with the air of an ill-used dog, his stump registering dejection.

We had not long to wait for the explanation. Shortly after tea Minna Minna Mowbray stalked upstairs and leisurely installed herself in the basket. By the time we turned off the radio and went upstairs to bed she was coiled up fast asleep (or ostensibly so) while Peter, squatting on the landing, regarded her balefully from a discreet distance.

That was the beginning of the basket war. The old Trojan War, the Hundred Years War, and the Great War faded into insignificance. Our household was promptly divided into two factions – the pro-Peterites, led by my wife, and the pro-Minnaites, which was me. The cook thought it was too bad, the parlourmaid echoed, 'Poor Peter.' It is true the postman grinned unsympathetically when he heard about it, but he and Peter are traditional enemies so that he was more anti-Peter than pro-Minna.

The fact that numbers were against her did not daunt my Minna. Her tiny stature was deceptive. In action she could give points to any Amazon. So that Peter's fugitive attempts to regain possession of his sleeping quarters are scarcely worth recording. Except perhaps the day when, bloated with tea and Dutch courage, he made a spirited attempt to get in while Minna dozed peacefully on the cushion. The battle was swiftly over; Peter emerged from the regions of the coal cellar only after an interval of two days and much coaxing.

Then other and more important domestic affairs took precedence over the Minna-Peter feud. While the rest of the household talked of other things it rumbled on in a state of trench warfare, with Minna securely dug in and Peter making occasional raids across no-man's-landing. Indeed, we all regarded the basket war as a permanent feature of our domestic life.

Actually it lasted for just over two years. Armistice was declared only when our baby daughter Shirley crawled out of the bedroom door, seized Minna by the scruff of her furry neck, neatly ejected her and solemnly climbed into the basket.

Peter was present at the ceremony and (presumably) gave a loud doggy guffaw. Minna withdrew with dignity. She then turned the day nursery into her sleeping quarters and Peter retired to the kitchen. The basket was 'reconstructed' after the war and for a long time was occupied by a teddy bear, a musical duck and a woolly rabbit. There was peace in our time.

The other occasion when Minna graciously surrendered was the advent of Charles O'Malley, my Siamese cat. I have written another book about Charles and I shall not say much about him here; although readers of that book may understand my feeling that this is Hamlet without the Prince of Denmark.

Charles O'Malley was the first Siamese I had had. Minna Minna Mowbray was furious when I brought him home and always looked upon him as an intruder. It was quite clear that she would never forgive me for adopting another cat. As for Charles himself, Minna at first swore and spat vigorously at his approach. But she soon decided to tolerate him and after a fortnight or so the two cats were drinking peaceably from the same saucer. Charles, as a ten-week-old kitten, was enormously impressed by Minna Minna Mowbray. No amount of bad language or threats deterred him from the pursuit of her tail but it was several weeks before Minna permitted him to play with her.

Charles O'Malley was aristocratically bred, and looked it. With his sapphire-blue eyes, delicate cream coat, chocolate-pointed ears, feet, tail and 'mask', he was a truly handsome creature.

There are differences between Siamese and other cats, apart from their shape and colouring. The Siamese voice is quite distinctive. When Minna first heard Charles's raucous squeak she visibly shuddered. Siamese cats have the reputation of being ferocious fighters; they are certainly stronger than ordinary cats. I do not think they are so graceful when walking or jumping. Indeed, Charles would land on his feet with a thud which was positively canine. Siamese are exquisite animals, however; sensitive, intelligent and responsive. Charles O'Malley (whom I confess I adopted partly to annoy Minna, who had been treating me very cavalierly at the time) was indeed a most lovable and charming cat and, as readers of his story* will know, he was destined to become my best loved cat.

However, no despot ever ruled his kingdom with more certainty of getting his own way than Minna Minna Mowbray did the house which we then lived in. It was a benevolent tyranny, this rule of Minna's; often amusing, never malicious, always sure and precise. She was clearly a believer in the divine right of cats, exercising her power with due regard to the niceties and obligations of her position.

To the uninitiated it may appear that I was merely foolish about my cat. However, I was not Minna's only subject. She bossed everyone in the house with the exception of my little daughter, Shirley, who occasionally did a bit of bossing herself. But Minna was quite happy about that. Shirley was privileged to stroke her fur the wrong way, to play with her tail and to carry her round the nursery suspended at all sorts of queer angles. I fancy that Minna rather enjoyed it all. Shirley was very fond of her and if Minna was accidentally hurt when they were playing together – this rarely happened, for Shirley knew she must be careful – the ensuing ceremony of contrite apology on the part of one and gracious forgiveness of the other was delightful to watch.

When Minna had kittens Shirley was a privileged visitor from the time of their birth. Minna allowed her to stroke them, knowing that Shirley would only touch them with gentleness. As soon as the babies reached the romping age Shirley was in her element. The nursery was transformed into an arena, in which young tigers leaped and raced swiftly in all directions, with Shirley's attempts at pursuit interrupted by her gurgles of excited laughter. Minna used to look on quite happily at these performances.

Like all cats who are happily accommodated in a human household Minna was a docile creature. But she insisted on having her own way. She would observe, with well-bred interest, my wife's painstaking preparations to provide her with a comfortable and secluded bed for her kittens. A large card-

board box, of the kind she loved, carefully lined with successive layers of newspaper, tissue paper and soft linen, and placed
in one of her favourite cupboards, which was conveniently
warm, well ventilated and discreetly dark – this was dutifully
prepared at certain times by one of us. Whoever prepared her
bed, however comfortably made and conveniently placed it
might be, we could be sure of one thing – Minna would not use
it.

Minna deceived several generations of interested cooks and
house-parlourmaids by her tactics on these occasions. It was
her custom to inspect at intervals the box or basket which had
been so thoughtfully made ready for her, even to occupy it for
forty winks every now and again as if to advertise her satisfaction. Many a beaming domestic servant announced the good
news that 'Minnie is very pleased with her new box.' But these
premature expectations were invariably disappointed. Minna
knew what she was about. The attention of our expectant
domestic staff being thus publicly drawn to a particular spot,
Minna had her kittens elsewhere.

In this respect most cats, I believe, behave in the same
independent way. Is it yet another survival of jungle instinct,
this hiding away from prying eyes at important times? Or
merely a gesture of independence, a rejection of our human
proprietorship, a challenge to man and his stupid ways?
Minna, although intensely secretive about her plans, made no
further attempt at concealment when her kittens were born.
She was then embarrassingly anxious that they should be seen
and admired. In this I think she may have differed from other
cats who, reasonably enough, do not like to be disturbed for
some days. Minna, however, scorned further camouflage. She
unmistakably invited us to pay our respects to the new arrivals.
Nor did she object to their being touched. Our praise was
clearly to her liking; she would purr loudly if we admired the
little, squealing, almost invisible babies.

Naturally enough she would resent it if we overstayed our
welcome, or if any stranger intruded on her privacy. And what
a calamity if there should be any attempt to move her family! In
that event, as soon as the coast was clear, Minna would remove
them methodically, one by one, to what she obviously trusted
would be a place less liable to disturbance. She was quite

capable of registering a protest if disturbed by strangers; this usually took the form of depositing her kittens under the cover of my bed. There were times when I arrived home to find the house in a state of agitation because Minna and her kittens had disappeared. Nearly always they were to be found huddled together at the end of my bed comfortably asleep under the warm and sheltering darkness of the eiderdown.

Minna brooked no interference in her private affairs. At an early age she began to take an active interest in the opposite sex and all our well-meant efforts to influence her in the direction of a more lady-like modesty were frustrated. If the doors were shut she climbed out of a window. Nor were our attempts to find her a worthy husband any more successful. Whether the so-called attraction of opposites is responsible or not, it is a lamentable fact that Minna invariably chose the most disreputable gentleman friends. Any ugly, one-eyed, torn-eared tom-cat seemed to have an irresistible attraction for our Minna Minna Mowbray.

The uglier they were, the more eligible they appeared to be. She had, I remember, a disgraceful passion for an old roué with a lacerated tail, fractional ears, a permanently closed left eye and a pronounced limp. At his approach Minna behaved in a shameless and otherwise indescribable fashion. On such occasions I used to pretend she was not my cat.

When we were living in Surrey we did our best to reform her. It was not successful. Within a few days of our arrival the news had spread in some mysterious fashion that a new and comely lady cat had taken up her residence and that she had a decided preference for experienced lovers. Somehow Minna had made it known to the cats of all Surrey (and part of Sussex, too, I fancy) that she liked to choose her followers from the ranks of the veterans and middle-aged. She had no use for boy friends, it appeared.

We discovered this, and were considerably humiliated thereby, when we introduced her to a young orange cat from a neighbouring house. As soon as we set eyes on this cat, we decided that here was an ideal husband for Minna. He was a strikingly handsome cat, young and, so far as we could see, perfectly eligible. Minna, however, thought not. She promptly spat at him in a most unladylike way. Our candidate let us down badly. He fled for his life. After that we left Minna to her own devices – and to the reprobate toms of the neighbourhood.

To look at Minna Minna Mowbray as she sat demurely on the arm of my chair, her little white paws set neatly together in a modest pose, you would never imagine that she favoured the toughs and tramps of the tom cat world. In every other respect she was fastidious to the point of absurdity. She would refuse to drink from a saucer that was not spotlessly clean; would spend hours industriously making her toilet, until every hair was in its proper place; insisted on her milk being at exactly the right temperature; and objected to being touched, making a pretence of exquisite discomfort if I happened to stroke her when she didn't feel like it or to lay hands, however gently, on any part of her sensitive anatomy. Yet, ten minutes later, she could be observed (if you cared to gaze on the unedifying spectacle) in the garden below, being rolled playfully about in the mud by a caveman lover from the slums of Camden Town.

The Slum Cat

ERNEST THOMPSON
SETON

LIFE I

THE LITTLE slum kitten was not six weeks old yet, but she was alone in the old junk-yard. Her mother had gone to seek food among the garbage-boxes the night before, and had never returned, so when the second evening came she was very hungry. A deep-laid instinct drove her forth from the old cracker-box to seek something to eat. Feeling her way silently among the rubbish she smelt everything that seemed eatable, but without finding food. At length she reached the wooden steps leading down into Jap Malee's bird store underground at the far end of the yard. The door was open a little, and she walked in. A Negro sitting idly on a box in a corner watched her curiously. She wandered past some rabbits; they paid no heed. She came to a wide-barred cage in which was a fox. He crouched low; his eyes glowed. The kitten wandered, sniffing, up to the bars, put her head in, sniffed again, then made straight toward the feed-pan, to be seized in a flash by the crouching fox. She gave a frightened 'mew', and the Negro also sprang forward, spitting with such copious vigour in the Fox's face that he dropped the kitten and returned to the corner, there to sit blinking his eyes in sullen fear.

The Negro pulled the kitten out. She tottered in a circle a few times, then revived, and a few minutes later, when Jap Malee

240

came back, she was purring in the Negro's lap, apparently none the worse.

Jap was not an Oriental; he was a full-blooded Cockney; but his eyes were such little accidental slits aslant in his round, flat face that his first name was forgotten in the highly descriptive title of 'Jap'. He was not especially unkind to the birds and beasts which furnished his living, but he did not want the slum kitten.

The Negro gave her all the food she could eat and then carried her to a distant block and dropped her in an iron-yard. Here she lived and somehow found food enough to grow till, weeks later, an extended exploration brought her back to her old quarters in the junk-yard and, glad to be at home, she at once settled down.

Kitty was now fully grown. She was a striking-looking cat of the tiger type. Her marks were black on a pale grey, and the four beauty spots of white, on nose, ears and tail-tip, lent a certain distinction. She was expert now at getting a living, yet she had some days of starvation and had so far failed in her ambition to catch a sparrow. She was quite alone, but a new force was coming into her life.

She was lying in the sun one September day when a large black cat came walking along the top of a wall in her direction. By his torn ear she recognized him at once as an old enemy. She slunk into her box and hid. He picked his way gingerly, bounded lightly to a shed that was at the end of the yard, and was crossing the roof when a yellow cat rose up. The black tom glared and growled; so did the yellow tom. Their tails lashed from side to side. Strong throats growled and yowled. They approached with ears laid back, with muscles a-tense.

'Yow – yow – ow,' said the black one.

'Wow – w – w –' was the slightly deeper answer.

'Ya – wow – wow – wow –' said the black one, edging up an inch nearer.

'Yow – w – w –' was the yellow answer, as the blond cat rose to full height and stepped with vast dignity a whole inch forward. 'Yow – w,' and he went another inch, while his tail went swish, thump, from one side to the other.

'Ya – wow – yow – w,' screamed the black in a rising tone,

and he backed the eighth of an inch as he marked the broad, unshrinking beast before him.

Windows opened all around, human voices were heard, but the cat scene went on.

'Yow – yow – ow,' rumbled the yellow peril, his voice deepening as the other's rose. 'Yow,' and he advanced another step.

Now their noses were but three inches apart; they stood sidewise, both ready to clinch, but each waiting for the other. They glared at each other for three minutes in silence, and like statues, except that each tail-tip was twisting.

The yellow began again. 'Yow – ow – ow,' in deep tone.

'Ya-a-a-a,' screamed the black with intent to strike terror by his yell, but he retreated one-sixteenth of an inch. The yellow walked up a whole long inch; their whiskers were mixing now; another advance, and their noses almost touched.

'Yo – w – w,' said yellow like a deep moan.

'Ya-a-a-a,' screamed black, but he retreated a thirty-second of an inch, and the yellow warrior closed and clinched like a demon.

Oh, how they rolled and bit and tore – especially the yellow one!

How they pitched and gripped and hugged – but especially the yellow one!

Over and over, sometimes one on top, sometimes the other, but usually the yellow one, and over they rolled till off the roof, amid cheers from all the windows. They lost not a second in that fall into the junk-yard; they tore and clawed all the way down, but especially the yellow one; and when they struck the ground, still fighting, the one on top was chiefly the yellow one; and before they separated both had had as much as they wanted, especially the black one! He scaled the wall and, bleeding and growling, disappeared, while the news was passed from window to window that Cayley's 'Nig' had been licked by 'Orange Billy'.

Either the yellow cat was a very clever seeker, or else slum Kitty did not hide very hard, for he discovered her among the boxes and she made no attempt to get away, probably because she had witnessed the fight. There is nothing like success in warfare to win the female heart, and thereafter the yellow tom and Kitty became very good friends, not sharing each other's lives or food – cats do not do that much – but recognizing each other as entitled to special friendly privileges.

When October's shortening days were on an event took place in the old cracker-box. If 'Orange Billy' had come he would have seen five little kittens curled up in the embrace of their mother, the little slum Kitty. It was a wonderful thing for her. She felt all the elation an animal mother can feel – all the delight – as she tenderly loved them and licked them.

She had added a joy to her joyless life, but she had also added a heavy burden. All her strength was taken now to find food. And one day, led by a tempting smell, she wandered into the bird cellar and into an open cage. Everything was still, there was meat ahead, and she reached forward to seize it; the cage door fell with a snap and she was a prisoner. That night the Negro put an end to the kittens and was about to do the same with the mother when her unusual markings attracted the attention of the bird man, who decided to keep her.

LIFE II

Jap Malee was as disreputable a little Cockney bantam as ever sold cheap canary birds in a cellar. He was extremely poor, and the Negro lived with him because the 'Henglishman' was willing to share bed and board. Jap was perfectly honest, according to his lights, but he had no lights and there is little doubt that his chief revenue was derived from storing and restoring stolen dogs and cats. The fox and the half a dozen canaries were mere blinds. The 'Lost and Found' columns of the papers were the only ones of interest to Jap, but he noticed and saved a clipping about breeding for fur. This was stuck on the wall of his den and, under its influence, he set about making an experiment with the slum cat. First he soaked her dirty fur with stuff to kill the two or three kinds of creepers she wore and, when it had done its work, he washed her thoroughly. Kitty was savagely indignant, but a warm and happy glow spread over her as she dried off in a cage near the stove, and her fur began to fluff out with wonderful softness and whiteness. Jap and his assistant were much pleased. But this was preparatory. 'Nothing is so good for growing fur as plenty of oily food and continued exposure to cold weather,' said the clipping. Winter was at hand, and Jap Malee put Kitty's cage out in the yard, protected only from the rain and the direct wind, and fed her with all the oil cake and fish heads she could eat. In a week the change began to show. She was rapidly getting fat. She had nothing to do but get fat and dress her fur. Her cage was kept clean, and Nature responded to the chill weather and oily food by making Kitty's coat thicker and glossier every day so that, by Christmas, she was an unusually beautiful cat in the fullest and finest of fur with markings that were at least a rarity.

Why not send the slum cat to the show now coming on?

"T'won't do, ye kneow, Sammy, to henter 'er as a Tramp Cat, ye kneow,' Jap observed to his help; 'but it kin be arranged to suit the Knickerbockers. Nothink like a good noime, ye kneow. Ye see now, it had orter be "Royal" somethink or other – nothink goes with the Knickerbockers like "Royal" anythink. Now, "Royal Dick" or "Royal Sam": 'ow's that? But 'owld on: them's tom names. Oi say, Sammy, wot's the noime of that island where you were born?'

'Analostan Island, sah, was my native vicinity, sah.'

'Oi say, now, that's good, ye kneow. "Royal Analostan," by Jove! The onliest pedigreed Royal Analostan in the howle sheow, ye kneow. Ain't that capital?' and they mingled their cackles.

'But we'll 'ave to 'ave a pedigree, ye kneow;' so a very long fake pedigree on the recognized lines was prepared.

One afternoon Sam, in a borrowed silk hat, delivered the cat and the pedigree at the show door. He had been a barber, and he could put on more pomp in five minutes than Jap Malee could have displayed in a lifetime, and this, doubtless, was one reason for the respectful reception awarded the Royal Analostan at the cat show.

Jap had all the Cockney's reverence for the upper class. He was proud to be an exhibitor but when, on the opening day, he went to the door he was overpowered to see the array of carriages and silk hats. The gateman looked at him sharply but passed him on his ticket, doubtless taking him for a stable boy to some exhibitor. The hall had velvet carpets before the long rows of cages. Jap was sneaking down the side row, glancing at the cats of all kinds, noting the blue ribbons and the reds, glancing about but not daring to ask for his own exhibit, inwardly trembling to think what the gorgeous gathering of fashion would say if they discovered the trick he was playing on them. But he saw no sign of slum Kitty.

In the middle of the centre aisle were the high-class cats. A great throng was there. The passage was roped and two policemen were there to keep the crowd moving. Jap wriggled in among them; he was too short to see over, but he gathered from the remarks that the gem of the show was there.

'Oh, isn't she a beauty!' said one tall woman.

'Ah! what distinction!' was the reply.

'One cannot mistake the air that comes only from ages of the most refined surroundings.'

'How I should like to own that superb creature!'

Jap pushed near enough to get a glimpse of the cage and read a placard which announced that 'The Blue Ribbon and Gold Medal of the Knickerbocker High Society Cat and Pet Show had been awarded to the thoroughbred pedigreed Royal Analostan, imported and exhibited by J. Malee, Esquire, the well-known fancier. Not for sale.' Jap caught his breath; he stared – yes, surely, there, high in a gilded cage on velvet cushions, with two policemen for guards, her fur bright black and pale grey, her bluish eyes slightly closed, was his slum Kitty, looking the picture of a cat that was bored to death.

Jap Malee lingered around that cage for hours, drinking a draught of glory such as he had never before known. But he saw that it would be wise for him to remain unknown; his 'butler' must do all the business.

It was slum Kitty who made that show a success. Each day her value went up in the owner's eye. He did not know what prices had been given for cats and thought that he was touching a record pitch when his 'butler' gave the director authority to sell the cat for $100.

This is how it came about that the slum cat found herself transferred to a Fifth Avenue mansion. She showed a most unaccountable wildness, as well as other peculiarities. Her retreat from the lap dog to the centre of the dinner-table was understood to express a deep-rooted, though mistaken, idea of avoiding a defiling touch. The patrician way in which she would get the cover off a milk-can was especially applauded, while her frequent wallowings in the garbage-pail were understood to be the manifestation of a little pardonable high-born eccentricity. She was fed and pampered, shown and praised, but she was not happy. She clawed at that blue ribbon around her neck till she got it off; she jumped against the plate glass because that seemed the road to outside; and she would sit and gaze out on the roofs and back yards at the other side of the window and wish she could be among them for a change.

She was strictly watched – was never allowed outside – so that all the happy garbage-pail moments occurred while these receptacles of joy were indoors. But one night in March, as they were being set out a-row for the early scavenger, the Royal Analostan saw her chance, slipped out of the door, and was lost to view.

Of course there was a grand stir, but pussy neither knew nor cared anything about that. Her one thought was to go home. A raw east wind had been rising and now it came to her with a particularly friendly message. Man would have called it an unpleasant smell of the docks, but to pussy it was a welcome message from her own country. She trotted on down the long street due east, threading the rails of front gardens, stopping like a statue for an instant, or crossing the street in search of the darkest side. She came at length to the docks and to the water, but the place was strange. She could go north or south; something turned her southward and, dodging among docks and dogs, carts and cats, crooked arms of the bay and straight board fences, she got in an hour or two into familiar scenes and smells and, before the sun came up, she crawled back, weary and footsore, through the same old hole in the same old fence, and over a wall into her junk-yard back of the bird cellar, yes, back into the very cracker-box where she was born.

After a long rest she came quietly down from the cracker-box towards the steps leading to the cellar, and engaged in her old-time pursuit of seeking for eatables. The door opened and there stood the Negro. He shouted to the bird-man inside:

'Say, Boss, come hyar! Ef dere ain't dat dar Royal Ankalostan comed back!'

Jap came in time to see the Cat jumping the wall. The Royal Analostan had been a windfall for him; had been the means of adding many comforts to the cellar and several prisoners to the cages. It was now of the utmost importance to recapture Her Majesty. Stale fish heads and other infallible lures were put out till pussy was induced to chew at a large fish head in a box trap. The Negro, in watching, pulled the string that dropped the lid, and a minute later the Analostan was again in a cage in the cellar. Meanwhile, Jap had been watching the 'Lost and Found' column. There it was: 'Twenty-five dollars reward,' etc. That night Mr Malee's 'butler' called at the Fifth Avenue mansion with the missing cat. 'Mr Malee's compliments, sah.' Of course, Mr Malee would not be rewarded, but the 'butler' was evidently open to any offer.

Kitty was guarded carefully after that but, so far from being disgusted with the old life of starving and glad of her care, she became wilder and more dissatisfied.

The spring was on in full power now and the Fifth Avenue family were thinking of their country residence. They packed up, closed house and moved off to the summer home some fifty miles away, and Pussy, in a basket, went with them.

The basket was put on the back seat of a carriage. New sounds and passing smells were entered and left. Then a roaring of many feet, more swinging of the basket, then some clicks, some bangs, a long, shrill whistle, and door-bells of a very big front door, a rumbling, a whizzling, an unpleasant smell; then there was a succession of jolts, roars, jars, stops, clicks, clacks, smells, jumps, shakes, more smells, more shakes, big shakes, little shakes, gases, smoke, screeches, door-bells, tremblings; roars, thunders, and some new smells, raps, taps, heavings, rumbling and more smells. When at last it all stopped the sun came twinkling through the basket lid. The Royal Cat was lifted into another carriage and they turned aside from their past course. Very soon the carriage swerved, the noises of its wheels were grittings and rattlings, a new and horrible sound was added – the barking of dogs, big and little, and dreadfully close. The basket was lifted, and slum Kitty had reached her country home.

Everyone was officiously kind. All wanted to please the Royal Cat, but, somehow, none of them did, except possibly the big, fat cook that Kitty discovered on wandering into the kitchen. That greasy woman smelt more like a slum than anything she had met for months and the Royal Analostan was proportionately attracted. The cook, when she learned that fears were entertained about the cat's staying, said: 'Shure, she'd 'tind to thot; wanst a cat licks her futs shure she's at home.' So she deftly caught the unapproachable Royalty in her apron and committed the horrible sacrilege of greasing the soles of her feet with pot grease. Of course, Kitty resented it; she resented everything in the place; but, on being set down, she began to dress her paws and found evident satisfaction in that grease. She licked all four feet for an hour, and the cook triumphantly announced that now 'shure she's be apt to sthay'; and stay she did, but she showed a most surprising and disgusting preference for the kitchen and the cook and the garbage-pail.

The family, though distressed by these high-born eccentricities, were glad to see the Royal Analostan more contented and approachable. They guarded her from every menace. The dogs were taught to respect her; no man or boy about the place would have dreamed of throwing a stone at the famous pedigreed cat, and she had all the food she wanted, but still she was not happy. She was hankering for many things, she scarcely knew what. She had everything – yes, but she wanted something else. Plenty to eat and drink – yes, but milk does not taste the same when you can go and drink all you want from a saucer; it has to be stolen out of a tin pail when one is pinched with hunger, or it does not have the tang – it is not milk.

How pussy did hate it all! True, there was one sweet smelling shrub in the whole horrible place – one that she did enjoy nipping and rubbing against it; it was the only bright spot in her country life.

One day, after a summer of discontent, a succession of things happened that stirred anew the slum instincts of the Royal prisoner. A great bundle of stuff from the docks had reached the country mansion. What it contained was of little moment, but it was rich with the most piquant of slum smells. The chords of memory surely dwell in the nose, and pussy's past was conjured up with dangerous force. Next day the cook left through some trouble. That evening the youngest boy of the house, a horrid little American with no proper appreciation of Royalty, was tying a tin to the blue-blooded one's tail, doubtless in furtherance of some altruistic project, when pussy resented it with a paw that wore five big fish-hooks for the occasion. The howl of down-trodden America roused America's mother; the deft and womanly blow she aimed with her book was miraculously avoided and pussy took flight, upstairs, of course. A hunted rat runs downstairs, a hunted dog goes on the level, a hunted cat runs up. She hid in the garret and waited till night came. Then, gliding downstairs, she tried the screen doors, found one unlatched and escaped into black August night. Pitch black to man's eyes, it was simply grey to her, and she glided through the disgusting shrubbery and flower-beds, had a final nip at that one little bush that had been an attractive spot in the garden, and boldly took her back track of the spring.

How could she take a back track that she never saw? There is in all animals some sense of direction. It is low in man and high in horses, but cats have a large gift, and this mysterious guide took her westward, not clearly and definitely, but with a general impulse that was made definite because the easiest travel was on the road. In an hour she had reached the Hudson River. Her nose had told her many times that the course was true. Smell after smell came back.

At the river was the railroad. She could not go on the water; she must go north or south. This was a case where her sense of direction was clear: it said 'go south'; and Kitty trotted down the footpath between the iron rails and the fence.

LIFE III

Cats can go very fast up a tree or over a wall, but when it comes to the long, steady trot that reels off mile after mile, hour after hour, it is not the cat-hop but the dog-trot that counts. She became tired and a little footsore. She was thinking of a rest when a dog came running to the fence near by and broke out into such a horrible barking close to her ear that pussy leaped in terror. She ran as hard as she could down the path. The barking seemed to grow into a low rumble – a louder rumble and roaring – a terrifying thunder. A light shone; Kitty glanced back to see, not the dog, but a huge black thing with a blazing eye, coming on yowling and spitting like a yard full of tom cats. She put forth all her power to run, made such time as she never had made before, but dared not leap the fence. She was running like a dog – was flying, but all in vain: the monstrous pursuer overtook her, but missed her in the darkness, and hurried past to be lost in the night, while Kitty sat gasping for breath.

This was only the first encounter with the strange monsters – strange to her eyes – her nose seemed to know them, and told her that this was another landmark on the home trail. But pussy learned that they were very stupid and could not find her at all if she hid by slipping quietly under a fence and lying still. Before morning she had encountered many of them, but escaped unharmed from all.

About sunrise she reached a nice little slum on her home trail and was lucky enough to find several unsterilized eatables in an ash-heap. She spent the day around a stable. It was very like home, but she had no idea of staying there. She was driven by an inner craving that was neither hunger nor fear, and next evening set out as before. She had seen the 'One-eyed Thunder-rollers' all day going by, and was getting used to them. That night passed much like the first one. The days went by in skulking in barns, hiding from dogs and small boys, and the nights in limping along the track, for she was getting footsore; but on she went, mile after mile, southward, ever southward – dogs, boys, roarers, hunger – dogs, boys, roarers, hunger – but day after day with increasing weariness on she went, and her nose from time to time cheered her by confidently reporting, 'This surely is a smell we passed last spring.'

So week after week went by, and pussy, dirty, ribbonless, footsore and weary, arrived at the Harlem Bridge. Though it was enveloped in delicious smells she did not like the look of that bridge. For half the night she wandered up and down the shore without discovering any other means of going south excepting some other bridges. Somehow she had to come back to it; not only its smells were familiar, but from time to time when a 'One-eye' ran over it there was the peculiar rumbling roar that was a sensation in the springtime trip. She leaped to the timber stringer and glided out over the water. She had got less than a third of the way over when a 'Thundering One-eye' came roaring at her from the opposite end. She was much frightened but, knowing their blindness, she dropped to a low side beam and there crouched in hiding. Of course, the stupid monster missed her and passed on, and all would have been well but it turned back, or another just like it, and came suddenly roaring behind her. Pussy leaped to the long track and made for the home shore. She might have got there, but a third of the red-eye terrors came roaring down at her from that side. She was running her hardest, but was caught between two foes. There was nothing for it but a desperate leap from the timbers into – she did not know what. Down – down – down— plop! splash! plunge – into the deep water, not cold, for it was August, but oh! so horrible. She spluttered and coughed and struck out for the shore. She had never learned to swim, and yet she swam, for the simple reason that a cat's position and attitude in swimming are the same as her position and attitude in walking. She had fallen into a place she did not like; naturally she tried to walk out, and the result was that she swam ashore. Which shore? It never fails – the south – the shore nearest home. She scrambled out all dripping wet, up the muddy bank and through coal-piles and dust-heaps, looking as black, dirty and unroyal as it was possible for a cat to look.

Once the shock was over the Royal pedigreed slummer began to feel better for the plunge. A genial glow without from the bath, a genial sense of triumph within, for had she not outwitted three of the big terrors?

Her nose, her memory and her instinct of direction inclined her to get on the track again, but the place was infested with the big thunder-rollers, and prudence led her to turn aside and follow the river bank with its musky home reminders.

She was more than two days learning the infinite dangers and complexities of the East River docks, and at length, on the third night, she reached familiar ground, the place she had passed the night of her first escape. From that her course was sure and rapid. She knew just where she was going and how to get there. She knew even the most prominent features in the dogscape now. She went faster, felt happier. In a little while she would be curled up in the old junk-yard. Another turn and the block was in sight –

But – what – it was gone. Kitty could not believe her eyes. There, where had stood, or leaned, or slouched, or straggled— the houses of the block – was a great broken wilderness of stone, lumber and holes in the ground.

Kitty walked all around it. She knew by the bearings and by the local colour of the pavement that she was in her home; that there had lived the bird-man, and there was the old junk-yard; but all were gone, completely gone, taking the familiar odours with them; and pussy turned sick at heart in the utter hopelessness of the case. Her home love was her master mood. She had given up all to come to a home that no longer existed, and for once her brave little spirit was cast down. She wandered over the silent heaps of rubbish and found neither consolation nor eatables. The ruin had covered several of the blocks and reached back from the water. It was not a fire. Kitty had seen one of these things once. Pussy knew nothing of the great bridge that was to rise from this very spot.

When the sun came up Kitty sought for cover. An adjoining block still stood with little change, and the Royal Analostan retired to that. She knew some of its trails, but once there was unpleasantly surprised to find the place swarming with cats that, like herself, were driven from their old grounds, and when the garbage-cans came out there were several cats to each. It meant a famine in the land and pussy, after standing it a few days, set out to find her other home in Fifth Avenue. She got there to find it shut up and deserted, and the next night she returned to the crowded slum.

September and October wore away. Many of the cats died of starvation or were too weak to escape their natural enemies. But Kitty, young and strong, still lived.

Great changes had come over the ruined blocks. Though silent the night she saw them, they were crowded with noisy workmen all day. A tall building was completed by the end of October, and slum Kitty, driven by hunger, went sneaking up to a pail that a Negro had set outside. The pail, unfortunately, was not garbage, but a new thing in that region, a scrubbing-pail – a sad disappointment, but it had a sense of comfort: there was a trace of a familiar touch on the handle. While she was studying it the Negro elevator boy came out again. In spite of his blue clothes his odorous person confirmed the good impression of the handle. Kitty had retreated across the street. He gazed at her.

'Sho ef dat don't look like de Royal Ankalostan – Hya, pussy – pussy – pussy – pus-s-s-y, co-o-ome – pus-s-s-y, hya! I specs she's sho hungry.'

Hungry! She had not had a real meal for a month. The Negro went into the hall and reappeared with a portion of his own lunch.

'Hya, pussy, puss – puss – puss.' At length he laid the meat on the pavement and went back to the door. Slum Kitty came, found it savoury; sniffed at the meat, seized it, and fled like a little tigress to eat her prize in peace.

LIFE IV

This was the beginning of a new era. Pussy came to the door of the building now when pinched by hunger, and the good feeling for the Negro grew. She had never understood that man before. Now he was her friend, the only one she had.

One week pussy caught a rat. She was crossing the street in front of the new building when her friend opened the door for a well-dressed man to come out.

'Hell, look at that for a cat,' said the man.

'Yes, sah,' answered the Negro; 'dat's ma cat, sah; she's a terror on rats, sah. Hez 'em 'bout cleaned up, sah; dat's why she so thin.'

'Well, don't let her starve,' said the man, with the air of a landlord. 'Can't you feed her?'

'De liver-meat man comes reg'lar, sah, quatah dollar a week, sah,' said the Negro, realizing that he was entitled to the extra fifteen cents for 'the idea'.

'That's all right; I'll stand it.'

Since then the Negro has sold her a number of times with a perfectly clear conscience, because he knows quite well that it is only a question of a few days before the Royal Analostan comes back again. She has learned to tolerate the elevator and even to ride up and down on it. The Negro stoutly maintains that once she heard the meat man while she was on the top floor and managed to press the button that called the elevator to take her down.

She is sleek and beautiful again. She is not only one of 400 that form the inner circle about the liverman's barrow, but she is recognized as the star pensioner as well.

But in spite of her prosperity, her social position, her Royal name and fake pedigree, the greatest pleasure of her life is to slip out and go a-slumming in the gloaming, for now, as in her previous lives, she is at heart, and likely to be, nothing but a dirty little slum cat.

Come, Lovely Cat

CHARLES BAUDELAIRE

Come, lovely cat, and rest upon my heart,
   And let my gaze dive in the cold
Live pools of thine enchanted eyes that dart
   Metallic rays of green and gold.

My fascinated hands caress at leisure
   Thy head and supple back, and when
Thy soft electric body fills with pleasure
   My thrilled and drunken fingers, then

Thou changest to my woman; for her glance,
   Like thine, most lovable of creatures,
Is icy, deep, and cleaving as a lance.

   And round her hair and sphinx-like features
And round her dusky form float, vaguely blent,
   A subtle air and dangerous scent.

ACKNOWLEDGMENTS

All possible care has been taken to make full acknowledgment in every case where material is still in copyright. If errors have occurred, they will be corrected in subsequent editions if notification is sent to the publisher. Grateful acknowledgment is made for permission to reprint the following:

'A Vet's Life' by John M Bower BVSc MRCVS, reproduced by permission of the author.

'Amours' from *Les Vrilles de la Vigne* by Colette, reproduced by permission of John Johnson Limited, translation copyright © 1992 by Michael O'Mara Books.

'Incident on East Ninth' by Jill Dower, reproduced by permission of the author.

'My Boss the Cat' by Paul Gallico, reproduced by permission of Aitken and Stone and Harold Ober Associates Incorporated.

'Gershwin' by Judy Gardiner, reproduced by permission of Rupert Crew Limited. Copyright © 1983 by Judy Gardiner.

'Minna Minna Mowbray' by Michael Joseph, reproduced by permission of Hugh Joseph and Richard Joseph Publishers Ltd.

'Rufus the Survivor' by Doris Lessing from *Particularly Cats and More Cats*, reproduced by permission of Michael Joseph Ltd and Jonathan Clowes Ltd, on behalf of Doris Lessing. Copyright © 1989 by Doris Lessing.

'Cat's Cruise' from *The Sacred Bullock and Other Stories of Animals* by Mazo de la Roche, reproduced by permission of Pan Macmillan Ltd.

'C Stands for Cuisine' from *Cats' A-Z* by Beverley Nichols, reproduced by permission of Eric Glass Ltd.

Extract from 'The Cherry Tree' by Derek Tangye, reproduced by permission of Michael Joseph Ltd. Copyright © 1986 by Derek Tangye.

'Solomon and Sheba' from *Cats in the Belfry* by Doreen Tovey, reproduced by permission of Serafina Clarke.

'The Cat that Could Fly' by Stella Whitelaw, reproduced by permission of Rupert Crew Limited. Copyright © 1983 by Stella Whitelaw.

'The Coat' by Mary Williams, reproduced by permission of Laurence Pollinger Limited. Copyright © 1976 by Mary Williams.

Grateful thanks also go to Joan Moore of Cat World and the librarians of Northcote Road Library, Wandsworth, London for their help in finding stories.